Tricks 'N' Treats

Jean Locke Holmes: Pornstar Detective
Book Two

John Luke Maxwell

DDP
DEEP DESIRES PRESS

Winnipeg, Canada

Developmental editor: Craig Gibb
Proofreader: Francisco Feliciano

Published Oct. 2023 by Deep Desires Press, an imprint of Story Perfect Inc.

Deep Desires Press
PO Box 51053 Tyndall Park
Winnipeg, Manitoba R2X 3B0
Canada

Visit http://www.deepdesirespress.com for more scorching hot erotica and erotic romance.

Subscribe to our email newsletter to get notified of all our hot new releases, sales, and giveaways! Visit deepdesirespress.com/newsletter to sign up today!

Special thanks to YouTuber Patrick Marano
for providing a ton of bathhouse etiquette.
Warning! NSFW!
https://patrickmarano.com/

And to Curt, who was also very helpful
with details about San Francisco sex club habits.

Tricks 'N' Treats

Chapter 1

"So, you're dating a porn star. What's that like?'"

This was a question that I had become well-acquainted with. Mostly, it came to me through Twitter. Like everyone else on the planet, I had an account that I was fairly active on. Nevertheless, I have been stopped on the street by total strangers more than once and they all wanted to know one thing.

What is he like in bed? Don't you get jealous? How long do you think the relationship will last? Does it count as cheating if he has sex in front of the camera? How many orgasms has he given you in one round? Can I borrow him for the weekend and will you take a check?

Yes, that was several questions, not just one. I was paraphrasing. One woman—yes, *woman*—blurted all of them out in a single breath while I was waiting at a bus stop. It looked like she was going to pass out afterward. I seized the opportunity and jumped on to the bus before she could recover.

It was definitely one of my more "salty bitch" moments, but I'd been having a bad day. She was being rude too, asking me all that without so much as an introduction.

First of all, though, my boyfriend has retired. I feel like we ought to get that out of the way right now. However, it is true. My boyfriend used to do gay porn—quite a lot of it, in fact.

His name is Jean Locke Holmes, and that is his actual name. He didn't do porn under a pseudonym like most performers. I've never been able to get the reason why out of him beyond the fact that he simply isn't ashamed and saw no reason to hide it.

My name, on the other hand, is Rafael Vásquez—"Raf" for short. Mine was the story of a poor gay Latino boy from The Mission who made good by getting a college scholarship out of several swimming championships in high school. I had actually known about Jean for many years, long before we ever met. Jean was my very first porn crush. His movies were my guide through the confusing adolescent period where I was figuring out who I was and what I found attractive.

A hairy, muscled, long-haired, gay, Greek-Italian-Puerto Rican man is a rare thing to behold. In the porn industry, it's practically a unicorn!

But yes, I watched Jean's movies through a free streaming service as a teenager, way before I was old enough to be viewing porn on the Internet. Lots of teens—gay and straight—watch porn at that age. I'm sure teenagers were looking at porn back when cable was the main way to view it. Before that, it was probably magazines.

The point is, teenagers get horny and they watch porn. That's the horrible truth, and we should probably all get on with our lives. Watching porn didn't turn me gay. It just made me realize that I *was* gay.

Someone once said that gay men take their porn way more seriously than straight men do. I think there's some truth in that. Name a Pride event that doesn't have gay porn stars at it. Sure, we have guest speakers and the odd gay celebrity show up.

But the ones who get the real rock star treatment—posters, red carpet, and all that? Those go to the men who spend their work hours in front of a camera showing off their dick and ass. The long and thick of it is, if gay men are honest, porn means something special to us all.

And I was no different. Long after getting into college, I remembered Jean's films. His earliest hits were back in the mid-nineties. They were campy, cheesy, pseudo-horror exploitation-style flicks. According to Jean, the budget was nonexistent, and the special effects had been put together by some poor slob living in his parent's garage.

And yet, I had loved them. They were what got me through my

lonely adolescent years. Seeing a half-Latino gay man on my computer screen gave me hope that I would find my way in the world after all.

Plus, Jean's body was to die for, and that did not change over the years!

However, real life isn't a porn movie, even though we might wish it could be some of the time. I got older and found my first boyfriend in college. We dated for a while and it got serious. After graduation, we found a small apartment and started making plans for the future.

Then, the quarantine happened.

One thing that got overlooked during the crisis was the effect that COVID-19 had on relationships. Intimacy hadn't been such a high-risk factor since the early days of HIV. Simply being near someone you loved put them in danger.

Months and months went by, with false reassurances that sounded hollow even to some of our then-president's most ardent defenders. One good thing that came from it was the veil being torn away. The next election was close, but enough people had seen the true face of horror in the walking Cheeto Cancer.

The empire had fallen, and many of us were glad of it.

In the meantime, however, life with Nik—my then-boyfriend—had become strained. I had studied to be a massage therapist. I liked helping people and the money seemed good. In California, wine mothers love their massages. Something catastrophic would have to happen to get that to stop.

And, it had.

Nik, my now-ex-boyfriend, had an office job downtown, but he was able to work from home most of the time. They only called him into the main building in the financial district when it was absolutely necessary. For myself and the rest of San Francisco, however, things looked dire.

The streets were deserted during the day, something once believed impossible. Businesses closed up left and right, many of which never reopened. People went mad from being locked away inside of their homes.

And yes, dear Karen needed a haircut.

The six-foot social distancing rule meant I could go nowhere near any of my clients. The spa I had been working for shut its doors. The government bailouts didn't trickle down that far, shockingly. This was just one of the many places that closed down and stayed that way.

I was left cooling my heels and running up high scores on the Nintendo Switch while Nik worked his ass off. I felt like garbage and hated how my life had turned out. Whatever may have happened between us, Nik didn't deserve to be crushed under the weight of so much responsibility.

In the end, I did find a job—working part-time in the Castro at a used bookstore, the Dog-Eared Doorstopper. It was really more of a used "whatever" store, since the second floor carried magazines, VHS tapes, and old DVDs. The owner was amazing and I got along very well with the rest of the staff.

Hell, if the pay wasn't so low, I'd have called it the best job ever.

During that time, Nik and I became strangers. We hardly ever saw one another anymore despite living in the same place. When he was home, Nik stayed locked up in the office—our spare bedroom—for hours at a time.

I used to ask myself if it was really all my fault. I could have tried harder, or done a better job of keeping the place clean, or gone out looking for jobs farther away. I didn't know it at the time, but Nik was in some financial trouble as well. The stress became too much for him and we broke up.

Actually, he dumped me via text message while I was on my way to work one morning.

Whether or not anyone believes I wasn't at fault, that was taking the coward's way out. Nik and I didn't speak again for several weeks. During that time, I met Jean Locke Holmes, retired porn star extraordinaire.

Jean had come into the Dog-Eared Doorstopper on a whim. I was upstairs placing used DVDs on the shelves and had come across several of his original porn titles—from before he made the jump to Internet videos in the Aughties. I was facing the possibility of homelessness soon, but couldn't resist picking up a few of my favorites.

Imagine my surprise when I came downstairs to find him standing beside the counter, calm as he pleased. I won't lie by saying that our first encounter was like something from an old movie. I made a right fool of myself, going so far as to drop the DVDs I'd been carrying.

I may have also fainted.

For whatever the reason, Jean saw something in me. That part was like a fairy tale. He came back to the bookstore again and again. We started talking, and not long afterward, he asked me out.

Jean was coming out of retirement to do a special performance at the Nob Hill Theater for a charity was hoping they could stir up interest in the old place. They wanted someone to invest and re-open the city's most famous male strip club for gay men. Jean agreed to do a one-night engagement since it was for charity and Pride month.

That, unfortunately, was when the trouble started.

One of the dancers was almost killed by a falling stage fixture. A fire broke out during a rehearsal not long afterward. Someone vandalized a poster featuring Jean's face.

And, one of the main acts of the charity event was murdered, leaving Jean as the main suspect.

It was not as bad as it sounds, though. Actually, on second thought, it was a lot worse than I made it sound, but there was one saving grace. Jean, it turned out, was quite the amateur sleuth. He demonstrated a keen eye for details and a razor-sharp mind when it came to unraveling the mystery.

We made it out alive in the end and the real culprit was caught. I ended up getting kidnapped—by Nik no less—who then committed suicide. He claimed that someone had paid him to hurt Jean.

Personally, I think he had lost his mind by that point. Nothing about what he said to me during the kidnapping made any kind of sense. He admitted that breaking up with me—via text message I wanna reiterate—was the wrong thing to do.

Nik wanted me to come back to him, but what we had was over.

The kidnapping was just the final nail in the coffin, and even if I hadn't been with Jean by that point, our relationship was finished. Jean had seemed worried at first, but things calmed down soon afterward, so I guess there wasn't anything to be made from Nik's crazy ramblings.

Since then, we have settled into a pretty comfortable life. Jean lives with a woman whom he has claimed as his aunt. Auntie Mags wrote best-selling murder mysteries in her spare time. She also played aggressively violent survival horror games online.

More than once, Jean and I were roused from our sleep late at night by unearthly wails. Jean always pulls the pillow down over his head and goes back to sleep. I usually end up getting dressed to go join her.

She always kicks my ass at *Death Mark IV: The Culling*.

Our lives have been peaceful. The cool temperatures of San Francisco June weather gave way to a hot summer. We all prayed for the survival of our extended surrogate gay families in Portland, who were in danger of melting like the Wicked Witch due to a severe heat wave.

October had come, bringing with it the promise that things would cool down again soon. The city was slowly recovering, inch by every snail's crawl of an inch. There was hope that life might one day return to what it once was.

But life has a way of being unpredictable. I learned that the hard way when Jean and I found ourselves face to face with a brand-new mystery. And it all started while we were out on a hunt for Halloween candy.

Even with the danger, though, I wouldn't trade the happiness that I've found with Jean for anything. Through him, I've come to understand with love really is. A part of me will cherish the time I spent with Nik—minus the stalking and kidnapping part, of course. It is with Jean, though, that I have found bliss and contentment.

And yes, the sex has been phenomenal.

Were you really expecting anything less?

· · ·

One thing that no one warned me about when it came to being a new couple was the adjustment period.

There are those early months—usually about two or so—where new couples are still getting used to one another. I have heard straight people call this the "nine-and-a-half weeks" phase. It's when things are all lovey-dovey and you feel like your new partner is just the greatest thing ever.

Then those rose-colored glasses come off and you start seeing the warts. Someone chews their food too loudly. Or they hog the covers in the wee hours of the morning. Maybe they don't know when to let the other person speak during a conversation.

Normally, when this kicks in, a couple has to decide whether or not they are in it for the long haul. Some choices have to be made. Some old living habits have to be tossed out. They might have to change their schedules to make time for one another.

Jean and I skipped most of that. With all that happened between Nik and I, including a kidnapping, I was left with no place to call home. Since I didn't have a roof over my head, Jean let me crash at his. I wound up living with him and his Auntie Mags. She was a godsend, welcoming me into her home with open arms.

Of course, we were also dealing with the Nob Hill Theater case and the fact that the police pinpointed Jean as the chief person-of-interest in the case. Thinking back, there was a lot happening during the early days of our courtship. Therefore, a lot of the things that normal couples go through got shuffled around.

I had to adjust to living in a new place with two other people, neither of whom I knew all that well, and one of whom I was in the early stages of a relationship with. As such, Jean and I tended to alternate between making goo-goo eyes at one another, which would typically then be followed by him getting on my nerves.

Of course, that meant we had great make-up sex afterward, so it wasn't as if this were a no-win situation for me.

One thing I learned about Jean in the wake of the murder was that he tended to be an early riser. Weekends were the days when we slept in. During the week, though, he would be up at the crack of dawn.

I, of course, had to fall in love with a morning person.

Even worse, he seemed to think that I should get up with him. The bed would be all cozy and warm from our shared body heat. The bed gravity would be nice and strong, further encouraging me to remain under the soft, silky covers.

All of that would end the moment Jean's eyes opened. He was a big man, so rolling out of bed created a seismic event on our mattress. I would be fast asleep when the quake started. The memory foam supporting my vertebrae even moved in the same pattern each time as though it had memorized it.

My body would bounce up and down. I was much smaller than Jean so it was easy for him to jostle me around like that. Once that happened, I would be awake, but in no way happy about the fact.

There was also Jean's morning routine. He did the usual shit, shower, and shave, but Jean also practiced yoga and calisthenics. I had a few minutes of peace while he dashed to the restroom down the hallway to relieve himself. My eyes would close each time. I would feel myself beginning to drift back to the serenity of dreamland where the fire-breathing cyclops was about to eat me.

And then, Jean's big size-fourteen feet would come stomping down the hallway, waking me up again. I knew each time that he would poke and prod me until I got out from under the covers. I knew that he would shoo me out the door toward the restroom so that I could do the same. I knew that he would come and find me if I didn't emerge from the restroom in a timely manner.

Knowing all of that didn't make going through it each morning any easier.

"Just a little bit more," Jean said insistently as I pushed.

"I can't…" My teeth grit together. "I can't take anymore."

"You can do it." Jean's voice was patient, but he never let up. "I know you can do it. You've just got to will yourself to."

He sounded like an instructor. It occurred to me that, given his profession, Jean most likely had given tutorials on this sort of thing before. I was most likely not his first pupil.

I tuned out the jealous spike that flared up inside of me and concentrated. "I really can't," I said after a moment more. "My body…just wasn't meant to take it."

"You can take it," Jean pressed, his voice never losing the persistent patience that I found so annoying. "I've been with other people who managed. Your body will adjust."

I opened my mouth to fire off a sarcastic retort, but Jean cut me off. "You just need to give it time," he added at that precise moment.

It was so hard to be rude when he was speaking so kindly. I suspected that was on purpose. If I lashed out, it made me look like the bad guy. Jean was only trying to help, after all.

"Fine," I relented, though I raised back up. "But we're taking a ten-minute break so I can recover."

Jean frowned, but didn't stop me when I moved to get a towel. "You're just giving your body time to tighten back up," he protested.

I dabbed the sweat away and scowled. "No," I insisted, refusing to give in to him this time. "I'm giving my body a reason to not hate me for ten minutes. We'll pick this up again once my leg muscles quit screaming."

Jean looked at me for a moment and shook his head. "You are the first massage therapist," he said, sounding amused, "that I've ever met who had this much trouble doing yoga."

I glared. "Not all massage therapists are new age retro-hippies looking for peace and love." I hesitated then, considering my words. "Not that I don't want peace and love, but that's beside the point."

Jean leveled his gaze at me. "You were the one who wanted to get in better shape," he reminded me.

Those words hung in the air. I actually cringed a little bit at them. It felt like Jean's eyes were trying to drill through me.

My shoulders slumped in defeat, mainly because I couldn't think of a valid argument. "You win," I said, moving back onto the expensive yoga mat that Jean insisted on using.

My boyfriend, whom I love dearly, practically radiated a smug confidence. "Good," he said, joining me on the mat next to mine. "We'll start over from the beginning."

"Oh, joy." My voice sounded as sour as I felt. "What fun!"

Nevertheless, I got down on my knees. The mat was admittedly very comfortable. I just hate sitting on my legs. The weight of my body pressing down on them caused my muscles to cramp up.

"I think your body needs more time to adjust," Jean advised, getting into the same position. "We'll go slower this time. Sorry for pushing you, by the way."

The apology helped. "Sorry for being such a bitch," I replied, meaning it. "You're right, just for the record. I did ask for this."

Back in high school, I was a skinny little twig. Puberty had not been kind to me. I joined the swim team because the guidance counselor thought I needed to be more social. The rat fink went so far as to contact my mother when I didn't warm to the idea right away. Mom heard the counselor out and decided that she was right.

The problem, however, was that I was ill-suited for most sports. Football was out of the question. I lacked the hand-eye coordination to play baseball. I didn't like to run, so that meant track and field were out as well.

I had always loved swimming, though. My younger brother and I practically lived at the community pool during the summers. Neither Mom nor the guidance counselor relented, so I signed up for the swim team.

It did have an effect on me. I wasn't the most popular jock in school, but I did make a couple of friends there. There were a couple nerdy gamers who shared my love of roleplaying and survival horror games. It was also how I was able to afford college. The scholarship paid just enough for me to attend a local university and get my massage therapy certification.

But I never fully developed the "swimmer's bod" that so many of my teammates did. That bothered me more than I cared to admit. Long after college ended, I still wasn't comfortable showing my body off to people.

Jean was patient with me. In the end, I opened up to him. We spent over an hour cuddling in bed. He ran his hands all over me, assuring me with his touch that he loved me, that he thought I was gorgeous.

I disagreed, of course. Jean was the gorgeous one. He was well over six feet tall with muscles in places that I could only fantasize about. A fantastic carpet of fur crowned his rich, brown skin. I loved running my fingers through it, and through the thick, curly mane of hair that cascaded down past his shoulders.

"One step at a time," Jean reminded me, bringing my mind back to the present. "Ready?"

I nodded, taking a deep breath to steel myself for the inevitable failure.

"Child's Pose," Jean said, holding his arms forward. "Knees wide in a V-shape. Make sure your toes touch and your ass rests on your heels."

I did as Jean instructed. Perhaps it was simply my acquiescence, but the weight resting on my legs didn't hurt as much this time. My feet fit into the curve of my butt much easier as well.

"Lengthen your spine," Jean went on, keeping my attention squarely on the present. "Then stretch forward between your thighs with your arms out in front of you."

True to his word, we went more slowly this time. I concentrated on my body, keeping my focus on doing this simple act. When I was nearly to the floor, something popped loudly in my vertebrae.

"Uh-oh!" I said, feeling a surge of panic.

"Ignore it," Jean advised, sensing my shift in mood. "Your body isn't used to it yet. That's all. If it needs to pop, it will."

I didn't move, despite how calm Jean sounded. "Keep going," he told me, using a gentler tone than last time. "You've got this."

My body complied after a moment of further protest. My lower thigh popped as well, sending a sharp pain up through me. I grit my teeth and focused. The pain vanished after a second. To my surprise, I was stretched out on my stomach with both legs curled up underneath me.

"You did it," Jean said, pleased. "Okay, hold that position for as long as you can. Up to sixty seconds, if you can make it."

I began counting, using "Mississippi" to space out each number. Jean counted aloud right alongside me. We had barely passed the tens when my body started spasming. I wanted out of this pose more than anything else in life.

"I used to swim laps every day," I grumbled aloud. "How am I this bad at yoga?"

"When was the last time you kept a regular workout regimen?" Jean asked.

I had to think about that for a moment. "Before quarantine," I confessed, not happy with the answer. "Back in college when I was still on the school's swim team."

"Tell me about it," Jean encouraged. "Also, let's move to the Downward-Facing Dog pose now."

Jean and I moved to our hands and knees. This felt a little bit more familiar to me. One did not fall for a porn star of Jean's caliber without becoming better acquainted with being on all fours.

"It was…" I paused long enough to move my body into an A-figure, mimicking Jean's movements. "Required. I had to stay in shape to stay on the team. Being on the team was what paid for school."

Sweat dripped down my face. Through the sheen, I saw Jean eyeing me.

"So you had to work out," he said thoughtfully. "It was a necessity—don't forget to count, remember?"

Counting in my head while carrying on a conversation as my body stretched past what felt like were its limits wasn't easy.

"Right." I wondered where Jean was going with this train of thought. "I would get up, go to the campus gym, work out for an hour and swim laps. Then it was time for classes."

"But you had a goal in mind—Upward-Facing Dog next!" Jean continued to talk while I brought my body down so that my arms were tight at my side and parallel with the bedroom wall. "You wanted to graduate and staying in shape helped you do that."

I hadn't thought of it that way. Granted, it was harder to concentrate while my spine was bent, and the upper half of my body was raised up off the floor. I powered through it anyhow while counting quietly to myself.

"I guess it did," I realized.

"Cobra," Jean said, which confused me. "I mean, move into the Cobra Pose next."

"Oh, of course." My face flushed slightly from embarrassment as I rested the lower half of my body onto the mat. Moving into his position was much easier. "Sorry, but where are you…?"

I made the mistake of turning toward Jean. Sweat was beading on his forehead. He had taken his shirt off at some point. I didn't know when, but the sight of him half-naked on the floor next to me made my brain go into four-oh-four blue screen mode.

"Ahhh…" My face burned brighter as I jerked my head away. "My bad. Had a brain fart there for a moment. You were saying?"

"Bridge Pose." Jean waited until I was resting on my shoulders with my body arched up off the mat using my toe tips. "It's all about motivation. About assessing what it is that you really want."

I was having a hard time following Jean's meaning. This position was usually when my body gave up. Muscles I didn't know I had—and I had to study human anatomy extensively for my degree—screamed in protest.

"What I want," I said, desperate for something to distract me, "is to not snap in half like a twig."

"Focus on my voice," Jean cooed. He knew this was the part that I struggled with the most. "You need to find that motivation again. You wanted something back when you were in college. You can find that again now if you look for it."

I breathed deep, tuned out the pain, and focused on Jean's words. "Makes sense, I guess," I said, thinking back. "I wanted…needed to do better. I saw what Mom went through, trying to raise two sons."

"Right," Jean encouraged. "Keep going. Follow that feeling. Verbalize it if you can."

He and I stood up and moved into the Chair Pose. I had never gotten this far before. It looked simple enough in the diagram that Jean showed me. The problem was that my body gave out beforehand.

I should have felt proud, but I was too busy thinking about what Jean said. "She worked her ass off," I continued, holding my arms and my upper body at a diagonal angle with my knees bent. "We had next to nothing. Growing up in the Mission... It was hard."

I remembered how hard everyone else had it in our old neighborhood. My brother and I got good enough grades to warrant being sent to a better school than the one the other kids in our area attended.

He and I were some of a few Latino students there. Most of the alumni were white. I saw how good everyone else had it. Nobody else wore second-hand clothes or cheap shoes. It was hard fitting in there.

"I wanted more out of life," I admitted. "Mom couldn't give me that. Maybe I resented her a little..."

"It's okay." Jean's voice stayed soothing and calm. "You were a kid. Let's move to Warrior One now."

"I was a spoiled teenager," I said, disgruntled with myself. My weight rested easily on one knee, stretching forward with both arms raised above my head. "I should've...known better."

Jean shook his head. "Wanting to do well in life isn't a sin, you know," he chided me tenderly. "People don't always find a way to make their dreams happen."

"Yeah, right." I shot Jean a look and made a face. "My 'dream' ended up being a tiny apartment. Then quarantine happened and I lost my job."

"So?" Jean pressed. "Warrior Two, please."

Each arm burned as I stretched them out in front and behind me. "Spent months sitting on my ass thinking things would improve on their own."

I didn't like where this was going. There were a lot of bad memories from that time. It was during the first year of COVID that my relationship with Nik fell apart.

"I told myself," I said, straining. "…there was nothing I could do but wait. But the whole time…" I hesitated, but Jean said nothing. "I wondered…if maybe I didn't try hard enough."

"Really?" Jean's voice sounded condescending. "Did you have the cure for COVID?"

"No," I snapped, irritated. "You know that. No one had a cure for COVID. Hell, it was another year before the vaccinations were available."

Jean and I had both gotten our vaccinations around the same time. We went to different pharmacies for them, but we were only a day apart from one another. I was surprised when I found that out.

"Then why do you punish yourself?" he asked me, looking me straight in the eye. "Tree Pose."

The conversation stalled for a bit. I had a hard time keeping my balance on one foot. As I wobbled there on the mat, Jean's question rattled in my mind.

"I don't know," I admitted at last once the sixty seconds were up.

"You worked hard," Jean pointed out. "Triangle."

The conversation stalled again. Jean had to help me get into the Triangle yoga position. I had never done this one before either. On the one hand, I got to use both of my legs. The problem was that I was little better at staying balanced while my body was twisted in such an awkward position.

"Maybe we should finish this later," I offered, worried I was becoming a pretzel—or a human centipede.

"You're doing great," Jean encouraged. "We've never gotten this far before. You should feel proud of yourself."

I hadn't let myself feel that way just yet. We were too busy going through an impromptu psych evaluation. Jean was right, though.

I was doing good, and that bothered me.

"I did work hard," I admitted, more to myself than him as we moved into the High Plank position—which was essentially a glorified push-up that didn't end. "I pushed myself to get good enough grades to go to college. I competed in swim tournaments to pay for school."

"You did all the right things," Jean said, putting it together for me. "Made all the right moves. Hell, you even found yourself a boyfriend while you were still in school."

"We got a place to live together." I was breathing hard, but it wasn't because of the yoga position I was in. "Everything was going great. So…"

"So," Jean finished. "Why did it end?"

I thought about his question while we stood on the mats in the Standing Fold, the last position in our routine. Blood rushed to my head from me bending my body in half. I felt dizzy from pointing my head toward the floor. My arms burned while Jean counted.

"I don't know," I confessed once the time was up. "I thought I did everything right. I thought everything was right. But…"

"That's life," Jean said, standing with me. "You can do everything right and still have everything go horribly wrong."

Hearing that was like having a load of bricks fall on me. In that moment, I wanted to cry. My face must have given that away. Jean was suddenly there, wrapping both arms securely around me.

"I just…" My body shook as I sobbed. "I thought I…was better than this."

"Shhh…" Jean said, rubbing my back with one hand. "You did good, my love. Hell, you survived through a pandemic."

He raised back, brushing my eyes clear with his thumbs so that I could see him. "Speaking as someone who grew up in the Dark Ages—when HIV was everywhere and the treatments were worse than the disease—that is saying something."

I was reminded again that Jean was twice my age. He had grown up when being gay was a death sentence. Coming out for him was far more traumatic than it had been for me. My mother just sort of hummed and hawed for a bit, then made me swear that I would use protection when I finally did have sex.

For a single Puerto Rican mom, she handled her oldest son's sexual orientation spectacularly.

"And you're coming back from all of that," he went on, holding me close to his chest again. I could feel his heart beating—such an amazing sound. "You have plenty to feel proud of, lover."

"Thanks." Gently, I pressed both hands against him. "But none of that means you're getting out of lunch today."

Speaking of my mother, she had been anxious to meet the new man in my life. The fact that she found out about him from reading that he was being accused of murder didn't go over well at first. Once the news died down, however, Mom was willing to hear my version of events.

It helped that Nik had turned out to be such a huge mistake. Mom had liked Nik a lot. They got along well before we were all forced inside of our homes for a year. I had to explain in painstaking detail how Nik dumped me via text and then spent a month stalking my new boyfriend.

The final nail in the coffin was when I explained to her how Nik kidnapped me. Mom spent the next half-hour cussing up a storm in Spanish. She must have forgotten that Jean was half-Puerto Rican himself. He was very impressed by her knowledge of swear words.

Mom had been so ashamed. Jean had understood every word she said, something she wasn't as accustomed to. She actually hung up on me!

Of course, she called right back to continue our conversation, but learning that Jean had rescued me earned him brownie points.

The problem with that, however, was she wanted to meet him. Jean seemed reluctant to make nice with my family. It took quite a bit of prodding to find out why.

"I told you," Jean said while we changed. "Parents don't like me. It's been like that for most of my life."

I was in the midst of selecting a shirt that Mom wouldn't hate. "Because you did porn?" I asked, turning halfway around to study Jean.

He was sliding into a pair of jeans. They fit over his hairy legs like a second skin. The sight of him, along with that perfect muscular ass disappearing out of sight, made me drool.

"That's a huge part of it," he answered, adjusting himself as he turned around to face me. "I didn't exactly date in high school. Not guys, anyway."

"No," I admitted, staring for too long at his bulge. "I imagine you wouldn't have."

Granted, I hadn't dated in high school either. Well, that wasn't entirely true. Rumors had circulated about me for a while. I had said that I would come out after graduation, but that plan fell through a month into my senior year.

A girl in my class was making tasteless jokes about gay guys. I had to sit in front of her every day and listen to the people around us laugh. Finally, I turned around in my seat and flat-out said to her face that she was wrong, that I was gay, and she could keep her collagen-soaked lips shut if she couldn't get her facts straight.

The teacher told the principal, who then called my mom. Fortunately, Mom already knew that I was gay. I had told her the truth after she found several of Jean's movies on my laptop.

It was going to be quite the experience having Jean over at her place for lunch. After all, the first time both of us saw him was on my laptop screen watching him plow some poor twink's ass senseless.

That wasn't something that a lot of gay men could brag about.

"Did you?" Jean asked, coming up behind me to wrap both of his arms around my smaller, skinnier frame.

"Mm?" I couldn't resist leaning back into him. "Sorry, someone is distracting me. I'm trying to pick the right shirt out."

Jean let go with one arm. His hand slid into the closet—into *my* side of the closet—pulling out a dark blue button-up with Pokémon characters printed all over it.

"This one," he declared with certainty. "If your mother doesn't know you by now, she never will."

I didn't take the shirt from him. "I want to look nice," I protested, giving Jean a glare. "Not like…"

"Like yourself?" Jean asked knowingly. He held the shirt close to me, insistently. "You should be comfortable around your mother. I am the one who is going to get grilled with questions, after all."

He had a good point there. "It's not like I haven't embarrassed her with my nerdiness before," I agreed at last, sliding the shirt over the light blue one I already had on. "Same goes for my brother."

"It suits you," Jean said, eyeing me up and down. "Now, what was this about you dating in high school?"

Jean sounded jealous, which was absurd. "It was my senior prom," I explained, reaching into the closet again to find a shirt for him to wear. "Samantha—the girlfriend of one of my buddies on the swim team—set me up. She had a cousin in college who was out."

"Dating an older man." Jean smirked at me as he took the black dress shirt from my hand. "I'm sensing a theme here."

"We kept in touch," I said while watching with lustful eyes as Jean slid the shirt over his white tank top, leaving it unbuttoned. "He wasn't interested in anything long-term, though."

"His loss," Jean said, checking himself in the mirror. "Did anyone give you a hard time?"

I shrugged, thinking back on that night. "Not really," I admitted. "I mean, we got a couple of looks, but nothing bad happened. Honestly, the prom was boring and we ended up leaving early."

The jealous look was back in Jean's eyes again. "To do what?" he teased, poking me in the ribs. "Go stargazing? Hang out by the lake?"

"Ow!" I recoiled from the assault on my poor sensitive ribs. "No fair! And no, it wasn't anything like that."

Jean clearly didn't believe me. "Right," he scoffed, pulling me back into his embrace. "Two gay teenagers—one of whom is older, I wanna point out—leave a chaperoned dance to be alone together. And nothing salacious at all happened?"

Jean leaned forward into me. I could feel his thick bush of a beard against the sensitive skin of my neck. A pair of moist, hot lips planted a kiss there, which sent shivers through me.

"Totally innocent," he whispered huskily between kisses. "I'm sure he was on his best behavior."

"You have an active imagination," I said, blushing from how

aroused Jean felt. His cock was snaking down one leg of his pants, and yet it still managed to poke me in the hip.

"I would've made a move," Jean replied unabashedly, moving his head around to kiss me properly on the lips. "You'd have gone home the next morning walking funny."

I reached down to feel the silk steel hiding in his jeans. "If you were packing this back in high school," I said, savoring the chance to tease him now. "I'd have gone to the emergency room."

"That would've taken some explaining," Jean admitted, chuckling.

I moved away, mainly because thinking while making out with Jean Locke Holmes didn't go well together.

"He didn't have your bravery," I revealed, somewhat disappointed in myself for cutting Jean off. "We got fake IDs and snuck into a beercade with some friends."

Jean smiled. I could see his mouth twitch underneath the thick beard he wore. Clearly, this story amused him.

"It's true," I insisted. "That's how I found out that I am not good at *Donkey Kong* when I'm drunk. We stayed there until they chased us out."

Jean wasn't willing to let the subject die. I suspected he was hoping to distract me so that we missed lunch. This was confirmed when he moved in close again, trying to kiss me.

"And?" he pressed, bending his head downward. He was so much taller than me. "What happened next?"

I held a hand up, cutting him off. "I'll tell you about it in the car," I said, stepping back so as not to fall into his sneaky, sexy trap. "You drive while I regale you about my teen years. Deal?"

Jean made a face, but didn't protest. "You drive a hard bargain," he said, going for his wallet and keys. "Fine, we'll do it your way."

I patted him on the back as we headed for the stairs. "You'll get through this," I assured him, taking each step at the same time he did. "Anyone who can win an award for a triple penetration scene can get through lunch with their boyfriend's mother."

Jean was still laughing when we walked out the front door. "Can I bring that up during the meal?" he asked teasingly. "There's a very funny story surrounding that, actually. See—"

"No," I said flatly, cutting him off. "Mom won't find it funny. No matter how good of a spin you put on it."

Jean and I lived with Auntie Mags on California Street. It was one of the sections of San Francisco where all of the nice townhouses were located. None of these were brightly colored, unlike the famous Painted Ladies in Alamo Square Park.

Our home was called Sherrinford House on account of the owner's surname. Auntie Mags had christened it as such long before Jean moved in with her. It was painted an off-white color and had dark shutters framing the windows.

The most impressive thing about it was the balcony located on the top floor. It jutted out slightly from a pair of French doors. I smiled at the sight while Jean and I made our way over to the garage. That was where Jean kept his studio. Since retiring from porn, he had taken up painting. Jean would post pictures of his work online and auction them off for sale. So far, he hadn't set the world on fire, but did well enough that neither of us were freeloaders.

The balcony was also the first place where Jean and I made love, so I had a certain sentimental attachment to it.

"Let's take the Prowler," Jean suggested as the garage door rumbled open.

I gave him a look.

"What?" Jean reacted as if I were insulting him. "You said it was important that we make a good impression."

"You wanna drive that..." I paused to point at the collector's item resting idly inside his aunt's garage. "...all the way out to The Mission. And leave it parked there?"

Jean opened his mouth to speak, but then hesitated. "I can't think of anything to say that isn't horribly classist. Which I'm guessing," he added while eyeing me shrewdly, "was the whole point."

"It was," I admitted, savoring that it was my turn to look smug.

Jean rolled his eyes. "Well-played," he contested. "But I would still like to drive it. It's been in mothballs for too long. The old girl could use a chance to stretch her wheels."

I shook my head at this. "Personifying your car as a woman," I said, walking over to climb in through the passenger door. "Sometimes I worry that deep down you're a straight guy."

"Impossible," Jean said haughtily as he slid in easily behind the wheel. "That would have made my own mother entirely too happy."

The roar of the engine starting drowned out my sarcastic snort. "Perish the thought," I retorted as we rolled out into the street.

In spite of my irritation, I reached out to take hold of Jean's hand, holding it as we drove down and over the rolling hills toward The Mission.

Chapter 2

It was only a little after nine-thirty as we made our way toward Mom's.

Jean and I left early in preparation for the usual morning grind of traffic. California Street was typically bumper-to-bumper, and things would only get worse once we hit Gough Street. Inwardly, I cringed at how long we would most likely be stuck at the turn near 101.

But there was another reason for us leaving so early. Auntie Mags had sent us on a quick fetch quest. Last night, she asked if we would pick up some Halloween candy. The holiday was coming up and Jean and I had both managed to put off shopping for trick-or-treaters.

Fortunately, Auntie Mags wasn't picky. "Just pick up a couple bags," she had said over one shoulder. Apparently, Auntie Mags had suffered an attack of nostalgia and cracked open her old copy of *Command & Conquer*—the one with Tim Curry in it.

"Get the cheap stuff," she'd added as several soldiers died on screen. "I've already got plenty of expensive chocolate for us to eat later."

I reiterated what Auntie Mags said while we crept uphill at a snail's pace. "Look at it this way," Jean pointed out, giving my hand a squeeze while we waited. "Neither one of us will have to hunt down the nearest Nippon-Ya for her."

I laughed, but Jean was deadly serious. "I've lived with her for close to fifteen years," he reminded me. "You haven't been there when she gets a craving for Strawberry Pocky at three in the morning."

His explanation didn't stop me from laughing. If anything, I was cackling like a lunatic. Jean let go of my hand to grip the steering wheel.

"I'm sorry," I said, taking his hand back into my own. "I didn't mean to hurt your feelings, love. Really. It's just…"

Jean eyed me as I trailed off. "Yes?" he asked, making it sound like a challenge.

"Well, you are a big guy," I pointed out, raking my eyes over him. "There's space in here for two of me, and at least three of her. The idea of her bossing you around… it is pretty funny, honestly."

Jean huffed, though he gave my hand a squeeze. "You've been with her long enough," he said, an edge creeping into the corner of his voice. "She doesn't like being told 'no'."

"Hmm, good point," I admitted after thinking about it for a moment. "Guess we both dodged a bullet after all."

"That DoorDash app has saved me so much heartache in the last couple years," he stated emphatically while the Prowler muddled along toward our destination, drawing a handful of awestruck and envious looks from the other motorists. "Nothing's more satisfying that pushing off an unwanted errand onto a total stranger."

"Looks like you've found the silver lining to the pandemic," I teased dryly.

Jean's eyes turned shockingly sincere. "You're my silver lining," he said softly, placing a kiss on my hand before turning his attention back to the road. "Now tell me about your prom night."

I sighed and began the whole sordid tale. "Like I said," I began, going back to that night in my mind. "We all piled into the limo and went to a beercade. One of my buddies had gotten us fake IDs beforehand. I had three beers and then failed spectacularly at *Donkey Kong.*"

There was a pregnant pause inside the Prowler. "At least," I added, "I think it was *Donkey Kong.* That was also the night where I learned I was a lightweight."

"What did your date do?" Jean asked curiously, still weaving the Prowler through the slow-ass traffic.

"Watched me make a fool of myself, mostly," I replied, shrugging. "He chit-chatted with my friends for a bit. And then…"

My face tinted a slight red as the memory of what came next rushed to the forefront of my mind. "Then," I went on before Jean could prod me, "we were thrown out."

"How come?"

I wasn't surprised by the question. Jean had been eager to hear this story. Naturally, he would insist on hearing the climax.

"The bartender that served us ended his shift," I explained. "And a different one took over. This one was more of a pro. I guess he had been serving longnecks for way longer because he spotted our fake IDs right away. Threatened to call the cops if we didn't leave immediately."

"Ahh," Jean commented, nodding once. "And being that you were all underage and new to the bar scene...?"

"We ran out like scared chickens," I confirmed, chuckling ruefully. "Or stumbled out, in my case. My date forgot that I was there and had to go back in after me."

"A good sign that it wasn't going to work out," Jean noted, looking pleased.

"It was," I agreed. "But I got over him."

Once upon a time, there had been a Walgreens on the way to The Mission. It would have served our needs perfectly. Sadly, though, the store closed down at some point.

It was just as well, since Auntie Mags preferred to do her shopping at Trader Joe's. It meant a slight detour, but that was the whole point of us leaving early. Cheap candy doesn't melt as quickly as the expensive stuff. So long as we kept it out of direct sunlight, it could stay in the car.

Hell, some of that stuff would survive a nuclear holocaust.

Jean rolled the Prowler into the parking lot, which garnered a few more avaricious glances. Trader Joe's attracted a variety of types from all over the surrounding area. Few of them drove rare vintage sports vehicles, however.

The insurance premiums alone on the thing were outlandish, but Jean refused to sell it. He had gotten the Prowler from a wealthy car collector. The man had paid Jean to spend a week together. Jean received the Prowler as a tip for, as he put it, "a job well done."

I never asked for the man's name, figuring it was better to leave that in the past.

The Prowler slid easily into an available parking space. We were nestled between an old Pontiac and a shiny new Tesla. Jean killed the engine before masking up. I did the same and we were off to the candy races.

Predictably enough, Trader Joe's was packed. We were nearly barreled over by a frantic mom pushing a grocery cart with two kids inside. An elderly woman took off out of the express lane as soon as the cashier had given her the receipt. We almost lost our toes because of that.

A couple nearby was arguing with one another in hushed tones, trying—and failing—to keep their voices low. A little girl, whom I presumed was theirs, was dumping boxes of sugary pink cereal into their cart in the meantime.

Two boys had gotten into a bag of chocolate bon bons. They were racing up and down the aisles yelling at the top of their lungs. I recognized the signs of a sugar rush at once, having experienced it a few times as a kid myself.

I sighed and kept moving. "Every year," I muttered as we passed a lady digging credit cards out of her purse. "It's the same damn thing every single year."

"I never want kids," Jean said suddenly, surprising me with the shift in topic. "I hope that's not a deal-breaker for you. We haven't talked about it before."

There was a horrific crash from behind us. One of the boys, riding high on his cocoa and sugar wave, had knocked down a display. A stocker saw this, but merely rolled her eyes and went back to what she was doing. I couldn't say I blamed her.

"I think I'll manage without them," I said, moving along.

Jean laughed. "Good," he said. "I'd rather keep you all to myself. And besides, I'm already having to face your mom today. Explaining to her that I had gotten you pregnant wouldn't endear me much."

I stopped dead in my tracks and doubled over. The comment,

especially the dry way that Jean said it, made me cackle. That drew a couple of looks, one from a father who had been trying to placate his three-year old son who was dressed in a skeleton costume.

"Sorry," I said, leaning over into Jean as we continued. "I was just imagining her face. That would definitely take some creative truth-telling."

Looking around, I made sure no one was watching us anymore. We were out of sight of the little munchkins racing about as well, so I felt safe. Reaching over, my hand took hold of Jean's sculpted behind and squeezed it.

"But feel free to keep trying," I added in a lower voice.

Jean snaked one arm around me to pull me even closer. "Don't worry," he said huskily. "I fully intend to!"

The candy aisle was easy enough to find. There were only banners and signs all over the store pointing toward it. Cheap decorations hung from above on fake spider webs. A couple of them had fallen and were trampled beneath the crowd of hungry holiday shoppers.

"Here we go," Jean said.

We were only a little ways into the aisle. The most expensive candy was near the middle. All of the inexpensive packs had been placed on the lower shelf near the mouth of the candy alley. The idea, I assumed, was that people would see other things that they liked on their way to the good stuff.

"Mission accomplished," I said as Jean cradled several bags in his left bicep. "Let's go!"

"Actually," Jean said, stopping me in mid-turn. "I'd like to get some new sandals. For both of us."

I could feel my forehead wrinkle as I looked back over my shoulder. "Why?" I asked, confused. "It's not like we're going to the beach."

"Not for the beach," Jean said, shaking his head. "For…"

He paused, remembering then that we weren't alone. Jean's eyes darted around at the various people cluttering up the candy aisle. There were a lot of kids there as well, which I was sure influenced his decision.

"C'mon," he said, motioning for me to follow. "This way."

I obliged, finding myself being led over to the health food section a few aisles down. "In here," he said, waving me on ahead. "Nobody ever comes here during Halloween."

"Okay," I said, slowing my pace once we were a few steps in. "What's going on? This is a bit weird even for you."

Jean walked ahead of me a few more steps, stopping about a third of the way down. "They're for the bathhouse party, remember?"

I had actually forgotten all about it. The lunch date with Mom had taken up much of my thought process over the last couple of weeks, primarily because of all the cajoling it took to get Jean to agree to go. Anything else had gone on the back burner.

A couple months ago, after Pride but before the end of our "grace" period, Jean and I each received an e-mail. It was an advertisement for a new bathhouse in the Castro. They were having a major event starting on Thursday night. It would continue all the way over into the Day of the Dead, which I was happy to see.

"We're still going," Jean said, though he phrased it more like a question. "We paid for the entry fee ahead of time. The tickets came yesterday."

We had, in fact, gotten the e-mail with our confirmations. I had completely forgotten about that.

"Is going really such a good idea, though?" I asked, keeping my voice down. "I mean, for health reasons."

"We're both fully vaccinated," Jean said, looking a little confused by my concern. "And they're only letting people with V-cards in that week."

"What about the latest booster?" I said.

We had both tried to get appointments. The trouble was that the new shots were in high demand. Pharmacies were booked solid for several months. This was, admittedly, good news in a way. People were taking the new vaccine boosters seriously, but having to wait so long was highly annoying.

"Neither one of us has gotten sick," Jean pointed out. "I mean, we're some of the only ones wearing masks now. And it isn't like the aisle we just left was practicing social distancing."

There hadn't been enough room in the candy row to sneeze, which was a good thing since it meant the threat of spreading disease was minimized.

"What's the matter?" Jean pressed, getting concerned now. "Did you change your mind?"

"I just…" I stammered, struggling with my words.

The truth was, I wasn't *that* worried about getting sick. It was cause for concern, sure, but Jean was right about our status and the safety procedures in place at the event. We could afford to let ourselves have a few nights of wild fun.

In theory, anyway. The e-mails promoting the event had come at a time when our relationship was in the early days. Back then, I had a difficult time saying "no" to Jean. The fact that I wound up dating—and living with—my old porn crush was still hard to believe.

I wanted to do whatever I could to please him. It was embarrassing because I wound up doing a lot of things simply for Jean's sake. Anybody could see that this was a red flag.

In the end, though, I began standing up for myself. It wasn't like Jean had been forcing the issue. I simply had to regrow a vertebrae and start speaking my mind.

Granted, I still had trouble doing that every now and again.

Case in point, I took a deep breath. "I've never been to a bathhouse before," I stated, looking Jean squarely in the eye as I carefully formed the words.

Jean's eyes widened slightly, but then something else called his attention. He was looking over my head—an easy feat given how tall he was. I turned and spotted what he was so focused on.

A woman was standing several feet away from us. She must have come down the aisle from the other side. My statement had stopped her dead in her tracks. She was looking at me now while holding on to her cart. Her other hand clutched a box of powdered fish. Clearly, she was unsure of what to do in this situation.

I must admit that I had some doubts about that myself.

"So much for privacy," Jean muttered, lowering his head somberly. "Maybe we should take this show on tour instead?"

"Anything that gets me out of this awkward situation," I replied, already walking past the lady with the powdered fish wearing a red face the whole time. "And by that, I mean life itself."

The lady let out a chuckle as I beat a hasty retreat. "I've never been in one either," she called out before I reached the end of the aisle. "A good friend of mine is a transman and he says they're loads of fun."

"Emphasis on the word 'loads'," Jean teased, making my face burn redder. "I couldn't have put it better myself."

I willed the floor to open up and swallow me. Unfortunately, Mother Earth was being uncooperative today. Jean took the lead, guiding me with one hand on my shoulder. The candy he had scrounged was still tucked underneath his other arm.

"I wish you had said something before," he said quietly while we navigated through the store, never stopping for more than a few seconds to allow someone else to pass by us.

"You would have thought I was lame," I confessed, revealing my fear right there in Trader Joe's. "That was what worried me, anyway."

"I don't think you're lame," he replied. "We didn't have the same experiences. I came out when I was twenty by doing…well, you know."

Jean was keenly aware of where we were still. I was grateful for that. A conversation about his porn career should not happen in a retail chain.

Conversations about bathhouses weren't such a great idea either. "And I was able to take a gay date to prom," I said, seeing where this was going. Unfortunately, it still made me a little uncomfortable. "Did you even date when you were…you know?"

"I mean, 'date' is probably the wrong word for it," he said, looking sheepish for the first time. "It wasn't just that I was a bit of a free agent, though."

"What do you mean?" I was genuinely curious. "Didn't people in your line of work still have relationships?"

"They did," Jean admitted, glancing down at me. "But, well…it's difficult to explain. We were in the middle of the HIV crisis and the government was still dragging their feet doing anything about it."

"Sounds familiar," I noted dryly.

"No kidding," Jean agreed as we turned a corner. His arm gave my shoulder a squeeze, which felt amazing. "Back then, everyone was angry. People wanted to fight back."

"I get that." I was starting to feel as though I were losing my grip on the conversation, though. "People today are still angry. That hasn't gone away."

"No, and that is good," Jean said softly in my ear. "But the anger was fresh. The best way to fight back was to *be* gay. To show the whole world who you were without compromise. Even if it means people would condemn you in the news or threaten your life in public."

A shudder went through me at the thought. "So…" I was hoping I understood what Jean was telling me. "Being gay, being overly sexual and promiscuous even though it was dangerous, was the way to fight back?"

"One of them, yes." Jean planted a quick kiss on the side of my head which got us a smile from a man shopping with his wife. "It's why p— why my job was so important in the nineteen-nineties."

I waited until the coast was clear before speaking again. "I can't imagine bathhouses were safe spaces in those days," I whispered to him once we were on a clear aisle.

"They weren't," Jean stated sharply. "But they were important nevertheless. People wanted them to be shut down. They had been trying that for years, so it felt like just another excuse."

I tried to think about what Jean was saying. It seemed unfathomable that I would not tell Mom about my sexuality. Yes, it was awkward and embarrassing, but I would have told her eventually. And yes, there were people who made fun of me in high school, but that wasn't new. The vast majority were surprisingly cool with it overall.

"Did you ever tell your family that you are gay?" I asked, almost afraid of the answer.

"Eventually, I did." Jean's face did not look happy. "It…wasn't a pleasant experience. There are other reasons, but that's the main one for why I don't have much contact with them."

I hugged Jean tightly. "I'm sorry," I said, meaning it.

Jean slowed his pace so he could pull me to him again. I felt him bury his face in my hair for a moment, breathing my scent in deeply. The warmth from his larger, muscular body seemed to wrap about me, protecting me.

"I have a better family now," he said huskily.

We stood there in each other's arms until we were forced to move. A couple wanted to drive their cart past us so they could reach the canned peaches. Trader Joe's wasn't the best place to have a moment together.

"We should have had this conversation in the car," I said.

Jean understood me even though my voice was muffled from pressing my face into his chest. "They'll live," he dismissed. "I'm glad we're having it now. Waiting until we reached the car would take too long."

He pushed on me slightly so that I raised back. "Have you seen the lines in this place?" he asked, staring down at me with heated eyes.

"I'm seeing something else I like better," I teased, kissing him once quickly on the lips before bringing him back into a fierce hug.

Jean's arms felt warm and strong around me. He could wrap me up in them and still have room for the bags of trick 'r treat candy. I would have stayed that forever, feeling the power in his curled biceps and the thickness of his chest.

Unfortunately, the mood was ruined when some punk twink shoved me. "Sorry," he said, not sounding remotely like it. "'Scuse me."

I pitched forward. Jean's body stopped me from sprawling face-down on the floor, but he was unprepared for the shift in my weight. It didn't send him careening into the jars of maraschino cherries, thankfully.

However, Jean did take a step backward right as an impatient new mother was racing her cart down the aisle. She managed to avoid mowing him over, but Jean proved too big a target to avoid getting clipped on the thigh.

"Ahh, dammit!" he cried out.

"Language," the lady barked, indicating the snoozing baby—a miracle in and of itself given that we were in a grocery store—in the basket.

Jean took stock of this as well. "Of course," he said dryly, rubbing the spot where her cart had bruised him. "What was I thinking? A thousand apologies, ma'am."

The last word had enough salt to have come from beneath the Red Sea. The insult did not go unnoticed, either. The woman bristled and gave both of us a thoroughly disapproving stare before storming off.

I should have been offended, but I was too busy searching the aisle for someone else. "Now where'd that little turd scamper off to?" I asked aloud.

Jean's face softened somewhat when he heard me. "Over there," he said, tapping me on the shoulder.

I turned and saw the direction he indicated. "Oh," I said, noticing that he was nearly to the mouth of the aisle. The wine mom who had almost committed vehicular homicide with a grocery cart was fast approaching him, and—I saw—wasn't paying attention.

"Should we warn them?" I asked.

"And spoil the fun?" Jean replied, enjoying himself. "And in three... two...one!"

The collision was hardly the stuff of legend, but it was entertaining all the same. The twink—a blond dye job dressed in a tank top and booty shorts—stepped back from the shelf with a box of raisins in his hand. The timing of this could not have been more perfect. The lady didn't look up until after she plowed her cart into him.

Two cans of peaches went flying out of his hands. They clattered onto the floor, rolling a few feet before stopping underneath the wheels of the cart. The box of raisins somehow came open at the same time. A shower of them rained down all over the wine mom.

Some landed inside the baby seat. Her child had managed to sleep through two collisions, but woke up spontaneously when pelted with health food.

That said a lot about the kid, I thought.

"Oh, thanks so very fucking much!" the woman yelled as her child proceeded to scream bloody murder, loud enough to be heard in the frozen food section on the far side. "See what you did?"

The twink had been bending over to pick something up off the floor. "Me?" he demanded indignantly. "Why don't you watch where you're going, Miss Thing!"

"Is 'Miss Thing' making a comeback?" I wondered, finding the whole comedy of errors funny.

"It isn't," Jean said, chuckling. "But we'll allow it. This isn't the first stripper I've come across who was trying to sound hip by using outdated slang."

"What?" I asked, looking from where the twink was over to my boyfriend. "How can you tell that—"

Jean was smiling as he pointed at the two who were arguing. "Short shorts and a tank top," he began explaining, having to talk louder. "He's comfortable showing off his body and being almost naked in public."

The outraged wine mom struggled in vain to get her cart to move around the canned peaches blocking the wheel. Jean continued to explain as she cursed in frustration. Despite the crying, I was sure her infant child heard her.

"Second," he went on, "his legs and arms are incredibly toned. Not only that, you can see that there's a lot of strength to them. He doesn't just work out. That boy has to use those muscles regularly."

"Meaning he's a dancer," I said, following along.

The wine mom, meanwhile, had begun trying to kick the canned peaches away from her cart. She had little success, as her feet kept coming in contact with the wheels instead. This did nothing to sage her temper, but it did clue the twink in that he should make his egress.

"Three," Jean was saying. "The blond dye job."

"Huh?" That part confused me. "What about it?"

"Blond hair shows up better in a dark room with minimal lighting," he explained, like he had been anticipating the question. "When you work for singles, you want to be seen."

All of his reasoning made sense. Plus, I knew that Jean had stripped in addition to doing porn during his career. Hell, our first date was at a temporarily re-opened gay club where I watched him perform.

"Anything else?" I asked, knowing how much Jean loved being right.

"He can also move," Jean added, wincing slightly as he brushed a hand across his thigh. "The kid managed to get ahead of the road-raging shopper. Quick movements and a good sense of balance are good tools to have when you're shaking your ass on a slippery bar top."

I looked again and saw that the angry wine mom had moved on. Raisins were scattered all over the mouth of the aisle. The cans of peaches had been left behind. Clearly, the stripping twink felt they weren't worth recovering.

"Let's get out of here," I decided. "That was more than enough drama for one morning. We still have to pay for our stuff before we head on to Mom's place."

Jean rolled his eyes. "If we're meeting your mother," he warned. "This won't be the last bit of drama you deal with today."

I ignored his bellyaching and pressed forward. The lines for the aisles were backed up, but that was hardly unexpected. To my surprise, we ended up standing behind the blond twink. I had half a mind to tell him off, but figured the wine mom had already done the job for me.

"Twizzlers," Jean whispered in my ear, pointing at the twink's sole surviving purchase he had brought with him. "Another clue that he works hard for the money. They're great for giving you energy without making you bloat."

My face turned into a scowl. "Okay," I hissed back. "I heard you the first time. He's a stripper. No need to pile-drive the point home."

The twink continued to ignore us. Most people would have been offended at having someone suggest they danced naked for a living. This guy didn't bat an eye, or even turn around.

As usual, Jean was right.

The twink was making an irritating crunching sound. A candy bar, half unwrapped, lay in one hand. He was munching on it noisily while we waited.

"Rude," Jean stated. "He could have waited. The line isn't that long."

I patted Jean's arm in response. "Don't be the grouchy old man who disparages today's youth for their life choices," I said softly. "So long as he pays for it, it's fine."

"He needs an attitude adjustment," Jean insisted, an edge creeping into his voice. "I'd sure love to give it to him."

"I'm sure you would." My voice took on a teasing note. "But you're retired and in a relationship now. So it's his loss."

I felt Jean's hand snake down the length of my arm. He was still rubbing the spot on his thigh where the cart grazed him. I worried momentarily, but trusted he would tell me if it was a serious injury. Instead, I focused on the warmth coming from his hand as he held mine.

We moved forward together, crawling toward the cashier. The twink went first, naturally, dropping his Twizzlers and a single can of peaches that he'd evidently salvaged from his own impact. The candy bar had already been consumed.

I watched him pocket the wrapper, not even bothering to hide the evidence. A smear of chocolate was spread across his lips. If the cashier noticed, she said nothing.

"Huh," I said, feeling a little let down. "I guess you were right after all."

The twink paid in cash. It took a moment for the cashier to count all of the bills. Jean seemed pleased by this.

"Singles," he said when I looked at him curiously. "What did I tell you?"

The cashier handed the twink his change. He accepted it, stuffed the coins into the pocket of his short shorts, and grabbed up the two items that he paid for. I ignored him as he made his way for the exit, wanting to get out of there. An embarrassing conversation followed by watching my boyfriend get injured by a rampaging wine mom were enough excitement for one day.

"Expecting a lot of trick-or-treaters this year?" the young woman in front of the register asked, giving her voluminous brown hair a quick shake.

"Something like that," I said. "And if we don't, there's more for us the next day."

"I hear you," she agreed, laughing as Jean drew out his card to pay with. "My kids are so excited. They love Halloween."

"I think I'm too old at this point," I joked. "But if I ever need a costume, Mom still has a few of mine in storage. We're on our way to see her for lunch."

I paused, nodding in the direction of Jean, who had gone stiff. "He's meeting the parents for the first time," I revealed in a none-too-subtle conspiratorial whisper.

Jean winced. "Pray for me," he asked the cashier as she passed the card back to him.

This earned him a light smack on his well-developed abs from me. "Quit your whining," I ordered, gathering up our things. "We're going."

The cashier was biting her lower lip as we walked toward the door. Jean had gone quiet, resolutely refusing to speak to me. I wasn't too upset as we walked out under the mother star, shielding our eyes momentarily from the bright light.

"Where did we—"

I was cut off by the dull roar of an electric motorcycle. It all happened so fast that my brain couldn't process. Someone came whizzing past us on the bike. A helmet concealed their face and the jacket they wore was bulky, making it hard to tell which gender they ascribed to.

I noticed that they were driving with one hand. The reason was because the other held a gun. Jean's hands fell down hard on my shoulders, taking hold of me. I felt myself being wrenched back away from the edge of the pavement as the driver took aim.

Pandemonium reigned. Shots were fired and people screamed. I could see none of what was happening. My body was falling backward, held tightly by Jean. Shock went through my body as we landed hard on the concrete.

I blinked, fighting to breathe against the fear and how tightly Jean was holding me to him. Dimly, as if in the distance, I could hear the motorcycle engine again. It was roaring away from the crime scene.

"Wha…" I breathed out, too stunned to form a complete word.

My heart was hammering in my chest. It felt like I couldn't breathe. My vision swam in front of me as I gazed around in a stupor. I realized I was crying.

I was also okay. The bullets hadn't so much as grazed me. I didn't even have a scrape thanks to Jean turning his body so that he fell first, cushioning my fall.

"Oh my god!" I screamed, struggling to free myself. "Jean! Jean, can you hear me? Baby, please tell me you're okay!"

I was frantic. Jean couldn't be hit. I couldn't live in a world where he died like this. It made no fucking sense whatsoever. He couldn't have taken a bullet.

"I'm okay," I thought I heard him say.

Even then, I was still caught in the grip of a wild panic. It took him shaking me before I started calming down.

"I'm okay," Jean repeated, looking me straight in the eye. "The biker wasn't aiming for us."

That helped me think a little more rationally. "They weren't?" I asked. "You mean, you're okay? Wait, how do you even know that?"

In answer, Jean pointed behind me. I was afraid to turn around in his arms and look. His expression was so grave. Whatever was behind me, it was bad.

I knew that before I saw. The twink was lying face-down. Half of his body had fallen onto the pavement. The other half, his lower half, was hanging on to the curb.

It was hard to tell where he had been hit. I couldn't see a bullet wound anywhere. There was no doubt that he was dead, though. His body wasn't moving, and a puddle of blood had already begun forming.

I watched as it washed over the concrete. A yellow candy bar wrapper was lying next to the dead young man. The blood pooled under it, soaking the plastic wrapper and dying it red.

It looked like we weren't going to make it to Mom's after all.

Chapter 3

The sign above the front door read *Treats*.

This was the name of the newest gay bathhouse to debut in the Castro District. Once upon a time, it would have been just one in a long list of such establishments taking up about half the area. Gay bathhouses used to be one of the things that this part of San Francisco was famous for.

But, a combination of the ongoing HIV pandemic, another, more recent pandemic that the world was still reeling from, and middle-class tourists coming to the wrong assumption that a gay ghetto must work like an animated musical meant businesses had to adjust their sales pitch a bit.

Some of the racier things about the Castro had been dialed back in recent years, or so I was told. This was one of the reasons why the Dog-Eared Doorstopper, where I was still currently employed, put its more indelicate material on the second floor. Visitors to the Golden Gate city wanted to bring their eight-year old kids here. A triple-X gay porn store with posters of naked men on the windows wasn't exactly family-friendly material.

The irony that one of the most famous gay neighborhoods on the planet had to dial back the very essence of what made it so that straight people would feel comfortable was not lost on anyone with half a brain cell.

The censorship didn't happen all at once, though. Up until several years ago, the Castro was one of the few areas left in San Francisco where clothing-optional laws applied. Two sex shops on Castro &

Market survived the purge as well. But the wilder days of the Castro that I'd only heard about through previous generations was long gone.

This was perhaps best reflected in the building. "This is it?" I wondered, standing at the street's edge with Jean's warm body radiating heat next to me. "I guess I was expecting something…"

Words failed me at that moment. "Grander?" I tried, embarrassed at my lack of loquaciousness. "Or at least something other than pale gray exterior."

Jean gave me that smile I found so annoying, like I'd just said something cute. "The important stuff is what goes on inside," he explained, taking me by the hand. "What's on the outside is irrelevant."

Together, we began making our way across the street. Our footsteps clip-clopped together across the asphalt path, creating a rhythm that made me smile. Treats had parking spaces available, but like most designated areas in the city, there wasn't space to put more than a dozen or so vehicles.

"Besides," Jean added as we reached the other side. "Places like this try not to draw too much attention to themselves. It's safer that way."

I shuddered a little at the implication, although that was only part of the problem. It was barely nighttime, but the cold winds from the coastline had found their way through the maze of city buildings. Instinctively, I moved in closer to Jean.

We both turned at the same time, continuing on past the Bank of America. It and the Wells Fargo helped illuminate Treats with their illustrious neon anthems to capitalism. Across from Treats was a Citibank, completing the unholy trinity.

"Shouldn't there at least be a line?" I asked as we drew up near the front entrance.

"Outside of a bathhouse?" Jean gave me a look this time. "Sweetie, I love you. But no one in the Castro—or out of it—would be caught dead waiting to get in."

I wasn't completely naive, and I said as much. "I get that," I replied, feeling aggravated, and wondering not for the first time if this was such a good idea. "But this is supposed to be a party. People should be outside chit-chatting or seeing if they can sneak a peek at one of their favorite adult celebrities."

I stopped outside the front door, only in part to help prove my point. "This looks like a party I tried to throw back in high school," I said, feeling apprehensive about what lay beyond the door in front of us. "Only about six people showed. I'd hate to think we paid money for something this…"

"Boring?" Jean offered when I hesitated.

"Yeah," I admitted as a blush crept up my neck. "I thought people would be excited. We're finally moving away from quarantine a little. Human contact isn't a death sentence anymore."

Jean placed a kiss on my temple gently. "I get your meaning," he assured me. "And I'm sorry that I made you feel smaller. That wasn't my intent."

Hearing him say as much helped. "Thank you," I replied, giving his thick forearm a meaningful squeeze.

"There's almost always a lobby inside the main entrance," he informed, nodding at the door ahead of us. "Guests will wait around in there. Or they'll come back later after the crowd thins out."

My nervousness had not abated yet. I was still shivering slightly from the cold. Feeling cold and scared at the same time was playing hell with the rest of my emotional state. I was seriously starting to regret this.

"I hadn't realized until now how excited I was for this," I said, swallowing my pride. "Having other people around who were also excited made me feel better, even if it was all in my head."

Jean hugged me, pouring his warmth into my bones. "We can go home if you want," he whispered in my ear. "There's no pressure. Just say the word."

I seriously considered it. It hadn't occurred to me until then how much I was looking forward to this. Nik and I missed out on our wild swinger days during college. I wasn't old enough before that to visit most of the "adult" gay things to do in town. I wasn't brave enough to sneak into them on my own either.

A part of me felt foolish. I had agreed to this because Jean was excited to go. It was also a chance to live a more adventurous lifestyle, the kind my boyfriend had when he was my age.

"I…" I began, but a thought interrupted me. I had been on the verge of telling Jean that I wanted to go home when an image flashed before my eyes. "Let's do it."

I was seeing the young twink outside Trader Joe's. More specifically, I was remembering how dead his eyes were after the bullets pierced his chest. One had gotten him right in the heart. He died almost instantly.

"Life is short," I went on, feeling a need to justify myself. "We never know how much time we have left. One night of fun won't kill us, right?"

"No, it won't." Jean was trying to hide it, but I could tell he was relieved. "But any time you feel like it's too much. Or if you're ready to leave—"

Smiling, I placed a finger on his lips. "I'll say the word," I promised. "Thank you for giving me the kill switch on the evening. It means a lot."

"We're here to have fun," Jean said, looping his arm through mine and walking me slowly over to the door. "That's not gonna happen if one of us is miserable. Especially you."

"Oh, such a smooth talker," I teased, going in first. "Keep that up and you'll have me wondering what your ulterior motives are."

Jean was smirking as he entered after me. "No ulterior motives here," he stated, not bothering to keep his voice down. "My motive is to have sex with you as much as possible and in as many places as we can."

My face must have taken on the shade of a tomato. It burned hot enough to feel like an overcooked one, at least. To take my mind off how bashful I was being, my gaze wandered around.

The walls had been painted different shades of red. Each hue crisscrossed with the other, forming block patterns. There was a streak of white as well, keeping the lobby from being too dark. Plenty of light shined down from track bulbs on the ceiling. It gave the space an artsy vibe, like I was at a museum or a studio.

Framed posters and pictures hung on the wall, helping to codify the illusion. All of them displayed nude artwork of men. In contrast with the poetic eloquence of the walls, these depictions looked as if they belonged in a temple.

There were men of all sizes, shapes, and body types. Each poster or framed photograph glorified the male figure. Staring at them made me think that the camera lens was worshiping the subjects. The intensity of it made the room hum with an unreleased energy that caused the hairs on my arm to rise.

Jean had been right about the lobby. It wasn't exactly packed, but there were plenty of people standing around waiting their turn. None of the faces were familiar to me, but I hadn't exactly been a social butterfly this year.

Jean and I spent the first couple months in our relationship being wrapped up in one another. Before that, I was struggling to make ends me and trying to salvage what turned out to be a dying relationship. There was also quarantine to factor in. Altogether, it wasn't shocking that so many new faces were in the Castro scene.

Something resembling a line was taking up the bulk of the lobby area. It didn't help that the lobby area was small. Everyone stood staring with the same anxious energy at a cashier window on the far wall. One poor soul had been left to check IDs, confirm vaccination statuses, and scan bank cards. He didn't exactly look frayed, but I could tell the young man had been at it for a while.

"Got everything we need?" Jean asked as we took our places at the back of the line—or the bulge of male flesh that passed for one.

"They have towels, you said," I began, listing off what I could remember. "We both have sandals. We brought our own lube—water-based since silicon lubricants aren't allowed. Everything we don't need can go in a locker."

I paused, thinking. "These places have lockers, right?" I added, asking the man who seemed to have all the answers this evening.

The tickets we bought gave us access to the special VIP area on the third floor. Everyone else was separate. Now that we were here, it felt like highway robbery.

"They do," he assured me. "But we'd be better off paying extra for a room."

"How come?" I wondered, taking a step forward as the guy at the front of the line moved aside so he could enter through the door next to the teller-style window. "Lockers are cheaper, aren't they?"

"They are," Jean confirmed. "But a room would be better."

I was confused. It felt like he wasn't telling me everything. I suppressed the annoyance bubbling up inside of me and resolved to approach this issue like an adult.

"How come?" I asked Jean insistently. "It's not like we're spending the night, right? What are you not telling me?"

A twitch pulled at the corner of my boyfriend's mouth. "I'm not entirely sure how...spontaneous you're feeling tonight," he began. "Rooms offer more privacy if you decide that you want to have some fun with me, but aren't interested in showing off."

He was keeping his voice down. We were standing in the lobby of a place where men came to have sex. And Jean, former porn star extraordinaire, was keeping his voice low to spare me from embarrassment.

"Too bad we didn't cultivate this ability to be discreet while we were shopping for candy," I muttered. "But you're right. It's unlikely that I'll suddenly develop an exhibition streak tonight."

For some reason, Jean chuckled. "Says the man," he whispered, bending down to tickle my ear, "who agreed to have sex on a balcony with me a few months ago."

My face was back to burning red. "I...that was..." No explanation for my behavior back then was forthcoming. "I was just going through a phase."

Jean was laughing low and huskily now. "Too bad," he replied, his words caressing the skin along my shirt collar. "I rather enjoyed our fun time in the backstage area of Nob Hill."

Once again, I wanted the earth to swallow me up. "You're horrible," I snapped, growing irritated at his teasing.

"And you're too sexy for words," he said as the line moved forward.

I ignored Jean until we reached the counter. It wasn't easy, either. I had to bite down on my lower lip to keep from responding when he began playing grab-ass with me. Worse, the line wasn't exactly moving forward at a steady pace.

The man behind the counter kept asking guests to pull more stuff out of their wallets. It seemed Treats personnel were serious about guests showing proof of vaccination. I was glad of that. Jean and I were all set, but I saw him turn away at least one person. The people who made it through, on the other hand, had to leave their identification at the desk to be picked up when they checked out.

"This must have been what getting a check cashed was like back in the day," I noted, watching while the next person up front removed an insurance card, a vaccination card, and what might have been a library card while hunting for his driver's license.

"It only feels like that," Jean replied, still keeping his voice lower. "Getting a check cashed was actually much, much worse!"

I laughed softly, feeling my anger with him abate. "I'll take your word for it," I said as the line moved further up.

Not everyone had paid for tickets ahead of time. So far, it looked like the people ahead of us were here for a good time, event or not. They were also getting restless. One fellow who was older than Jean moved out of the line and brushed past us, going for the exit. Another, the one who had been behind him, kept tapping his foot impatiently.

"Feels like we're in line for train tickets," I whispered to Jean as we again took a step forward. "Or for *Frozen: The Musical*."

"No one is this excited for that," Jean retorted sarcastically. But then he thought for a moment. "I mean about train tickets. Speaking of—"

"Maybe," I said, cutting him off as we trudged along closer to the window. "My job doesn't pay much. And, no offense, but your paintings barely help Auntie Mags out."

His strong hands were on my shoulders suddenly, massaging them. "We can afford to be good to ourselves," he insisted softly. "Once in a while."

I sighed, feeling like the bad guy. "I just don't want to end up in the same situation like I was before," I confessed, trying to resist how good his hands felt. "Struggling every month. Fighting to stay afloat. And living in fear of what the next couple months will be like."

Jean gave both shoulders a tender squeeze. "It's not going to be like that," he said, keeping his voice low and his head close to mine. "Lover, you're still dealing with a lot of PTSD from quarantine."

I went still, tensing up in preparation for a lecture. "And that's okay," Jean went on, surprising me. "But I'm here now and you're not going to go through anything alone."

It was several deep breaths before I was calm. The last thing I needed was to break down and cry in the lobby of a gay bathhouse. That would have ruined the mood. I didn't want to be a killjoy. Hell, the whole reason we were here was to have fun, and I wasn't being a very fun person for some reason.

"I'm sorry," I said softly.

"Stop apologizing," Jean said, giving my shoulders another squeeze. "You're not a bad person. And you didn't do anything wrong."

I wasn't convinced right away. "I feel like I'm bringing the mood down," I explained, keeping my head low and my eyes pointed at the ground. "We're here to have fun and I'm worried about money."

His arms were around me in a second. I felt the itch of his thick beard against my neck. Jean squeezed me tightly, as if willing the anxiety to leave my body. I let myself fall back against his strength. He was always holding me up like this.

"We can have fun anytime," he said, giving my ear a nip to emphasize his point. "The offer still stands. You wanna leave?"

Before I could give Jean an answer, we had arrived. The man in front of us turned to the right and marched through the double doors leading to the back. I found myself staring past the slightly stained glass of the window at the young man behind it.

He looked to be a couple years older than I was. A round, innocent-looking face was framed by a pair of ears that were just a little bit too large for the rest of his body. His hair was cut short, but a long pair of bangs fell forward into his face.

Those bangs couldn't quite hide the dark eyes that stared out at me. In that moment, I felt like this guy had seen a lot. He was young with a compact, sexy body, but a maturity lurked beyond the seemingly-wholesome face he wore.

"Welcome to Treats," he said in a tone that would not have sounded out of place coming out of an old drive-thru speaker. Standing there, I felt like I was hearing the Gobi desert dry out. "Membership is fifty dollars for six months, card or cash. Lockers are an additional five dollars. Bedrooms are—"

"We ordered ahead of time," I jumped in with, cutting the guy off before my soul died from how utterly bored he sounded. "Two tickets, for the event?"

As I was speaking, my hand went south—not that way—into my jeans pocket. I managed to retrieve my phone without dropping it and quickly tapped out the unlock code on the screen. Once it was working, I pulled up the two tickets that Jean and I bought months ago.

"See?" I asked, holding the screen up in front of the glass.

The dark-eyed young man stared past his bangs and the glass. "Right," he said crisply after confirming that I was being honest. "Sorry about that. Not everyone here tonight bought tickets."

There was only a modicum of life in his voice now. He seemed to perk up for a second while apologizing. Every word afterward, though, slipped further and further back into tedium.

"Tickets?" someone behind Jean and I called out. "We're supposed to have tickets?"

"Is this place throwing a party?" another asked, back near the wall.

"Can we order them online if they're already here?" shouted a third from somewhere in the cluster of bodies near the middle.

I gave Jean a very droll look. "It feels like we made a bigger deal out of this than it deserves," I muttered.

"Don't worry about it," the ticket booth operator informed, still speaking in the utterly bored tone he had been using the whole time.

I watched him scan the screen again. My phone was still pressed up against the glass. It only took him a moment to search for the ID numbers we were sent.

"Got 'em," he said, stifling a yawn. "Just need your state-issued IDs and vaccination cards."

Jean had already retrieved his. I stepped out of the way so that he could slide both underneath the window. As I was fishing my wallet out, something caught my attention. The ticket booth guy was staring straight ahead. His eyes had opened wide.

For the first time since I laid eyes on the young man properly, he looked wide awake. Furthermore, he was staring up at my boyfriend. One hand had fallen on top of the two cards Jean had given him, but it lay idle.

"You," he breathed out. I watched as his chest rose and fell quickly. "Oh, Jesus! Do…do you know who you are?"

Jean went very still then. "I have a feeling you're going to tell me," my boyfriend retorted, trying to make light of the situation. "But do me a favor and keep it down, would you?"

"I…" It didn't look like the ticket booth guy had heard. "You're Jean Locke Holmes, aren't you?"

His eyes turned from Jean over to me. "Isn't he?" the young man demanded. "Is that who he really is?"

A part of me felt pleased by this turn of events. "He is," I said while Jean gave me a look. "But my boyfriend is retired. Do me a favor and don't pass out. That was how we ended up dating and I'd hate for it to be the reason why he leaves me for you. Deal?"

I handed him my V-card and state ID. The movement seemed to snap him somewhat out of his trance. I was just grateful that the guy was finally injecting some emotion into his voice.

Unfortunately, he seemed unwilling to take his eyes off Jean. We stood there a moment longer while he fumbled around. All of our cards wound up scattering to the floor. It took him even longer to gather them all up as he kept banging his head on the counter top.

"Here," he said, sliding them back along with two keys with our room number looped into the ring. "You can go in. I don't need to see anything. My boss will flip when he finds out about this. And don't worry. The rooms are on the house!"

"Thanks," Jean said, putting our cards in his pocket. "I'm...very flattered and a little surprised that you know about my work."

That earned him an elbow to the side. "Hey," I reminded sternly. "I knew about your work too and we're practically the same age."

Jean threw some side-eye my way before clearing his throat. "Ahh, no. This fellow is nowhere near the same age as you. There's a pale spot on his left ring finger, indicating that he is or recently was married. His shirt is also neatly pressed, but a place like this wouldn't have that strict of a dress code. So he either has someone do it for him or is pressing it himself to get attention."

To think that only a few short months ago, I found this routine of Jean's charming. "Let's go," I said, taking hold of his hand. "And stop showing off. You're going to give someone a serious freak-out one of these days."

The young man turned like he was going to follow us. As we passed through the double doors, I saw him standing at a second booth. Moving with the speed of someone who was used to rushing, the young man seized two towels for us.

"My name's Justin!" he said, practically salivating as he held both white towels out to Jean. "The boss introduced me to your movies. He's gonna want your autograph."

Jean merely accepted the towels and kept going without a word. "Hey, call me!" I could hear Justin calling out with frantic adoration as Jean and I walked away. "My number's on the wall of Room 201. I have weekends off, y'know, in case you're interested."

The corridor past the double doors was similar to the lobby. Each wall was painted the same crisscrossing shades of red with white streaks. The framed photographs had been replaced by flatscreen televisions. Each was playing advertisements for strip shows. A cash machine stood off to the side in case guests found themselves low on funds. There were posters as well, for everything from warnings about mixing poppers with Viagra to advertisements for condoms and PrEP. All around us, a PA system wired into the building blared a techno mix that was just the same six beats played on a loop.

My hunch was that it was to help guests maintain a steady rhythm.

The lighting in the corridor was a great deal darker. I held on to Jean the whole time. The last thing I needed was to get lost wandering around a semi-dark gay bathhouse without an escort.

This sounded stranger in my head than I expected it to.

None of this could keep me from breaking down into a giggle fit. "Damn," I said, laughing once we were far enough away. "Of course you would be recognized at a gay bathhouse. What was I thinking?"

"This'll be all over the gossip websites come morning," Jean said. He didn't exactly sound happy about it either. "Half the community will be calling for my blood because they swear I'm encouraging unsafe sex practices."

I was used to this rhetoric by now. "And the other half," I finished sympathetically, knowing his feelings were justified, "will be wishing they had shown up."

A smile tugged at the corners of Jean's mouth. "True enough," he acknowledged while we rounded the bend in the corner. "Anyway, we came here to have fun. Not worry about what people think."

"If we were worried about what people think," I said as we passed by the locker area, "then we should've picked a better place than 'gay bathhouse' for our date."

My feet slowed to a stop.

"Say," I called out, getting Jean's attention. "Can we…"

Hearing me hesitate, Jean walked backward to my side. "See something you like?" he teased, placing a protective arm around my shoulders. "Or just browsing?"

Very lightly, I elbowed him in the side. "Nothing like that," I told him, meaning it. "I was just…wondering if we could…" My face flushed. "Make a quick pass through the locker area."

Jean frowned, but in a very comical way, which told me he was gearing up to give me a serious ribbing. "I suppose we could," he agreed amicably. "A little window shopping before the all-out orgy."

This time, the blow to his ribs was a great deal sharper. "Hush, you!" I ordered, steeling my nerves. If I was this apprehensive about looking around at men undressing, gods only knew what would happen when we came across men having sex.

And that was assuming they weren't having sex in the locker area. I had no prior experience to base this date on. For all I knew, we'd have to step lightly around the piles of screwing bodies in the hallways.

"Ow," Jean said, bringing me back to earth. "What gives? You okay, lover?"

I sighed, feeling the pangs of guilt stab at me deserving. "I'm nervous," I admitted. "And scared. I don't want to seem uncool during all of…"

My arms made wild, random gestures at the pictures on the wall. "This!" I finished helplessly.

Jean chuckled. "You're doing fine," he said, taking me gently by the hand. "Let's take things slow. A quick tour of the locker area is a great way to get your feet wet."

I felt considerably better thanks to the encouragement. With his hand in mine, we each turned and walked forward.

This part of the bathhouse was well lit, much better than the hallway. Several rows of bright red lockers stood before us. A number of men had found theirs and were in various stages of undress. None of them recognized Jean—or, if they did, they gave no obvious indication.

"One, shut up," Jean said when I pointed this out, borrowing a phrase he had heard me use as we strode past several locker corridors. "Two, you're right—"

"And three," I finished for him, "still shut up. Yes, yes. Heard it before. You had it coming after all the teasing you've put me through."

"I'd like to think I've more than paid my due after that elbow strike," he muttered back, rubbing one side with his free hand. "Sheesh, it still hurts!"

I refused to feel pity for him.

We turned at the last row, placed against what I presumed was the outer wall. Out of habit, I counted the numbers as we walked down between the two-tier stacks of storage units. A Chinese-American man with amazing eyes and a body that looked like it had less than two percent of fat looked up at the sound of our footsteps.

Our eyes met and at once I felt a chill run through me. It was powerful enough to make me slow to a stop. Blinking, I took a second glance.

He was shorter than me, which was saying something, but only by a couple of inches. A mop of hair, dark brown and cut short everywhere but the bangs in the front, concealed most of his forehead. The tips along his bangs had been dyed a bright red, bright enough to seem like it shone in the florescent light.

He was wearing a red speedo that left nothing to the imagination. Judging by the bulge there, this guy was packing some impressive heat. Twin dragons, colored gold, framed that impressive package. I found this an odd choice, but if he was okay with it, it wasn't my place to comment.

The rest of him was all muscle. Every curve and juncture looked like it had been carved out of marble. I could count the eight-stack of abs he sported as easily as I could the numbers on the lockers. Each one stood out prominently—again, as if they had been carved. Those things looked like they could crack walnuts.

"Sorry," I mumbled, embarrassed. He had been looking at me for a while, and I only just realized that I had been staring. "Excuse me."

I hurried off before I could make a bigger fool of myself. Jean was up ahead, about halfway down, leaning against the last couple of lockers. He was watching me the whole time I did my walk of shame.

"You know," he said as I hurried past, keeping my eyes firmly on the floor. "I came in here with the understanding that you'd see something you liked sooner or later."

"No talking," I uttered out, fighting off the urge to bury my head inside my shirt. "Not until we get to our room."

"What's the rush?" Jean's footsteps hurried as he came after me. "We've got all night."

The thought of spending the rest of the night in a perpetual state of bashful humiliation didn't help. I had yet to see what room we were staying in. This, of all things, got me to stop.

I was fishing around in my pocket when Jean bumped into me. Given how dim the corridor was, it wasn't a surprise. The problem was that I dropped my ring on the floor.

"Dammit," I groaned, feeling like an immature teenager at that moment. "Do you see where my key went? It has our room number on it."

"Three-zero-eight," Jean said, though he bent over with me to look. "I already checked."

Of course, he would have. Jean was an expert at this. I was the one fumbling around in the dark—literally at the moment—trying to find my way.

"I'm just not good at this," I said, raising up with the key in one hand. "Maybe…we should go home after all."

Jean didn't answer me right away. He was giving me a curious expression.

"Here," he said after a second more. "Lemme see your key. For just a second."

I frowned, but didn't fight when he reached for it. "Take the tab with the room number off," he explained, doing so with the key ring in front of my face so I could see. "Put the tab in your pocket and leave it somewhere you will see it once we get to the room."

"How come?" I wondered, confused at where this was going.

"So you can keep your key with you," Jean explained, passing mine back to me. "Towels are the dress code here, if that, and those don't come with pockets."

I watched Jean pause and look thoughtful. "Although," he added, "that wouldn't be a bad idea. But they're probably expensive, if they exist at all, so your best bet is to take the tab off."

"In case I lose the key," I said, following along his train of thought finally.

"Or someone steals it," Jean said darkly. "That does happen in these places. But without the tab, no one will know what room we're staying in. Unless you tell them, which also happens."

I gave Jean a shrewd look then. "I have the sneaky suspicion," I told him playfully, "that there are several stories behind why you have this habit."

"No comment," was all Jean would say, which was saying more than enough.

We went a bit further in, passing more flatscreens hanging from the walls. These were playing hardcore gay porn. I even recognized a couple of the studios that Jean did movies for

"It is a bit nostalgic," Jean admitted when I pointed this out.

We stopped together at an intersection in the hallway. To the right was a room with more dim florescent lights. A light whiff of steam waved down our way, tickling my nose. I could smell chlorine as well.

"Must be the steam room," Jean surmised. "Or the whirlpool room."

"Let's check it out," I suggested. "Maybe I'll calm down once I'm more familiar with this place."

Jean had no objections, taking my hand to guide me. We were only a few steps in when the steam grew thicker. I winced, feeling the denseness of the air in my lungs, as we walked through the door frame.

This space was much brighter compared to the corridors. It was still low-lit, but the light reflected better. Blue tiles covered the walls and ceilings, giving the space a very ambient vibe.

The whirlpool was in the center of the space. It wasn't all that different from what a high-dollar gym might offer. The water churned as the jets sprayed, causing the surface to bubble like a cauldron.

It was big too, large enough to fit five or six people. That capacity was being tested at the moment. Once my eyes adjusted to the steam, I counted somewhere between seven or eight men. All of them were naked and in the midst of a very hot and heavy makeout session.

Jean and I had just found our first orgy of the night.

Chapter 4

"Um, sorry!" I blurted out, beyond embarrassment at that point. "We didn't mean…I mean, I wasn't…not interrupting, I hope…"

My words trailed off. None of the men heard me. They were too preoccupied with getting as many of their limbs tangled up with each other. Hands were traveling all over, sliding in and out of orifices and places that rarely saw the light of day.

Above them, hanging on the back wall, was a sign. *No Physical Contact In The Whirlpool* was on display prominently. This rule was being flagrantly ignored.

"You're overreacting," Jean warned, though not unkindly. "Chances are, this was completely spontaneous."

I was too busy staring to take his words into consideration. The thing that struck me as odd was how *ordinary* all of the men look. Advertisements for bathhouses always depicted the guests as gym bunnies, the kind of men who worked out for several hours each day.

These guys could have come right off the street. Most of them, I realized, probably had.

They were of different ages as well. That was another thing I noticed. One or two might have been around my age. Another looked old enough to be married with kids. At least three were in their twilight years, sporting thinning silver hair and wrinkles on way more than their face.

"Wow," I breathed out, still not able to look away. "I guess, maybe… I expected an orgy to be louder."

Jean, of course, was nonplussed. "They're just getting started," he replied with a wave, not bothering to avert his gaze. "And, it varies from group to group."

It was then he became aware of my predicament. "Don't worry," he said while I struggled to find a place to put my eyes that wasn't rude. "If they didn't want to be watched, they'd get a room."

"But, still!" I insisted, which unfortunately meant that I stopped looking around and focused on Jean. That meant I turned back in time to see one of the guys bending over while another began eating his ass out. "Damn, this *is* just getting started."

Jean looked over his shoulder. "Pretty much," he told me. "They'll get really wild once the drugs start being passed around."

I blinked. "How?" I wondered. "I mean, how do you know that? About them just getting started, not the part about illegal substances."

Jean smirked at me. "There's no jizz in the pool," he stated plainly, loud enough that the others could have heard him.

"Ew." I made a face. "Well, I guess that's one thing we can cross off me trying tonight. No sense in going into the whirlpool if there's a splooge ball clogging up the pipes."

Jean laughed. "We can come earlier tomorrow night," he said, still sounding sure of himself. "They'll have drained the whirlpool and cleaned it by then."

"You're sure?" I asked, even though I believed him. I wanted to be reassured, and Jean seemed to know everything about how bathhouses worked. "I mean, really sure?"

"Positive," Jean insisted, getting slightly annoyed at my paranoia. "A bathhouse gets cleaned constantly. People come here to have sex, and sex—if you will recall—is very messy. So they have to maintain a constant cleaning schedule."

That made me feel a lot better, oddly enough. "Okay," I said, turning to leave. "We've seen, and I got more of an eyeful than I thought I would. Let's find our rooms now."

Jean followed, but didn't take me by the hand. He was acting offended. Having been in the sex worker industry for years, he had a right to be. There was tremendous prejudice against people in that line of work. Dating Jean had opened my eyes to so much of what was wrong with the way people were treated.

Granted, I was doing the same thing. A part of me felt bothered by that. However, I also felt that I had a right to know. It was important for both of us to be safe. I couldn't do that without asking the right questions.

This wasn't the sort of thing I wanted to show up on my Google search history either, though.

As we exited through the cloud of steam, someone collided with us. Specifically, they managed to avoid me somehow and slammed face-first into my boyfriend's chest.

"Oh, sorry!" Jean exclaimed, meaning it.

"Ah, watch where you're going," a man's voice barked. "Some of us are trying to w—"

His voice cut off unexpectedly. I heard the rude stranger gasp and take a step back. Curious, I followed his lead by moving forward, walking back into the dark corridor.

There was less light, but I could still see his face. The man was short, but still had an inch or two on me. His hair was a natural blond color, cut short and crisp. It told me he was busy a lot and didn't have time to manage it beyond a simple comb.

The most surprising thing about him was that he was fully dressed. A pair of dress slacks covered his legs. They might have been brown, but it was hard to tell in the darkened hallway. A blue shirt, buttoned up all the way to the top, covered his chest and sleeves.

He held a small tablet in one hand, but his face was staring straight ahead at Jean. "It's you!" he exclaimed.

I laughed. "Second one tonight," I told Jean, enjoying myself. "I wonder if we'll make it to our room without anyone else recognizing you."

The fellow with the tablet shook his head. "Sorry about that," he apologized. "I couldn't see very well and I was…well, it's been a rough night." A hand reached out to shake Jean's first, then mine. "My name is Michael Shaffeur," he introduced.

I gave the offered hand a shake. To my surprise, his fingers were ice cold. Going by the way Jean was flexing his fingers, he noticed too.

"I'm the talent coordinator," Michael added. I stared back, having no idea what he was talking about. "With Stud Stable, the male strip revue. They're hosting the party upstairs."

Michael's pale face turned downward into a frown, so I decided to play along.

"Right," I said, nodding. "Of course. That was on the website, right?"

"It had better have been," Michael muttered darkly. "Anyway, I didn't realize you two were guests. Please accept my apology."

"It's no problem," Jean said, although he looked toward me next. "Is it?"

"Not at all," I agreed. "We shouldn't be taking up your work time."

Michael shook his head, waving the tablet in my face in the process. "Don't worry about that," he insisted cheerfully. "Actually, I could use a break right now. Want me to give you the tour?"

I took a step back to get away from the steam Michael was fanning into my face. This put me closer to Jean, who reached out with one arm. I felt him pull me close to his side.

"That's not really necessary," I said, losing focus as the warmth from Jean's body chased away the remains of the chill in my fingers. "Is it, baby?"

"I mean," Jean protested. "You were wanting to have a look around. And we just met someone that's been working here all day."

Michael went still very suddenly. "How did you know that?" he pressed, staring at Jean hard.

"He does this," I explained to Michael, hoping it would calm him down. "All the time. He did it to me on our first date, even. He likes to show off."

Jean pointed down at Michael's feet. "Your shoes are untied," he began, listing off the reasons he knew Michael's work schedule and possibly even his birth sign. "Your shirt is very business-like, but you're soaked with sweat."

My boyfriend was right on both points. I could see the stains underneath Michael's pits. They were harder to notice in the dim light, but once Jean pointed them out, I spotted where the blue fabric was darker from absorbing all the moisture.

"The sweat says that you've been here a while," Jean went on. "And since you're fully dressed, that means you haven't been having fun. The fact that your shoelace is untied means you've been too busy running back and forth to take care of it."

Michael kicked one foot out reflexively, snapping the loose shoelaces like whips against the leather of his sneakers.

"You got me," he said, throwing both hands up. "That's pretty impressive, honestly. Have you taken up police work in your porn retirement?"

"Nothing so austintatious," Jean answered. "I have a history of not doing as I'm told. It makes for a poor police inspector."

"I see." Michael stroked his chin, looking thoughtful. "Well, come this way. I've had to be here since the crack of dawn so I know every part of this place like Chris Pratt's well-sculpted ass."

I held back just a moment. "I'm more partial to Chris Hemsworth myself," I called out.

Jean moved when I did, following along in Michael's footsteps. "Down there and to the left are the restrooms," he explained, pointing at the corridor we came from. "And the lockers. You've probably seen those already."

"We did," Jean affirmed. "But, we opted to pay extra for a room instead."

Michael gave Jean a thumbs-up. "Good man," he said, sounding pleased. "Lockers are far too risky."

"And they don't offer the privacy a room does," Jean added as we moved deeper into the building, away from the orgy in the whirlpool.

"Very true," Michael went on. "The shower area is up here, on the right. I have it on good authority that they were cleaned less than an hour ago. But you should still wear flip-flops if you have them."

"Way ahead of you," I said, holding ours up.

"Excellent." Michael gave me an appreciative nod before moving on. "Up here are the stairs. This complex does have an elevator, but it's for staff only."

It was hard to see in the darkened hallway. I spent a moment squinting through the gloom, fearful that I was going to trip over a step and land on my face. When we passed the showers, light spilled out from the open frame.

Chlorine and cleaneing chemicals assaulted my olfactory sense. The intensity of the light blinded me momentarily. However, I was still grateful for it. Once the initial lens flare faded, I was able to blink away the dots.

Standing there, it was much easier to see where we were. "I'm guessing that's the elevator?" I said, pointing at a set of sliding doors on the left next to the stairway entrance.

"Yup, goes all the way to the basement," Michael informed, playing his part as the tour guide well. "But, like I said, it's for employees of the bathhouse only. The rest of us slobs have to get in our cardio before we have fun."

Jean and I began ascending each step, keeping close to Michael the whole time. The stairway was narrow, giving it a claustrophobic feeling not unlike the entrance hallway. My shoulder would periodically brush against Jean's side—although that wasn't exactly a detriment.

Thankfully, we didn't meet anyone coming down. "They don't let you in either?" I wondered, offended on Michael's behalf. "That's rude."

"I'm the talent coordinator," Michael explained as we rounded the halfway point. "Technically, I rank higher than a guest, which means I have access to things like the front office and the VIP area."

"But for security reasons, they still keep you sectioned off from certain areas?" Jean asked, speaking up.

"That," Michael said as we neared the top. "And the basement is being renovated. Not sure what they've got planned for it. But I've instructed all dancers to stay out of there so no one gets hurt."

Michael paused as we all entered the second floor, one after another. The hallway we stood in was a repeat of the ones below. Each wall was painted black and adorned with erotic art. The framed paintings and posters were all of nude men in even more complicated sexual acts.

"We should think about hiring whoever did this place to redecorate the house," Jean mused humorously.

I made a face. "And what," I asked him dryly, "would Auntie Mags think?"

Jean laughed at my question. "She'd love it," he told me, being one-hundred percent serious.

I thought about that for a second. "You're right," I admitted, consigning defeat as usual.

Michael seemed amused by the two of us. "She sounds like fun," he said, turning around in a full circle on the spot. "Okay, straight ahead of us is the dark maze. If you keep going and turn to the right, the hallway will take you to your rooms."

"Just what we wanted to know," I said happily.

"And in the other direction," Michael went on, gesturing back behind us, "on the left is the dungeon. That's where you'll find the sex sling, padded sawhorse, and St. Andrew's Cross."

A knowing smirk was smeared across his face when his eyes met mine. "No judgment," Michael added, giving me a wink. "Just so you both know. In case you're into the kinky stuff."

"We're moving slowly," Jean explained unabashed.

I was far less confident. "Anything else?" I asked through my embarrassment.

Michael pointed one finger up toward the ceiling. "VIP area is on the third flood at the pool and outdoor deck," he said, nodding toward a second set of stairs beside the ones we came up. "That's where Stud Stable is set up too. I'm obligated to tell you that for business purposes."

"No harm there," Jean replied, looking at me. "What do you think? Want to check it out once we're settled in?"

"A pool sounds fun," I said. "Hopefully they didn't start the orgy without us."

Jean and Michael each raised an eyebrow at this. "A pool can hold more people than a hot tub," I explained, feeling defensive. "If that may guests have descended into debauchery, I'll have to declare sanction."

"It's possible," Jean admitted earnestly. "I've seen it before."

Michael was intrigued. "You can ask," I warned, touching his shoulder lightly. "But be forewarned. He *will* tell you. And once you know, there can be no turning back."

Michael didn't appear alarmed. "I've been a coordinator for a stripper company for a few years now," he replied, smiling. "There's very little that would shock me."

"They always say that," Jean warned. "And they're always wrong in the end."

Michael waved my boyfriend's concern away with a grin. "I'll take your word for it," he said, stepping away. "I've got to get back to work. Have a great time here, though. It was nice meeting you both."

"Nice meeting you," I said, meaning it.

"Likewise," Jean agreed.

Michael took a couple of steps and then halted abruptly. As he did, his left hand snaked down the back of his jeans. I watched as he snatched something from his back pocket.

A crinkle of paper echoed down the narrow corridor we stood in, followed by a crunch that could have broken glass. "Oh, and one other thing," Michael said, walking backward as he chewed on what I realized was a candy bar.

Confused, I watched as he leaned in conspiratorially. "Yes?" I asked, smelling a strange combination of chocolate on coffee in his breath.

Michael's cocoa-covered smirk was easily visible in the dim light. "Down there, past the dungeon, is the Slurp Room," he said, giggling as he smacked me heartily on the back. "Have fun, boys!"

Jean and I watched Michael skip merrily away, still crunching on his snack bar. "I'm gonna regret asking," I said, turning to face my boyfriend. "Aren't I?"

"You might," Jean admitted without hesitation. "But I can tell you still want to know."

I winced at the accuracy. "Yes," I grumbled. "Fine, what is a Slurp Room?"

"Let's find our rooms," Jean suggested, taking my hand. "I can show you along the way."

That seemed like the sensible thing to do. This meant that I couldn't think of a sensible excuse to get myself out of the mess I was in. The thought of a sex dungeon in this place wasn't out of the ordinary, but it still made me tremble.

Whatever a Slurp Room was, it was probably much worse.

"That," Jean explained, stopping in front of a doorway to point inside, "is the Slurp Room."

I stood in the door frame, unsure of how to react. This room, unlike the hallway, was much better lit. It didn't have the glaring brightness of the showers. The florescent lights were dim, but they provided enough illumination without blinding me.

This room was much higher. Ascending steps stood on either side of the door. They formed a sort of balcony that encircled the room on all four walls.

The partition was protected by a railing. As I stepped tentatively into the room, I saw that the gaps were actually holes—gloryholes to be precise. Row after row of gloryholes, vertical in shape and descending low to avoid harming the more fantastically endowed, were carved into the balcony.

The floor was devoid of furniture or decoration. Padded mats were lain out in the style of a traditional Japanese house. I could guess their purpose.

"Slurp Room," I said aloud, making sure Jean could hear. "Accurate, if nothing else."

This was the room for guests to line up for blowjobs. "At least they designed it with the giver in mind," I added, walking back.

"The knees hurt after a while," Jean replied, pulling me to him.

"This way, the giver can stay upright while the receiver enjoys themselves."

"How entrepreneurial of them," I said sarcastically as we walked away and around the corner. "It's a wonder they haven't made a fast-food chain by now."

"I think 'tire and lube' makes for the better analogy," Jean argued, guiding me in the gloom toward the bedrooms. "Pull in, get head, and then drive right out."

"You're right," I admitted. "And somehow, that is both better and worse than what I pictured."

Jean was enjoying himself again. "Although," he added teasingly. "Your version gives a whole new meaning to the term 'happy meal'."

"Ew." I made a face and smacked Jean's arm. "Bad retired porn star. No Scooby Snack for you!"

Jean behaved himself while we looked for the right room. All of the doors on this side of the bathhouse were marked with a number. Room three-oh-eight was down a hallway near the back. We passed by a couple of doors that were open. I slowed down as we walked by, catching an eyeful of a couple going at it on a small bed.

"I'm beginning to think you have a voyeuristic side," Jean noted. "That's a feature, by the way. Not a bug."

"I'm coming," I said, turning away from the spectacle.

Jean chuckled as I slid the key into the lock. "Not yet, you aren't," he said in a husky tone.

I might have been in a hurry to get the door open. This was the excuse for my fumble with the lock. I managed to turn it on the second try, but the door didn't swing out. Trying again, I found it didn't go inward either.

"What the…?" I wondered aloud, getting impatient. "Is it stuck?"

Jean resolved the situation by reaching out with one hand. "Here," he said, tapping the side of the door with his open palm. "Try this."

The door slid to the side at once. It worked like a sliding glass door, moving on rollers attached to the top and bottom. I had been trying to push in on a door that wasn't built that way.

"In my defense," I said, burning brightly with shame. "It is very hard to see in here."

"True," Jean agreed, stepping inside. "C'mon, let's give the room a quick sweep."

I was frowning as I pulled the door closed. "Why?" I wondered, placing the few meager possessions we had on the table. Per Jean's instructions, we were traveling—such as it were—light.

Jean had already raised up the mattress. "Just in case," he said, checking the space between the two cushions.

Though bewildered, I nevertheless complied. "Bathhouses are supposed to clean their rooms thoroughly," Jean explained while I opened all the drawers on the desk. "But sometimes…"

I jumped slightly when Jean let the mattress fall back down. "Employees get lazy," Jean went on, moving over to the flatscreen mounted on the wall. "Rooms get skipped over. Or they're busy and don't get to a used room in time."

"Bathhouses have lost their enchantment for me," I said, continuing to search the desk drawers. "Not blaming you. Just stating a fact."

"Noted," Jean replied, unperturbed by the revelation. "It was going to happen sooner or later."

"Of course it was." I finished searching the drawers and looked around, wondering where to look next. "It would help if I knew what we were looking for. I'm assuming you don't think the CIA bugged this space in advance."

Jean snorted. "The CIA?" he asked dismissively. "No one would trust that bunch to monitor a Pride parade. Much less bug a gay hotel."

"How…" My brain went into four-oh-four mode briefly. "How do you even know—never mind, what are we looking for?"

"Drugs," Jean answered plainly. "Used needles. That kind of thing. People lose track of their stuff while their minds are in altered states."

"Wow, drugs lead to poor life choices," I joked back, peering behind the desk next. "The DARE program was right after all."

"Only by accident," Jean said derisively. "You should also look for used condoms."

I made a sour face. "Gross," I said. "And here I was thinking we'd covered the worst with 'used needles'. Plural!"

"Never underestimate what people will forget to take with them when they're finished with a bathhouse room," he instructed. "They'll always surprise you."

"'Surprises' seem to be the order of the night," I grumbled, settling onto the bed. "Find anything?"

Jean finished by looking over the floor from corner to corner. "Nothing we didn't bring with us," he said, satisfied. "We lucked out. This room was cleaned before we got here."

"I'm so happy," I said dryly. "And I really am, for the record. But a part of me wishes I hadn't heard anything that came out of your mouth for the last couple of minutes."

"Better you know than learn the hard way," Jean warned me seriously. "Like I did."

A part of me did understand what was going on. Jean was right, of course. The last thing I wanted was to stumble upon someone's leftover heroin addiction.

I was in a sour mood at the moment, though. When Jean first proposed the idea of coming here, it sounded fantastical. I was excited, thrilled by the chance to have fun.

My college years weren't the wild, rebellious times that most people expect. I was too young to get into bars. Granted, I slipped into one on prom night, but that had ended disastrously. That experience shook me enough to keep me on the straight and narrow as far as bar-crawling went. I dated, drank occasionally at parties, but was already in a committed relationship by the time my twenty-first birthday rolled around.

"I guess I was expecting this to be a non-stop party," I said, sounding like a disappointed child. "You know, people dancing and getting naked and having a great time."

Jean's hands slid tenderly over my shoulders, bringing with them the warmth and strength of his presence.

"Oh, it will be," he assured. "Make no mistake of that. But the problem is you have to accept the good with the bad. Wild parties mean people making poor decisions or having sex with somebody they wouldn't look at twice in the light of day."

I smiled, then. "Well, we came here to have fun with each other," I reminded, sliding one hand up to grasp his. "Not anybody else."

"Too true," Jean agreed. "You've managed to make an honest man out of me."

I turned in my chair, which wasn't easy, but I was determined. "And the hearts of millions break simultaneously," I teased, standing so I could pull my boyfriend close.

Jean wrapped his arms around me. I felt the power in his embrace, how strong he was and the willingness to use it. Looking up into his eyes, I saw the heat take hold.

He bent down. Jean was always having to bend at the back. He was well over six feet tall, towering above me. I felt his mouth crash against mine in a wild, eager kiss. His beard was thick and dark, rubbing against my face like soft sandpaper.

I loved it. Jean used to trim his beard before we met, keeping it neater and more refined. I managed to convince him to let it grow out. He was always desirable to me, but there was something about him sporting a wild, untamed bushel of facial hair that drove my lust over the edge.

"Let them," Jean whispered, breathing the words into my face. "I'm right where I wanna be."

His arms roamed all over my back, kneading the muscles there. Tension I didn't know was there slipped away, evaporating into the aether. My own hands slid underneath the shirt Jean had on, raising it up. I could feel the strength in his back muscles as well. They were built like a bronco's, as if Jean had been some massive beast of burden in a former life.

Much as I loved this part of him, in particular when he was on top of me, my hands inevitably worked their way around to Jean's front. I absolutely adored how hairy he was. In the past, so Jean had told me, other lovers complained about the thick, dark carpet covering his chest and abs. It was the reason why, in all his earliest films, Jean performed on camera while shaved smooth.

I didn't understand it. His hair was glorious. It felt amazing between my fingers. I loved how it hid so much of his body, turning each touch into a playful game of hide-and-seek.

"I love you," Jean murmured into my mouth, making me swallow his words.

"Mmm," I groaned, kissing him back hungrily. "Love you too."

His grip on me tightened. Jean pulled me against his body so hard that my hands were squashed between us. The movement caught me off-guard. I felt the air rush out of my lungs.

"But I need to fuck you," he went on, still kissing me. "Right the fuck now!"

Jean took a step forward, pushing me back in the process. I was still held tight in his grip, a captive. My tender, sweet boyfriend was long gone. A hungry, primal animal had taken his place.

Fortunately, I knew how to tame this particular creature. And it wasn't as if the process were unpleasant. Rather than resist, I stepped back in time with Jean's movements, complying with them.

Jean moaned, kissing me harder on the mouth. His tongue forced past my lips urgently, needfully. Nothing turned my boyfriend on more than compliance. He loved being with me, knowing I wouldn't reject him.

We were separated briefly. Jean pushed me away long enough to yank the shirt I was wearing over my head. A shiver went through me as gooseflesh appeared on my arms.

They were banished as soon as Jean wrapped his arms around me. I felt him fumble with one hand, trying to undo the belt around his waist. Sensing his problem, my own hands reached down, making space between us so I could free his cock—first by tossing the offending piece of clothing aside, and then by popping the buttons loose on his fly.

Jean's cock was a marvel to behold. It was not for nothing that he had been a renowned porn star for over a decade. Thirteen inches of thick, uncut cock swung out, already hard and dribbling precum onto the floor.

My hands wrapped around the length of it. He always needed both of them. The fingers barely touched despite my best efforts. I immediately went into a familiar rhythm, stroking him up and down so that the precum lubed him up.

Unlike in porn, Jean was too much man for most men. He had been too much for me at first. It took time and a lot of prep work for the living legend, as I liked to call it, to fit inside of me.

It helped that we had done the groundwork ahead of time. I was stretched and lubed already. We left a trail of clothing across the short expanse of the room, stopping only when my back touched something smooth and cold.

"Ahh!" I exclaimed, shocked by the sensation. "Sorry, I didn't expect for the wall to be—"

Jean didn't let me finish. His mouth was still crushed against mine. I could feel his kisses becoming more intense, more urgent.

"Plasmascreen," he managed to get out.

Naked, Jean reached down. I felt his legs cup underneath my thighs, lifting me up. I was hefted up off the ground and into his arms, feeling that thick forest of virile fur rub sensually against me.

My legs wrapped securely around his waist. I could feel his arms hold me tight, forming a loop around my shoulder blades. He never stopped kissing me, continuing to murmur words of lust and love into my body.

"Love you…" he said between kisses. "So much. Just…can't hold back…anymore."

"Don't," I struggled to get out. It was hard to talk while I was nursing on his tongue like a tit. "Just…do it. You know…I trust you."

Jean moaned into my mouth. He was trying to say something, but his words never formed. My tongue stayed lodged inside his mouth, blocking the way. I could taste them, though, and feel the weight of them.

Something hot and hard nudged against the crack of my ass. I knew the feel of Jean's cock. Hot steel wrapped in warm silk. It was slick from the fountain of precum drizzling out of the head.

This was the cock I fantasized about for years. I would dream of it, imagining what it might feel like pushing inside of me. Jean was my ultimate dream man. As a teen, I would have done anything he asked me to.

As a grown adult, it was still hard for me to resist that impulse. "Wanna try," Jean managed to speak around my mouth. "Something kinky?"

I laughed, forcing the sound into his throat. "We're naked in a bathhouse room where gods know how many men have fucked each other before," I pointed out, raising back slightly. "I think we're already pretty far into the kinky zone."

A leer spread across Jean's face. "You think so?" he asked, making it a challenge. "I bet we can still turn things up a little. Hold on to me."

Jean let go of me with one arm. I had no clue where he was going with this, but held on tightly anyway. A noisy "click" rang in my ear, followed by the sound of the plasmascreen coming to life.

"Ever wondered what people watch in these places?" Jean asked, setting me down slowly.

"No," I admitted, bewildered. "Doesn't seem like people would have much time to sign into Netflix. What with all the screwing they—"

I was cut off then—not by Jean, but by the familiar sounds of sex. Turning around, I saw a video playing on the screen. Two muscle studs were going at it. One had his cock buried all the way up the other's hole. They were rocking back and forth into one another, pounding loud enough to test the springs of the bed they lay across.

"Porn," Jean said simply. "There's always porn playing in these places. Either in the rooms or in one of the recreational areas."

This wasn't one I had seen before. I didn't recognize the performers. Their bodies were the standard "gym" look that most studios went for.

Even their faces seemed plain somehow. There wasn't an ounce of hair to be found anywhere besides the tops of their heads.

The urgency with which the two fucked each other was something to behold, however. It looked as if they were starved for touch, aching to feel each other as much as possible. I stood there for a second while Jean positioned himself behind me, watching as one plowed the other senseless.

"Everyone comes here for the same reason," Jean said, whispering in my ear softly. "If you're not already horny when you walk through the door, they've got just the thing to fix that."

I felt Jean push me forward. My hands came up automatically, landing on the slick surface of the screen. They were splayed out apart from one another, far enough that I could watch what was happening in front of me.

"It's all about getting off," Jean went on. I could feel one massive foot work its way between my legs, nudging them open wider. "About finding what you want."

That thick slab of muscle, hard and aching, slid up underneath my cheeks, running back and forth along my taint. It left a thick trail of fluid. Droplets ended up on my balls, making them throb with a hungry need.

"At the end of the day," Jean whispered as the plum-sized head of his cock nudged at my entrance, "everyone comes here…"

There was a pause, just long enough for him to push past that tight ring serving as my gatekeeper. "…to fuck!"

As always, the first impulse was to scream. It was impossible to not feel pain the first time Jean entered me. I learned this the hard way. He wasn't even being brutal in his entry. The sad fact was that Jean existed in a class by himself. His cock was a thing to behold, and taking it always proved to be a challenge.

"Fuck!" I shouted at the top of my lungs once I was able to take in enough air.

A deep, masculine rumble traveled from Jean's thick chest down to his cock and into me. "That's what I'm doing to you," he crowed in a low, husky voice. "Feel me inside of you right now."

I could. There was no way in hell anyone could miss that. We weren't even at the halfway mark. I had taken Jean enough times to be able to gauge how far along he was inside of me. There was a thick vein that throbbed against the walls of my inner canal. I could feel it the moment he was far enough in me.

That was how I knew we were a third of the way in. "Keep going," I croaked out, trying in vain to claw at the screen while the two performers in front of me switched positions.

"Like I would stop now," Jean replied, pushing a fresh few inches in me further. "So tight. You are always…fuck, so tight!"

One would think my hole looked like the Miami Tunnel after so many months. "Then make…Ah, dammit, make me looser," I challenged. "Stop holding back."

I felt Jean squeeze my hips. "Nice try," he told me. "But I want this…ugh, fuck! I wanna last. Want you to feel me…mmm, deep inside!"

In response, I braced myself against the screen. The two actors were facing each other now. One lay on his back, legs spread wide. The other was positioned between them, slowly working his way back inside.

A good hard push was all it took, for them and for me. Using the wall in front of me, I held my body fast. Jean was expecting me to give a little when he entered me. My body would automatically move toward the wall, driven by the short spurt of momentum.

"How deep?" I asked, forcing myself back onto his cock. "This deep?"

It hurt like hell, but in a sweet sort of way. Jean's cock had taught me a lot about pain, about the many different types. I had never been one for the S&M crowd. Those thirteen inches did something to me, though. I didn't mind it so much when Jean hurt me, so long as he was hurting me the right way.

Feeling my hole struggle to accommodate as my body slid down on all thirteen of those inches was hurting just right.

"Mmm, fuck!" Jean gasped out. "Oh, mutherfucker!"

"I won't break," I assured him, squeezing down hard with the muscles in my anus. "You know me better than that by now."

A dangerous growl came sliding out of Jean's chest, surprising me. "You little shit," he snapped, digging his fingers deeper into my hips. "Fine, you're gonna get it now!"

The next thrust came fast. Jean slammed himself against me, burying the last of his cock balls-deep inside. I felt my teeth chatter from the blow. The side of my face landed hard against the screen.

Light exploded before my eyes. I couldn't tell if it was from being so close to the set, or if it was because Jean knocked the wind out of me. Either way, there was a moment where I couldn't see.

Being deprived of my primary sense kicked the others into overdrive. I was suddenly assaulted with fragrances from all around. I could smell the cleaning chemicals used to scrub the room. There was a slight hint of chlorine coming from behind the door. Someone was making use of the showers, enough that the smell of water drifted upstairs and down the hall.

"This is what you deserve!" Jean growled in my ear, beginning the first of what would be many, many thrusts inside of me.

Heat radiated off his body in waves. It was like being drilled by a space heater. I could feel it wash over me, bathing me in sweaty warmth. Jean's hands roamed all over my body as he pounded me without mercy or restraint.

"Teasing me all the time," he continued, biting my ear as he spoke. "Being so sexy without even realizing it."

I could taste the sweat from his body. It poured down over me, spilling like raindrops. Each fast-paced thrust shook more free. They pelted against my skin, mingling with my own moisture. My tongue flew out, aching to catch as much as it could, like a kid on a snowy winter morning.

"If I had my way," Jean swore on his next entry, "you'd never leave the house. Spend all day...fuck, taking my cock. Being bent over whenever I get hard."

Most of all, however, I could hear the need in Jean's voice. "You

make me hard all the time," he revealed. "Every single fucking second…
goddammit! Of every damn day!"

I reached back with one arm, curving it into a hook. It snaked
around the back of Jean's neck, pulling him even closer. I couldn't stand
the thought of us being apart. My body craved being close to him, to
touch him with every fiber of my being.

"Do it," I said between gasps. My lungs ached but I wasn't about to
quit now. "Take me however you want. Use me whenever you need to."

"Right now," Jean grunted back, doubling down on his thrusts. "I
need you right now. I need…fuck, I need you always, love!"

There was no hesitation anymore, no holding back from either of
us. My body lunged backward, meeting his cock halfway. Both arms
ached from bracing against the wall. I tuned the pain out and keep
working, determined to fit as much of Jean inside of me as I could each
time. There was no way in hell I would pass on having his cock inside
me. Even if it permanently rearranged my organs, I welcomed the
change.

"I love you so much," I revealed, turning away from the porn
playing to look him in the eye. "You're all I've dreamed about. Oh, fuck
me! For years…"

One arm pulled me against him again. "You're all I could have
hoped for," he whispered, still drilling me as best we could.

We kissed, our tongues dancing in circles around one another.
There would be plenty of time for kissing later, though. Right then, and
right there, I needed Jean to claim me. I wanted him to pound me until
I couldn't walk straight.

"Fuck me like I was in one of your movies," I said, breaking the kiss
to brace against the wall again. "Use me like you did all those men
before."

"Shit," Jean cussed, gripping me by the hips once more. "None of
them hold a candle to you, lover. Your ass loves this cock more than
theirs ever did."

I highly doubted that, but it felt good hearing him say it all the
same.

"Do it," I coached, needing him to fully claim me. "Harder, please!"

"Gonna mark you as mine tonight," Jean declared as his cock touched that spot that only he could reach, making my knees buckle. "Make sure everybody else keeps their distance."

"I'm yours," I swore. "There's nobody else for me but you."

"Damn fucking right," Jean said, digging fresh bruises into my hips from gripping me so hard. "Doesn't matter who else has been inside this hole before. It's mine now!"

I was surprised, but not angry, when Jean brought his hand down on my ass. "Hear me?" he snarled. "Nobody but me owns this."

"All yours," I told him. "Fuck me like you own me."

"Fuck yeah!" I could feel the handprint that Jean left behind sting as he picked up speed, fast approaching the point of no return. "Gonna breed you right here, lover. Here where fuck knows how many men have been bred before."

"Yeah, breed me in this filthy little room." I was really getting into the roleplay now. "Doesn't matter how many times they clean it. You can... Ahhh!, smell the sweat and cum."

"In the rooms," Jean agreed, picking up on where I was going. "Out in the hallway. Nothing but non-stop sex here. Dirty little men like you who need to get their rocks...fuck, off!"

"Do it!"

I was practically screaming. Half the people on this floor could hear me. I was too far gone to feel embarrassment anymore. My balls had begun churning, signaling that they were getting ready to release their payload. Jean was the only man who had ever been able to make me cum hands-free.

"Cumming!" Jean said loudly, tossing his thick, curly mane of dark hair back. "Fuck! Oh, I'm cumming...cumming!"

Thick ropes of cum exploded out of my cock. I felt my piss slit expand and burn. Hot streaks splattered against the wall, staining the paint. It made my balls sore, cumming so hard.

That was nothing compared to Jean, of course. His cock felt like it was trying to double in size. I felt him give one final thrust. It was powerful enough to rattle the bones in my skull. I slammed hard against the wall, feeling my knees bang against the sticky warmth of my own seed.

Jean, meanwhile, roared loud enough to make the door rattle. I felt his load unleash inside of me. There was so much of it too, enough that my guts struggled to hold all of it in. My sphincter clamped down reflexively, wanting to hold all of it in.

"Shit!" Jean screamed, pinning me to the wall with the weight of his own body. "Fuck! Goddamit! Son of a bitch! Fuck!"

He had a potty mouth during sex. It most likely came from all those years of working in the industry. Jean only swore during sex when it was really good, however.

He had been swearing a lot since we started dating.

"Fuck," I breathed out, leaning into his thick, muscular frame.

"So good," Jean breathed out, using the wall I was still pinned against for support. "So amazing. I love you so much."

"I love you too." To illustrate my point, I squeezed his cock with my hole. "Do you still feel like going to the party?"

Jean thought about that for a moment—or maybe he was just catching his breath.

"Maybe later," he said, slowly moving in and out of me once more, which elicited soft whimpers from my chest. "I'm in the middle of something right now."

Chapter 5

"Now, this is more of what I had in mind."

We did eventually emerge from our room. *Treats* was starting to fill up now that some time had passed. The hallways were a little more crowded. Guests were roaming in and out of the various recreational areas sporting towels, skimpy underwear, and a whole lot less.

As warned, most of the guests didn't quite fit the gym bunny look. There were men of average builds, men who were overweight, men who were trans, men who fit the burly bear look, a few that were drop-dead gorgeous, and a couple of poor souls who looked as if they had hit every branch on the way down after falling out of the Ugly Tree.

I wasn't feeling bold enough yet to wander around in the nude, so Jean and I made use of the sexy jock straps we'd packed. They fit securely and cradled my balls just right. I had wrapped my towel around my waist as well, but Jean was marching securely around with his plump, hairy ass hanging out for everyone to ogle.

More than a few people reached out to cop a feel. I had to shoot a few dirty looks at the hands' owners before they took the hint.

"Yeah, same here," Jean admitted as we surveyed the scene before us. "Even though I knew what to expect, the ads made it seem like this was going to be more of a club."

Jean and I had definitely found the "party" part of the bathhouse bash. We had decided to visit the third floor. This was the only area of the bathhouse that I was unfamiliar with so far. It turned out to be where the pool was kept.

Treats had converted the top floor into a deck area. The pool itself was covered by a roof to keep the rain off and hold in the heat. Anyone could swim there, even in the cold months. There were doors that opened up into a rooftop patio area. It offered a gorgeous view of the Castro and a bit of San Francisco beyond.

"Is that…?" I asked, stopping Jean to point. "DJ Chrissy Sinz?"

Jean turned to where I was gesturing and peered through the dimness. "Yeah, I think it is," he said, smiling. "He was in that wild west porno, right?"

"He was," I affirmed.

Chrissy Sinz had been a rather notorious figure in the gay porn industry. A former gang member of the Chicago streets who got cleaned up, joined the military, and then went on to star in a major adult mini-series about gay gunslingers in the Old West.

"I was almost in that movie," Jean said idly, watching as DJ Chrissy worked the turn tables, spinning beats for the dancing crowd on the deck area.

I almost didn't hear him at first. "What, really?" I was surprised, thinking I knew most of Jean's career. "I didn't know that."

Jean shrugged. "They sent me a script," he explained. "It was different from the finished product, but the premise was essentially the same."

"What made you change your mind?" I asked.

The conversation paused so we could move. A handful of people were moving through in an attempt to leave the deck area. Two of them still sported towels, but one seemed to have misplaced his. His eyes met mine as he walked past. I could tell there was nobody at home.

"Tweeker," Jean said once they were out of earshot, which wasn't more than a couple steps. The beats from the speakers hit hard enough to vibrate the air around us. "He's checked out for the night."

"Here's hoping he'll be okay," I said, looking back over my shoulder with a worried expression.

"You can't save everybody," Jean reminded. "He's an adult and can make his own choices. We're here to have fun, remember?"

"Right." I turned back to face Jean. "You were telling me about your illustrious career. A part of it I wasn't aware of, it turns out. What else are you keeping secret?"

Jean smiled. "Stick around and find out," he teased, poking me gently. "But there's nothing secret about that. It came down to scheduling conflicts. I was with another studio at the time."

"Ahh!" We were having to yell to be heard. I could already feel my throat getting sore, but that could have been due to the screaming from earlier. "Not as interesting as I had hoped, but still good to know."

Jean nodded. "I'll try to think of something more scandalous later," he told me. "Also, Mustang Studios, who produced the series, wanted me to sign an exclusive contract. Meaning I couldn't work anywhere else but with them."

"Yikes," I said. "Yeah, probably best you turned them down. Even if you did retire not long afterward."

"I enjoyed being a free agent," he revealed, smirking at the double entendre. "Studios were getting real possessive with their performers. It's one reason why I got out."

It was his turn to point to DJ Chrissy. "They got him with an exclusive contract," he explained. "Saturated the market with films about him, then put him on a shelf. Poor guy couldn't get out of his contract, so his career dried up after a few years."

I watched DJ Chrissy spin the turntables. It looked as if he were having the time of his life. The dark lights made the tattoos on his body shimmer. He was famous for them, having adorned nearly every part of his body, including his cock, with body ink. DJ Chrissy was shirtless, wearing only a pair of cut-off jeans.

"Looks as if he's bounced back," I noted.

"He's one of the lucky ones," Jean said sadly. "But enough of that."

I turned to find Jean extending a hand toward me. "May I have this dance?" he yelled with as much seriousness as the situation allowed for.

"Sure," I said, placing mine in his. "But promise not to laugh when you find out that I have two left feet."

Jean began to lead me out deeper into the deck area where people were gyrating. "My feet are big," he reminded me. "They make for easy targets."

I hung back, following along after my boyfriend. Jean went into the sea of bodies first, cutting a path through them for me with his size and presence. I thought he would stop after a couple of feet. Instead, he kept going until we were in the dead center.

He never let go of my hand the whole time. I felt him squeeze it tightly. He was my lifeline into this world, a place of uninhibited sexual freedom and libertinism. I was afraid to let go, but letting go was the whole point.

No one around us cared. They were all dancing joyously to the house music. People French kissed and rubbed up against each other, committing acts that would have gotten them arrested in any other place. We must have passed thirteen health code violations alone before Jean stopped and pulled me into his embrace.

"Relax," he said, gazing deep into my eyes. "Let go."

In that moment, I was afraid. "Promise you'll catch me?" I called out, begging to be understood above the din surrounding us. "If I fall too far."

Jean placed a secure hand against my back. "You'll never fall," he said, somehow making himself heard. "Not while I'm here. Now come flying with me."

We began to move together. I wasn't secure enough in myself to take the lead. Jean was guiding my movements, helping me find the rhythm and keep it. His hand continued traveling sound down along my back while we danced. I kept my eyes locked on his, forgetting to look around.

The rest of the party slipped away the longer I looked into those beautiful blue eyes. I wanted to stare into them forever, to forget about the rest of the world. The music thrummed as we moved in unison.

I felt Jean make his hand into a fist when he reached the small of my back. There was a slight tug, followed by a cool breeze. Something went sailing up high over our heads. I broke the spell Jean's eyes had on me and looked up.

A white towel was fluttering down fast into the crowd. Confused, I stared at myself and realized that I was now clad only in the red jock strap. My ass was hanging out almost as much as Jean's was.

It should have made me angry, but in that instant, I felt relieved. It was like a weight had been taken off me, or maybe a set of chains had been unlocked. I reached up and seized hold of Jean by his hair with both of my fists, yanking him down hard. Our mouths locked as we resumed our dance, kissing deeply while the music took us into the night.

I could feel his hardness between us. It was impossible not to. Despite having fucked me senseless less than an hour ago, Jean was hard again. His thick cudgel strained against the elastic straps, spreading a wide stain of pre-jizz on the front.

My own hardon was having difficulty staying contained. Dancing with Jean while making out meant that each thrust pushed us against each other. I could feel the slick stickiness on the front of his jock spread into mine.

It made me groan. The sound traveled from my body into his, competing with the music. I wanted him to feel the effect he was having on me. I wanted Jean to know what he was doing, how I felt about it, and how good all of this was.

We weren't alone. The illusion that Jean and I were the last two people on earth had broken. Bodies surrounded us on all sides. Men rubbed up against us from every angle. Any other time, it would have been a huge violation of personal space.

Now, though, it was like everyone was celebrating along with Jean and me—rejoicing in me having stepped out of my shell at last.

Something clicked in my brain. It felt as though I had some kind of breakthrough, a revelation at that moment. Everything about the bathhouse thus far had been far from ideal. A lot of what I had seen ranged from seedy to outright unpleasant.

This, however, was different. I was beginning to finally see the appeal. It was a place where anything could happen. People brought their wildest fantasies here to be lived out. They could let go and stop hiding, stop playing by the rules of society.

As gay men, we were always being judged by the world. Here, in this paradise, we were all free to be ourselves. I understood what Jean had said before about being "aggressively gay". My sexuality was my power. It gave me freedom from expectations. I could be whomever I wanted to be, however I wanted to be it. There was no boss of me other than myself.

And it was high time I started enjoying it!

"This is fucking incredible!" I screamed, loud enough to startle a couple of people near us.

Jean merely laughed, and I laughed along with him. "Now you're getting into it," he said cheerfully, pulling me back into him.

"I am," I said openly, throwing both arms around his neck to kiss him hard on the mouth. "Thank you for doing this!"

It was hard to tell how long we were dancing for. Faces moved in and out of my field of vision. I saw the young and the old thrust together. Men traded dance partners and brushed their bodies against each other in pairs of three, four, or even five.

I grew really bold at once point and spun around. Jean had been in the midst of shoving his groin against mine. His barely-concealed cock slid in-between the crack of my ass. I bent myself over, wigging my rear as I went, and let him hump me right there on the dance floor.

Jean got into it immediately. I ground back against him while he continued to hump me. A couple of people cheered and pointed. I simply smiled and gave them a thumbs up.

We were being moved around. The music had shifted to some kind of fast-paced reggaeton beat. The crowd around us danced even faster, determined to keep up.

Trying to grind against my boyfriend while bent over and simultaneously moving with a crowd wasn't easy. I was starting to get back pain, a reminder that I wasn't a teenager anymore. Jean's thrusts weren't quite filling me up the way they had before, either. I raised up, deciding to call it quits, and turned around.

That was when I got what felt like the latest in a long series of shocks for the night.

Jean was nowhere to be found. A large, Black bear dressed to the nines in leather kink gear was standing behind me. I had been shoving my ass into his crotch—which was covered by a skimpy leather thing that had become unfastened at some point. His cock was laid out for everyone on the dance floor to see.

"Don't stop now," he said to me above the hammering island rhythm, grinning from ear to ear. "I'm almost there!"

"Um, sorry!" I yelled, hearing my voice crack from embarrassment. "Thought you were someone else."

The bear laughed, loud enough to drown out the music, if only momentarily. "Look around," he said. "Nobody here cares!"

This was true enough. The dance floor looked even more packed than when Jean and I first started. I couldn't stand still for more than a second before someone elbowed me in the ribs. It was turning into a low-key mosh pit at this point.

"Maybe I oughta—"

I had been on the verge of excusing myself when someone brushed past me from behind. The contact was brief, but hard enough to pitch me forward. I wound up right in the leather bear's thick, muscular arms.

"Your boyfriend's over there," he told me, jerking his head back over his left shoulder. "A couple of thirsty bitches cornered him when you two first got separated."

I looked and saw that Jean was indeed surrounded on three sides by a trio of otters. They didn't look like much, pretty standard in terms of attractiveness. One had his cock out, though, a short but very impressive chode whose thickness stood out even at a distance.

Something came over me in that moment. I wasn't sure what I was feeling. A part of me wanted to go over there and break the scene up. And yet, there wasn't really much for me to interrupt. Jean was only dancing. It looked as though he was having a good time, but as far as lewdness went, the scene was fairly tame.

Was I jealous? I didn't want to be jealous. A part of me enjoyed seeing that he was having a good time without me. Somewhere deep down, I was also upset that he hadn't made more of an effort to come to my rescue.

Then again, I wasn't in any danger myself. It was a party and we were dancing, just not with each other. That was all right, after all.

Plus, seeing him surrounded by three guys who were obviously into him triggered something in my brain. For a moment, a blinding instant, I was taken back to my teen years, watching Jean in action on my laptop while pulling on my cock.

"Okay," I decided then and there, turning my attention back to the stud bear in front of me. "So long as he's all right. Let's dance!"

The Black bear didn't need further encouragement. We moved together on the floor, grinding against each other. My jockstrap kept me from feeling his cock against mine. He didn't seem to care—at least, he made no comment about it being there.

"What's your name?" I asked, figuring I should at least know the person I was being lewd with on the dance floor in front of everyone.

"M' real name is Bobby," he said, never missing a beat. "I'm originally from Alabama. Moved out here a couple years back."

"Welcome to the Castro," I said. "Having a good time?"

Bobby grinned. "Always," he replied. "Folks nowadays call me by my Chaturbate handle, ThiccBlackDaddy."

It wasn't every day that I got hit on by a webcam entertainer— which isn't the same thing as a porn star, for the record. "Can't imagine why!" I laughed. "Name's Rafael. Most people who know me call me Raf. You were right about that guy over there being my boyfriend. We came here together."

"No worries," Bobby said easily. "ThiccBlackDaddy don't go nowhere he ain't invited."

Bobby and I danced for a bit. His hands wandered downward a time or two. I felt him run a finger down the length of my crack, which made me shiver. When he made a play for my hole, though, I had to cut him off.

"Sorry," I told him, "but that's private property." He didn't seem all that upset, and even backed off without protest. "Besides," I added, "my boyfriend may have left something in there. Not sure how you feel about sloppy seconds."

"Maybe I should ask him for permission," Bobby teased, still grinding his cock against me. "Then you can find out for yourself, eh?"

This was getting a little bit too intense for me. I decided to excuse myself. Dancing for so long without a break had left me dehydrated. I worked my way through the excited mass of bodies, eventually pushing my way through the border to freedom.

It felt weird being out in the open space. I had nearly forgotten what it felt like to move without rubbing up against somebody. The air was chilly as well. I could feel goosebumps raising up on my arms as I worked my way toward the dividing glass wall that separated the deck from the pool area.

A vending machine stood up against said wall. The soft blue florescent light cast an eerie glow out into the area, mingling with the floor that was already graced with black lights and some strange patterns on the ground. I honestly could not tell whether the splatters were intentional or if someone had just used too much lubricant.

Either way, it didn't matter. There was no line in front of the machine, so I raced over to it. Reaching into my jock strap, I pulled out a rolled-up wad of bills. This was another tip Jean had given me.

"I just hope the machine doesn't mind the jizz stains on them," I muttered, rolling out a couple of singles.

In addition to water, there were also several other items available for purchase. I saw condoms, lubricant, and dick pills to aid with erections. Unsurprisingly, the bottled water inside the machine was ridiculously overpriced.

"Beggars can't be choosers," I reminded myself, sliding the bills through the slot.

The machine made several disgruntled grunts and groans before a bottle of Aquafina clunked its way down through the shoot. I heard it land with an even noisier "thud" in the dispenser, loud enough to drown out DJ Chrissy's latest electronic house track, but only for a second.

"Here's to my health," I said, tossing my head back to a long pull from the bottle.

The water was cold, but it felt glorious going down. I drank over half the bottle before stopping. The cool temperature made me shiver. I looked around to see if any of the other guests had left a towel behind that I could borrow.

There were plenty of naked bodies on the dance floor now, but I couldn't find so much as a towel to use. "Just my luck," I said, taking another swig.

I could always warm up by going back into the dancing crowd. That many bodies rubbing up against one another would have me sweating in a few minutes. My legs were sore from getting my freak on for so long, though.

"Maybe I should just go back to the room and wait," I said to myself thoughtfully. "Jean will come and find me there eventually."

I didn't really want to be alone in our room for long, not when there was a party going on. Looking around, I scanned the deck to see if there was anything else happening. Most of the space was taken up by the dancing crowd. There was hardly enough space left for the DJ booth anymore. All of the deck chairs that would have normally occupied this space had been removed.

Turning around, I peered through the glass wall. The pool lay beyond, glowing a softer shade of blue in the dimness. Several people were swimming laps in it. I could see another crowd on the other side.

"Huh," I said, squinting. "What's going on there?"

A clump of men stood in a semi-circle. They appeared to be cheering someone on. I wondered if maybe they had come across a couple having sex.

"Must be some damn good fucking," I mused, "if they can draw a crowd like that without trying."

My curiosity was aroused more than anything else. I decided to take my icy water inside and investigate. The pool was heated so the space inside would be a little bit warmer.

"Ahh," I said, finishing off the last drop in my bottle as I pushed through the doors. "That's better."

It was indeed warmer on the inside. Jean and I hadn't done more than taken a cursory glance around this space. The pool was large enough to fit in a suburban family's backyard. It was also not very deep. I suspected this was to keep guests from drowning.

Still, the fact that this place had a pool made it infinitely cooler to my mind. I was a former swim team champion, after all.

"Now let's see what they're so excited for," I said, dropping off my water bottle in a recycling bin. "Sheesh, a few minutes away from Jean and I've fallen back into the bad habit of talking to myself."

It was a short trek across the front of the pool to where the crowd was. I could hear a different music track playing than the one outside. Several men cheered, holding their fists up high.

As I drew closer, I could see several singles clutched there and began to get an inkling of what was going on. "Of course," I said, feeling naive at that moment. "What else?"

Someone had climbed up on top of a deck table. Fortunately, the legs were thick and sturdy enough to hold the weight of a human body. He was twisting his body while moving around in a circle, shaking his ass at the gathered throngs in exchange for dollar bills.

It was hard to see what was happening from a distance because the dancer wasn't very tall. A mop of dark hair whipped back and forth whenever he shook his head to the beat. A red speedo with twin dragons painted on the front shined under the low light.

As I drew closer, easing my way into the crowd for a closer look, a jolt hit me. I realized that I recognized him. This was the same guy I saw coming out of the locker area when Jean and I first arrived.

The dancer took notice of me when he turned back around. I was surprised to see him smile. To my utter bafflement, he winked.

Not wishing to snub a patron of the arts, I pulled out a couple of singles from my jock strap. The dancer kept his eyes on me the whole time. When I waved them at him, he began gyrating across the table toward me.

"You probably don't remember me," I said. It was easier to talk inside the pool area since the source of the music was a simple boombox. "We met downstairs in the hall right outside the lobby."

The dancer locked eyes with me. One hand reached out to take hold of mine as I moved to insert a bill into his speedo. A spark of something that might have been static raced from his fingers into mine. I felt my cock spring to life at once.

"I remember you," he said, eyes shining as he placed my hand on his chest, moving it down slowly to his groin. "You were so cute."

A blush crept up my face, staring at my neck and stopping just below my eyebrows. "I…thank you," I said, unsure of what else to say. "You're amazing."

He was a very good dancer. The movements were simple, but he had a grace and style that was impossible to deny. Each turn was expertly done. The muscles in his arms and legs flexed ever so slightly, showing that he knew what his body was capable of. If I didn't know better, I would have sworn this guy had been on stage before.

A theatrical stage, not a stripping stage—although, that was likely as well.

"Believe me, I am." He stopped my hand just below the navel. "Do you wanna see how amazing?"

I swallowed the lump that formed in my throat. "I have…" I stammered. "I mean, I'm with…I don't know…"

Words were a foreign concept. I had completely lost the ability to make full sentences. This only made me blush harder. I wanted to slide the bill into his speedo, but only to pay him and then make a run for it.

Sadly, he was still holding my hand tightly, which meant any chance of escape was futile. I could still feel the electric current running between us. It made my heart race.

"My name's Brandon," he whispered, bending forward so that I would hear. "What's yours, handsome?"

I gulped "Raf," I said thickly. "Rafael Vásquez. It's, ahh…very, very nice to meet you, I think."

"Very nice," Brandon agreed, gazing down. "From where I'm standing, at least."

My legs went together, but concealing the hardon tenting my jock was an exercise in futility. All this did was squash my balls and make it stand out more. I wished fervently for a hole to open up underneath me and take me away from this situation.

"C'mere," Brandon said as the bill slipped at last into his speedo. "And I'll show you how amazing I really am."

Brandon hadn't let go of my hand. I found myself being pulled forward. A spike of panic raced through me once I realized what he intended to do.

"No," I protested, trying to pull away. "I can't. I have a boyfriend. I'm a terrible dancer. No one wants to see this…" I hesitated just long enough to gesture to myself. "…up there with you!"

"I beg to differ," Brandon said, smiling. "I saw you dancing outside on the floor. You had half the deck drooling after you. Doesn't surprise me that it took three guys to steal your boyfriend away."

Brandon released my hand. I was free, but the suddenness of his movement caught me by surprise. I wound up pitching forward, nearly falling forward on top of the table. My hands reached out to catch myself, grabbing hold of the edges. This gave me balance, but it also left me vulnerable.

I felt a pair of warm hands reach down. They grabbed hold of me under the arms and lifted. Brandon was deceptively strong. He may have been short and compact, but his body was strong. I felt him lift me up as though I were nothing but a sack of potatoes.

"Hey, ask first!" I chided, but went quiet when my feet touched solid ground again—or what passed for it when standing on a deck table. "You could get us both in trouble!"

Brandon held me close and began to dance, guiding my body with his. "No one here is gonna care," he stated flatly, sounding sure of himself. "My boss sure as hell won't so long as I bring him half of my tips."

"I…" It clicked together for me. "Oh, you must be with Stud Stable. I met Michael earlier when my…when we were looking for our room."

Brandon didn't seem to mind the slip, but leaving out Jean sent a pang of guilt through me. "Yup," he said. "That would be our laborious taskmaster. Funny you caught him wandering around the bathhouse, though."

The fact that he used "laborious" in a sentence correctly made me smile. "How long have you been a dancer for?" I asked as the crowd around us cheered.

It was such a surreal experience. Being out on the dance floor was one thing. Everyone was dancing and having a good time there. These men couldn't take their eyes off us.

Even stranger, they couldn't take their eyes off *me*!

"A few years," Brandon replied, moving behind me so that our hips thrust together. "I used to strip for parties in college. This ass paid for all of my schooling, way past the college level."

"I'm impressed," I said, meaning it.

Brandon's warm hands slid around me, moving slowly up my front. I gasped, unable to ignore the way my cock leaped in my jock from his touch. His fingers sent that same electrical current up and along through my limbs.

"I joined Stud Stable a couple of months back," he went on.

"What happened to school?" I asked, wanting something to take my mind off the way my body was betraying me. "Or is that too personal a question?"

"Nothing worth hiding here." To illustrate his point, Brandon pressed his cock between my cheeks. "I passed everything with flying colors."

I could feel his slick heat. It moved in and out of the crack of my ass with ease, like it was born to be there. My hole, still spasming from Jean's cock, was kept safe by the sheer material of his speedo. It was the only thing keeping Brandon out of me.

"Just got bored of the working world after a while," Brandon added, his voice sounding much thicker. "And needed a change."

I should have felt mortified. Worse, I was thinking about my boyfriend and how he had plowed my hole into a gaping tunnel while another man—a stripper and a total stranger—dry humped me in front of a crowd.

Speaking of, the crowd was going nuts. Singles poured out of their hands. There was hardly any space left to dance on the table's surface. A wrong move would send both of us spilling onto the floor, brought to our doom by Washington's pasty mug.

Their faces were awestruck. These guys acted as if they were the luckiest queers in the world right now. Brandon was the one doing most of the work. His hips moved with expert precision, thrusting in time to the beat while working his upper body as well.

As for me, I was in hog heaven. It should have been degrading. I was putting on a show while my boyfriend was elsewhere having fun. This wasn't like me. I'd never come close to being this big of a slut in public before. The shame should have killed me right there on the spot.

I wouldn't even have booze or drugs to fall back on afterward for explaining my behavior tonight.

But tonight was about letting go. I could apologize to Jean later if need be. He wasn't even around to watch me turn into the Whore of Babylon anyway. Some pretty faces and hairy bodies had swept him off. If the boys around me wanted a show, that was fine too!

"What about yourself?" Brandon asked as I was coming back down from my own moral jump to conclusions.

He must have taken my silence for nerves, or maybe he was worried I was losing interest. Then again, he could have just as easily thought I was getting too into the moment and wanted to bring me back.

Either way, I surprised both him and the crowd by shaking my hips a bit. Brandon let out an audible gasp. His cock had been wedged in my crack and wound up getting a bit of a massage. Luckily, he didn't lose his load on my back. I could feel his body go tense, though.

"Sorry about that," I apologized.

"Fuck, you almost made me cum," he said, breathing hard. "But... no apologizes necessary. Just save it for the finale, okay?"

I laughed a little. "To answer your question," I went on, keeping my voice down so the crowd wouldn't hear. "I'm letting loose a little tonight. Lost my job because of the quarantine. Spent a long time feeling depressed and miserable—something I'm only just beginning to realize."

"I get that," Brandon said, meaning it.

I could see it in his eyes when I turned to face him. Our bodies fit together almost perfectly, like two halves. I was taller by an inch or two up close, but we were equal enough in height for me to stare into his beautiful golden-brown eyes. It was strangely intimate, especially since I could see what lay behind them.

Life had dealt him a few hard blows as well. "For once," I finished, sliding both arms underneath his pits to close what little gap there was. "I'm not holding myself back as much."

"Good," Brandon said, surprising me with a quick kiss. "Don't hold back at all. Not with me. I'm liking what I see so far."

I should have put a stop to things there, should have reminded him that I had a boyfriend. The same boldness from before was back, though. Instead of running away, I held tightly and took the lead. My hips began swaying, guiding Brandon into a *perreo*.

Brandon wasn't familiar with it, I could tell, but he caught on quickly. Of course, my dance moves weren't nearly on par with his. In a few minutes, it felt like he was outdoing me.

No one in the crowd cared. Their howls reached the top of the pool room, echoing back down to ring in mine and Brandon's ears. Fresh singles went sailing through the air. There was no more room on top of the table for them, however. Quite a bit spilled down onto the floor.

No one was making a move to collect them. They had already been claimed.

"You're very good at this," I said, keeping my eyes locked with his.

"You're amazing," Brandon cheered me on, running his hands along my body. "A real natural."

I was trying to not smile, but it was impossible. Brandon was having an effect on me similar to the one that the crowd on the dance floor had. My inhibitions were falling away. We danced together on top of that table and it felt glorious.

"I've never done this before," I confessed. "Not at all."

Brandon grinned. "Feels great," he said knowingly. "Doesn't it?"

"It feels like I've missed out on a lot," I told him earnestly. "But yeah, this does feel incredible!"

I wanted this night to never end, wanted to keep dancing forever. But then, the music stopped. Brandon's body quit moving automatically, as if a switch had been thrown. I didn't resist when he pulled away, but a part of me wanted to. I wanted us to keep dancing, to keep the crowd's eyes on us—for them to cheer and shower us both with their cash.

"That was great," Brandon said, sliding down off the table. "Follow me. It's time for my break."

I was suddenly aware that I was on top of the table, a table that didn't seem nearly as sturdy now as it did before. Brandon seemed to instantly know what my predicament was. Immediately, he reached out with one hand, helping me down.

My fingers tingled long after he let me go, having helped me plant my feet back down on the tile floor. I shook my hand, trying to free myself of the sensation.

"Oops!" Brandon added, bending over. "One sec. Can't forget my earnings!"

I reached over and collected the singles on top of the table. A lot of them had scattered, but there were a few stragglers left behind. In a moment, I had two hands full of one-dollar bills. It was undoubtedly not as much as it looked, but this was still a lot of cash I was holding.

"Here," I said, passing it along into Brandon's hands. "These are yours."

Brandon accepted them with a gracious smile. "Thanks," he said, stuffing the wad down the front of his speedo. "I was worried you might ask me to split them with you."

"No thanks," I replied. "This was me getting out of control for a moment. You do this for a living. And you're way better at it than I was."

"I beg to differ," Brandon said, raising back up with a speedo bulging at the seams from all the cash he'd earned. "And so does the crowd."

Brandon was right about that. The crowd had yet to disperse. The throngs of admirers began moving in now that Brandon and I were finished collecting the money they'd wasted. Hands reached out, eager to touch our bare flesh.

I could understand the appeal of Brandon. He moved like sex on two legs, almost as good as Jean did the one time I saw him on stage. But their hands touched my body as much as Brandon's. I felt fingers caress my skin, hungry and slick with need.

It hadn't occurred to me before now that my body could have power over someone. I'd never considered myself attractive enough to draw men to me. These men couldn't get enough. Their eyes shined in the dim light, alert and starving for more.

"This way," Brandon said, taking my hand. "Sorry, guys! Show's over for now. Feel free to come back in an hour."

None of them moved away, but Brandon wasn't fazed. He pulled me along, forcing an opening in the small knot of hard and hairy bodies. Several men tried to make me stay. I felt one seize me by my free arm in an attempt to pull me back. I jerked it out of his grip on reflex.

"Good move there," Brandon said, having seen what I did. "Don't let them own you. Establish some ground rules and stick with them. Exceptions will only encourage them to try harder."

I blushed as we pushed ahead, freeing ourselves. "It's not like I'll be doing this again," I muttered.

Several men from the crowd were following us. "Are they serious?" I asked, glancing back. "I figured they'd go join the party or take a swim."

"The price of fame." Brandon didn't sound surprised or particularly worried. "Some fall into lust and have a hard time shaking it. These are the type that can get persistent."

"It's a little scary," I admitted as we fled the pool area together. Their footsteps weren't far behind us. "I've never been stalked before."

That wasn't entirely true, actually. "Except for that one time after my ex-boyfriend broke up with me," I added hastily as Brandon led me to a dark staircase. "He tried to kill my current boyfriend by dropping a light fixture on him."

Brandon laughed. "And I thought my ex was crazy," he said, assuming I had been joking.

"It's less funny than it sounds," I replied irritably. "The ex in question kidnapped me and held me hostage in our old apartment. I nearly died."

Brandon slowed his steps, but only long enough for me to gain enough speed so that we moved side-by-side. Our "admirers" were still behind us. Granted, none of them had exactly done anything in the last minute. They had been keeping a distance of several feet away on the staircase.

Still, while I respected their persistence, it was getting me spooked. "Any place we can go to get away?" I asked.

"I was actually about to ask you the same thing," Brandon said as we reached the end of the stairs.

The second floor stood before us. All of the corridors were dark, even more so than before. Footsteps thundered behind us, warning that our crowd of fans was fast on our heels.

This was the last place I wanted to be cornered in. Even if they meant well, those guys were breaking some personal space boundaries. I imagined them swarming Brandon and I, pinning us up against a wall.

Sure, it sounded hot as a porn scene, but since dating Jean, I had learned that real life wasn't anything like a porno.

"I know a place where we can hide." Giving his hand a squeeze, I pulled Brandon along behind me, taking the lead. "This way."

Brandon didn't resist. We moved along together up the darkened corridor. I spotted the door frame leading into the Slurp Room out the corner of my eye. It looked as though several of the guests were making use of it now. I could hear the sounds as we ran past, grunts and moans as those kneeling on the padded floor serviced the cocks of everyone on the raised platform.

Sadly, taking refuge there was out of the question since those groans were quickly accompanied by the sound of someone retching all over the padded floor.

"Nope, not there!" I declared.

We kept moving, turning a sharp left at the intersection. Brandon kept pace with me as we fled down the hallway, heading for the area where the rooms were. It took a second for me to remember which number mine and Jean's was.

Fortunately, I still had the key. Jean's advice proved invaluable. Taking the number tag off meant no one from the crowd knew which room I was staying in. They might have spotted it while Brandon and I were dancing on the table together. Without the tag, though, it was just a key on a rubber coil that glowed slightly in the dark.

"It's right down here," I told Brandon, guiding him through a lingering cloud of cigarette smoke. Apparently, one of the guests hadn't noticed the "No Smoking" signs. "I think…"

This part of the bathhouse was especially confusing. The rooms were divided up, roughly two per square, meaning we had to move through a grid made up of doors and walls. Fortunately, this also meant that the crowd behind us was just as lost, if not more so.

"I think we're almost there," I said, feeling more confident now. "It's just around this—"

We both collided with what felt like a wall. Someone was coming around the corner from the opposite direction. They slammed into us moving at a slower velocity, but the fact that they were essentially a walking monument made up of muscle and sinew meant that Brandon and I were thrown back.

"Sorry about that."

I recovered myself and stared through the gloom into the face of Bobby, the man I had mistaken for Jean earlier.

"No problem," I said. "Wasn't paying attention myself. We were just trying to escape from a few unwanted admirers."

"Mm, one of those, huh?" Bobby the ThiccBlackDaddy said knowingly. "Yeah, I've a couple of those myself."

"Think you can hold them off?" Brandon asked, jerking a thumb back the way we came.

Bobby looked Brandon up and down, thinking it over. "For you," he decided, turning his head to me. "And you, sure thing."

Bobby moved past us, putting on a game face that could've rattled a linebacker. Brandon watched him go, impressed.

"Friend of yours?" he asked me, wearing a smirk.

Before I could answer, a second figure strode up, startling me by wrapping a pair of thick, muscular arms around my chest. "What's this?" a familiar voice asked teasingly. "Your first night at a bathhouse and you're already trying to sneak a stripper back to our room?"

I shook my head and stared straight ahead, finding Jean staring cheekily at me. "I'm impressed," he said.

"It's not what you think," I protested. "We were dancing and some of the crowd got a little possessive."

"I saw," Jean replied with a knowing wink. "The dancing part, I mean. Thought it would be okay to leave you be, but now…"

His eyes turned serious for a moment. "Do I need to be worried?" Jean asked me, all humor leaving his tone. "Is he my competition?"

"No," I stated, growing agitated.

"Maybe," Brandon spoke up, having recovered already. "Your boyfriend is a great dancer. He oughta be doing this professionally."

My lips pursed. "I'm not looking for a new job," I replied. "And really, can we take this conversation somewhere more private. I hear the pitter-patter of stalkerish feet coming closer."

"Not a bad idea." Brandon said. "I hope your room is close. Because this is a bad place to get cornered in."

"Too true." Jean seemed amicable enough all of a sudden. "This way."

Jean whipped his key out and took the lead. I had been right in that our room was just up ahead. A figure came down the hallway from the other side as we slid to a stop.

"Found 'em!" they called out. "They're down here."

"Shit," Jean uttered, sliding the key inside. "Why is it that these kinds of events always bring out the love-struck crazies, huh?"

"Occupational hazard," Brandon stated. "Care to work a bit faster there."

The door slid open just as Brandon finished speaking. "Got it," Jean said, stepping aside to let us pass first. "Last one in is the bottom bitch for the night."

I laughed in spite of the situation and so did Brandon. "He says that like it's a bad thing," Brandon quipped, holding the door so that Jean could rush in after us.

Brandon shut the door once Jean was in the clear. My boyfriend reached a hand out as he hurried inside, switching the light on. Light spilled into the room as I reached over to lock the door, feeling my heart race the whole time. The knob rattled immediately, indicating that my newfound fanbase wasn't about to give up so quickly.

"Can they get in?" I asked, feeling oddly more afraid now that we were locked in a room with no other way out.

"Bathhouse locks aren't known for their sturdiness," Jean said as the person on the other side rapped at the door with their knuckles, demanding to be let in. "But give it a minute."

"Uh, guys?" Brandon asked from behind us.

"Relax," Jean said, paying Brandon little attention. "I've seen this sort of thing before. People get high and feel the rush of touching someone. Those two things send the Miss Manners booklet right out the window."

My heart was still rattling against the ribs in my chest. "I haven't had a fright that big for a while," I said. "You neglected to mention that some guys don't like taking 'no' for an answer."

"Guys?" Brandon called out again.

"It's why you always get a room," Jean said simply. "C'mere. You're shaking like a leaf in the wind right now."

I went for Jean at once, needing to feel his arms around me. Jean pulled me into his embrace, holding me to him. I buried my face in his chest and breathed deep. His scent suffused me, making me feel warm and loved.

"Sorry to interrupt the little love fest you've got going on right now," Brandon called out, irritated. "But you two really oughta take a look around."

Jean rose up. I did the same, sensing that my boyfriend was prepared to read Brandon the riot act. I was feeling something along the same lines as well, but any shade I might have thrown stopped dead in my throat. Instead, I pulled away from Jean slightly so as to take in the state of our room.

It was completely trashed.

Jean let out a whistle. "Looks like somebody threw a rave in here while we were out," he said softly. "And stuck us with the clean-up."

"So this didn't happen because you guys are into really rough sex?" Brandon quipped, placing both hands on his bulging hips, still swollen thanks to the singles stuffed inside his speedo. "Good to know."

"This wasn't us," I said, shocked by what I was seeing. "The room was fine when we left."

"Despite that," Brandon said, giving Jean a strange look then. "I get the feeling that the management is gonna want to have a word."

I almost felt like crying. What few possessions we had were strewn everywhere. The mattress had been flipped over and cut into. Someone had tried to tear the flatscreen off the wall. Speaking of, there were cracks in the walls as well, like someone had hit them hard enough to break through the sheetrock.

Jean was studying everything closely, as he often did during a crisis. "Take pictures," he advised. "Assuming we still have our phones. I'll do the same."

It took a moment more for us to find our phones. Brandon helped by asking for our numbers. Apparently, he kept his phone secured inside of his shoes. I tried not to stare while Brandon bent over, drawing it out of his sole with one hand.

"Smart thinking," Jean complimented. "They made those too bulky back in the day. Now, just about anything will fit inside of a pair of socks."

"Back in the stone age, maybe," I heard Brandon mutter.

His plan worked, however. Brandon was able to dial both of our numbers after we gave them to him. Jean followed the sound of the Twilight Zone theme blaring from his. Mine was set on vibrate, but I could nevertheless hear it rattle over against a wall.

"Okay," I said wearily while opening up the camera feature. "Let's take stock of the damage so we can find out how much they're gonna charge us."

"It shouldn't be so bad," Jean assured me, holding his own phone in front of him. "I'm pretty sure I can convince the owners that this wasn't us."

"The door wasn't broken, though," Brandon pointed out, moving so that I could snap pictures of the bed. "That's the weird part."

"The lock was probably picked," Jean dismissed, keeping his back to Brandon the whole time.

"Strange that a couple of tweekers could have enough sense of mind to pick a lock," Brandon pointed out, standing by the door now. "When they could've just broken it."

Brandon fiddled with the lock—I assumed so he could confirm it wasn't broken. The door slid sideways and he stuck his head out.

"Coast is clear," he said, leaving the door open. "Guess they got bored and left to chase tail somewhere else."

"Good," I said, feeling relieved. I heard Jean pause and turn around, spinning on the heel of his foot. "You know," he admitted thoughtfully. "That's a good point."

"Glad you think so." Brandon didn't sound happy. "Which part are you talking about, exactly?" I was about to tell him to cool it, but he slithered over to stand next to me. "I guess now is not a good time to tell you I was serious about you signing up for Stud Stable, huh?"

That made my jaw drop. "What?" I asked once I had picked my mandible up off the floor.

"A job offer?" Jean asked, having overheard. "That's not a bad idea, honestly."

"What?"

"You're not going to get jealous, are you?" Brandon challenged before returning his focus to me. "But seriously, I'll put in a good word to my boss for you if you want."

"What?"

"And I can coach him," Jean said, moving over to stand beside me. "I've shaken my ass on a few stages. Teaching him how to wow a crowd won't be hard."

"What?" I was really on a roll with that one word. "Seriously, what?"

At that moment, a figure appeared in the doorway. For a moment, panic seized me. I was afraid one of my supposed fans was back. This was the last place I wanted to be cornered right now.

"There you are," said a voice I recognized as Michael's. "Brandon, I've been looking all over for you. We need you to do another set right—" Michael cut himself off in mid-sentence. "Sweet mother of Ga-Ga!" he cried out, noticing the destroyed room for the first time. "What the hell happened in here?"

Chapter 6

"I can't believe that this is happening," I muttered in a daze. "I can't believe I'm actually doing this. I can't believe that you're doing this. I can't believe we're going to do this."

Jean was as patient as ever, which annoyed me in this situation. "Just relax," he said encouragingly. "Be calm and take your time. It's not so different from yoga."

I wasn't reassured. "If you'll recall," I said, giving him a dirty glare, "I'm not so great at yoga either. Being a stripper won't translate so well once I'm naked in front of a crowd of horny madmen."

The trip home was not a pleasant one. Jean and I argued the whole time, something we didn't do very often. I was not happy that he had agreed to put me naked on stage in my stead—while I was in the room and without even consulting with me first.

You can bet I gave him an earful.

Admittedly, I might have gone a little too far. Before all of that, we had to inform the manager of what happened. Brandon was very sweet, sticking around long enough to corroborate our story. We explained that we came back from the third floor to our room and found it trashed.

The manager had been upset, of course. I got the distinct impression that he wasn't entirely convinced in the beginning. Something told me that this kind of thing wasn't uncommon.

Fortunately, several people had seen Jean and I upstairs. Brandon was working at *Treats* all week long. The fact that his story matched ours went a long way. In the end, the manager gave Jean and I a refund.

We were also offered the option of calling the police to report any damages, but Jean begged off. Neither of us had brought much in the way of worldly possessions to the bathhouse that night, per Jean's instructions.

Plus, for some reason, he seemed anxious to leave. I might have found out why, but I was too busy being mad at him for signing me on to be a stripper without my consent. Thus, the remainder of the night was spent with me yelling at him right up until we fell asleep.

"Why do you even want me to do this?" I demanded. We were in our bedroom because Jean wanted to teach me a few basic routines. I flat-out refused to do this in any room where Auntie Mags might walk in on us. "You still haven't explained that."

Jean took a deep breath. "I think there's something fishy going on at that bathhouse," he said, looking me dead in the eye. "There a few things that don't add up."

"What, like the break-in?" That didn't seem particularly suspicious to me, even though I did upload pictures of the state of our room afterward to Instagram. "I thought you said that kind of stuff happens all the time."

"It does," Jean said, nodding. "That's not what I'm talking about."

I waited, but he said nothing else. "What?" I demanded, getting impatient. "Now is really not the time for you to be cryptic with me."

"Sorry," Jean said immediately. "I was deep in thought."

Clearing his throat, he sat down on the foot of the bed. Taking refuge in here had only made me slightly less uneasy. Giving Jean something to distract himself from teaching me how to strip was doing a better job of calming my nerves.

Besides that, much as I hated to admit it, I was curious to hear what he had to say.

"One," Jean began, ticking off on his fingers. "There's the fact that you were recommended."

"Thank you," I muttered. "I thought that was weird too."

"Not so much that," Jean went on, smirking. "You weren't bad up there on the table. I was watching for some of it."

I blushed, though heaven help me if I understood why. Jean and I had engaged in some pretty deep things during our brief period together. I definitely got more "recreational" with him than I ever did with Nik. A big part of my embarrassment had to do with the fact that I was dancing so salaciously with someone else while he watched.

"Then what?" I wondered, trying to will the flush in my cheeks away.

"It's more the eagerness to hire you," Jean added. "The whole situation is a little bit Hollywood."

"The nobody that gets discovered by the talent agent and becomes a big star?" I thought about where his train of thought was going. "Yeah, that does sound shady. I mean, if Hollywood filmed porn."

"Who says they don't?" Jean asked seriously. "But anyway, this is supposed to be a big company. Touring in different cities with a large cast. Why do they need an amateur on such short notice?"

I bit my lower lip. "Isn't that a good reason to not take the job?" I pointed out.

"It brings me to my second point," Jean said, adding a finger to the count. "Where were all of the strippers last night?"

I thought back to when we arrived on the third floor of the bathhouse. "Brandon was on a table with me in the pool area," I said, flushing again. Some deeply shameful part of myself had been waiting for Jean to be angry about that and was confused by the fact that he wasn't. "I think there was another one…"

"By the DJ booth," Jean confirmed. "On the outer deck area."

"That was it," I said, agreeing with him. "But I can't recall seeing anyone else there. I mean, who was there to work and not play."

"Exactly my point." Jean stood up. "Why only two? This is supposed to be a big event for Treats. Shouldn't there be more?"

"Maybe because it was the first night?" I offered. "They'll probably have more as Halloween creeps closer."

"I don't think so," Jean said, shaking his head gravely. "And then, lastly, there's that young man who was shot outside the store."

I shuddered involuntarily as Jean added a third finger. "I wonder if he wasn't a part of the same company," Jean insisted. "Could he have been with Stud Stable?"

Automatically, I reached over to retrieve my phone off the table. "It shouldn't be too hard to figure out," I said, doing a search on my phone. "They probably have the dancers listed on the website."

Jean was smiling while the page loaded. "Quick thinking," he applauded as a glint sparkled in his eye. "I would have called someone."

"It's because you're old," I teased. "And don't think this gets you off the hook. Even if there is something shady going on at *Treats*, it doesn't give you the right t—well, that was fast."

I stared down at the front page of the Stud Stable website for a moment. "I didn't even have to scroll down," I said, turning the phone around so Jean could see. "It's right here."

Gently, Jean took the phone from me. "It's the same guy," he said, his voice growing thicker. "We were standing right next to him when he was shot."

"Kind of makes him hard to forget," I said sadly, thinking back.

A photo had been added to the homepage of the Stud Stable website. It was a memorial commemorating the death of one Blu Harlow. The same handsome blond face staring coyly up from my phone had died a few short days ago. Fans and fellow dancers alike offered up their sympathies. No details were given on how he died, but Jean and I didn't require that.

"Guess that solves the mystery of how and why they are short-staffed," I said as Jean handed the phone back to me.

"Not really," Jean said. "They should have booked more dancers for an event this big."

I frowned, thinking that over. "Maybe the other dancers bowed out," I offered. "Out of respect for their friend."

"Not a chance," Jean said, utterly convinced. "Dancers live and die by tips, remember? If they don't shake their ass, they don't get paid. Plus, this guy—"

Jean hesitated. I would have scolded him for forgetting the young man's name, but I had to check my phone again.

"Blu," I said, lowering the phone again.

"Probably a stage name," Jean said thoughtfully. "Anyway, he didn't die at *Treats*. Blu was shot outside a grocery store chain."

"Meaning they're probably not connected," I pointed out. "Right?"

"I can't be certain yet." Jean reached over and pulled me to him. "But the company should have replaced him. Why was bringing in another of their dancers impossible?"

I hated to, but pushed Jean away. "In that case," I told him, putting my foot squarely down. "Why don't we go to the police?"

"And tell them what?" Jean countered with. "That something suspicious is happening in a gay bathhouse. Cops won't buy that. Something shady is always going down in places like that." Jean made a face. "And then," he added grimly, "there's the fact that bathhouses have a tenuous relationship with the authorities at best. A lot of raids went down back in the day for reasons that were flimsy at best."

"And let me guess," I added, realizing something. "The last time there was a dead body and we were involved, you almost got hit with a murder charge. Am I right?"

Jean looked away. "I do seem to have issues with the police as well," he murmured softly.

"Can't argue with you there," I said sadly. "Okay, so we don't go to the police. Why not call Wendy?"

Wendy was a—well, "friend" seemed like a bit of a stretch. Jean and I met her on our first date after a light fixture almost crushed a porn star to death. She was a journalist for an online leftist news media site. Her dream had been to be a reporter for a major San Francisco newspaper. That fell through when they made her a coffee girl, so she struck out somewhat on her own writing for a website that most people hadn't heard of yet.

"It's a gay bathhouse," Jean reminded me. "She wouldn't exactly blend in."

"And we don't exactly have a lot of friends on the force to talk to either," I acknowledged, hating that Jean's logic made a weird kind of sense. "So you want to know if something strange is happening there and that is worth throwing your boyfriend to the wolves, right?"

Jean pulled me to him again and I didn't resist this time. "You won't get thrown to the wolves," he told me seriously. "I'll be there with you every step of the way."

That, oddly enough, did make me feel a little better. "I think it's sweet that you want to do something to help," I said, looking up into his gorgeous face. "And I hate how this sounds, but…why me?"

"They asked you," Jean answered, plainly and simply. "The dance troupe is looking for young blood. I'm a little too over the hill for their tastes."

"You've danced before," I countered, not willing to give up just yet.

"Once," Jean insisted. "For a brief period, and for charity. Before that, I was retired and it had been years since I got up on a bar to wiggle my butt at strangers for dollar bills."

"People recognized you while we were there last night."

"One," Jean reminded, growing impatient with me. "Maybe two, tops. Sweetheart, I know you were a fan of mine, but I just do not have the star power that I used to."

Carefully, Jean took my hands into his. "Time for someone new to take center stage," he encouraged. "I'll be with you every step of the way, figuratively and otherwise."

The man could always make my heart melt, even when asking me to do the impossible. I could feel the warmth from him seep into my arms. It traveled up to the rest of my body with every beat of my heart.

"I love you," I told him, meaning every word. "But you're asking me to dance. Wearing next to nothing. While people stare at me."

"You seemed okay with it last night," he kidded, kissing the back of one hand. "To be honest, it made me just a little bit jealous."

"I wasn't the one who got dragged off by three hunky boytoys," I poked back playfully. "And what happened on the table was a one-time thing. That was just the heat of the moment."

"Then we need to figure out how to get you back into that state of mind," Jean said, turning serious again. "So you can trigger it whenever you want."

I took my time, longer than was necessary, to come to a decision. "I'm not saying you're right about my dancing skills," I told him, giving my boyfriend a real jab with an index figure this time. "But if there is something weird happening at *Treats*—something that got a young man killed—then you're right. Let's see if we can find out anything and then we'll call either Wendy or the police."

"Deal," Jean said, grinning. "Ready to start?"

"Not even remotely." I moved away from Jean a little. "But here we go anyway!"

My assumption was that Jean would have me start on a stripper pole. Granted, we didn't have one of those. There wasn't anything in Auntie Mags' townhouse that would substitute for it either.

"Stripper poles are overrated," Jean replied dismissively when I voiced my concern. "And highly unsanitary."

I thought back to our first date and couldn't recall Jean having touched the pole on stage at the Nob Hill Theater. "No arguments here," I said, nodding emphatically. "So where do we start, then?"

"You won't have to worry about doing anything overly complicated," Jean reassured me, sensing that my apprehension about performing hadn't abated. "Remember, bathhouses are about getting laid and—" Jean paused briefly. "—*maybe* making use of the sauna."

I laughed. "For an actual steam bath, you mean?"

"Exactly." Jean had on his traditional knowing smirk. "But if you decide to use the sauna while you're on break and find two or more guys fucking in there, don't take it personally."

"I love how casual you sound," I retorted, giving him the eye. "It makes me think you've done that more than once."

Jean's response was to shrug nonchalantly. "Men who go there like spontaneity," he said. "Getting back to my point, there won't be any stripper poles at *Treats*. It's best if we focus on your moves instead."

I waited while Jean went for his phone. He spent several minutes scrolling through a playlist while I stood by anxiously. I bounced on the balls of my feet, going over the various reasons why we were doing this. It felt like I needed to reinforce that this was all for a good cause.

After all, what kind of person did it make me if I was getting involved simply for the thrill of dancing for strangers?

"I found a couple of songs to start off with," Jean revealed, snapping me out of the moral spiral I'd begun sinking into. "Okay, get naked."

For some reason, I balked at that. "Um, couldn't we start off with me clothed?" I asked anxiously. "I mean, the whole point is to take my clothes off slowly, right?"

"Not really," Jean answered plainly.

"That was how you did it," I pointed out, making it sound like a challenge.

"Yes, but my style is different," Jean argued gently. "And that was for a stage show. Bathhouses are a different sort of environment. Very rarely do guests stay clothed for very long."

I gulped. "So the idea is for me to get up on a table, in front of a crowd of hungry older men, and shake my ass in a thong?" The apprehension I felt before was back in spades. "Right off the cuff?"

"'Fraid so," Jean admitted, trying not to laugh at my embarrassment.

I was quivering too much on the inside to be mad. "How do you do it?" I asked, wanting to shift gears a little. "How does anyone do that?"

Jean didn't answer right away, cluing me in that I wouldn't like what he had to offer. "Most do drugs," he admitted. "GHB is typically the substance of choice."

I must have made quite the face in response to that. "No thanks," I replied. "This is sounding less and less like a good idea."

"I didn't think you'd want to," Jean said quickly. "That's why I have something a little different in mind."

In spite of my anxiety, I was intrigued. "Like what?" I asked.

Jean tapped the screen of his phone with one thumb, queuing up the first track. "Later," he said. "Let's practice your moves first. First things first, the key is all in the shoulders and the hips."

What sounded like a very generic house sample began playing.

"Keep your body moving at all times," he instructed, placing his hands on my hips to guide me. "It's what the audience has come to see."

I tried to do as Jean asked, but it wasn't easy. His hands had to guide me through the entirety of the first song. Whenever I felt him let go, my body faltered. I couldn't seem to keep the beat on my own.

"Relax," Jean said. "Confidence is everything in this game."

To illustrate his point, Jean proceeded to dance. I was instantly star-struck by his movements, how he seemed to command attention with effortless ease. It made my apprehension rise to a new level.

"How are you…?" I struggled to come up with a way to voice what I was feeling. "It's like you turn it on and off with a switch."

"Practice," Jean answered, still dancing as the second track played, a slower number with a bit more genuine rhythm to it. "I've done this for years."

I went still as Jean locked his gaze with mine. "Dance with me," he breathed out, sliding both hands up my sides to cup both shoulders. "Please?"

It was impossible to say no. He was asking me to, not making me. My body complied at once, going along with the rhythm. Having Jean there to guide me helped. Also, the music was easier to follow since this was a slower song.

"You're getting there," Jean said, encouraging me.

"This isn't as bad," I said, breaking the gaze for a moment. It surprised me that I was able to keep up without Jean holding me with his eyes. "I think it helps that the beat isn't as fast."

"Slow songs are fine," Jean said while I watched our feet move. "They are more sensual. Less hard and heavy. More erotic."

I looked back up. "Could we dance to a few more like this?" I asked. "I feel more comfortable with this kind of music."

"We can do whatever you like." Jean's voice was low and husky. "In this situation, you are the one who is in control. Never let that thought slip from your mind."

Jean moved his hands from my shoulders down to my chest, making me shiver. "If someone touches you in a way you don't like, make them stop." His thumbs flicked across my nipples. "If they don't respect you, send them away."

I placed a hand on Jean's chest, feeling the muscles there. It wasn't something Jean wanted me to do. I was acting of my own accord now.

"Always remember," Jean whispered, leaning in close. "You have the power."

The time was never more right. My hand left his chest, sliding easily across the surface of Jean's hairy skin. A sigh slipped out of him as my fingers cupped the back of his neck.

It was me who pulled Jean down, making his back bend. I had the power to bring our faces close. I was in control, bringing him in to claim his mouth.

Right before our lips met, the door banged open, shooting the mood in the kneecaps.

"Hey, boys!" Auntie Mags' voice rang out, causing me to jump. "Have either one of you seen my old memory c—"

I leaped back. Jean whirled around, eyes wide as he stared across as his surrogate aunt. She was standing just inside the door frame. It looked like Auntie Mags had stopped in mid-step.

To her credit, she looked embarrassed. "You two are in the middle of something," Auntie Mags decided right then and there, backing up. "I'll come back later."

The door clicked shut. Jean's mouth was stretched thin as he turned back to face me. I did not look happy.

"At least it wasn't my mother," he mused. "I've been caught like that before and it wasn't fun."

My eyes narrowed then. "I thought you locked that door," I said pointedly.

"Minor miscalculation," Jean admitted, holding both of his hands face-up at me. "Shall we try again?"

Chapter 7

"I've changed my mind."

We were sitting in our new room at the bathhouse. Checking in took longer this time around. The line was much longer and they were short-handed for some reason. Thankfully, no one at the booth downstairs recognized us. Word apparently hadn't gotten far enough around for Jean and I to be easily recognized as the two people with the trashed room.

"You're doing fine."

Jean kept busy by putting our stuff away while I settled down on the bed. We decided to get there early so I could warm up. It had been Jean's suggestion. I wasn't sure how much "warming up" was going to help.

At present, I was dressed in my "stripping" wardrobe. This consisted of a single string bikini brief. Jean went out and bought it for me during one of my practice sessions, and I confessed that it showed off my package nicely.

Getting into it was easy too. All I had to do was wear it underneath my street clothing. Jean had dropped trou as well and now had a towel secured around his waist. It did nothing to hide the ample bulge showing there. Even only semi-hard, there were few men walking the earth who could compare with him.

"I'm not doing fine," I protested, staring straight at a spot on the wall. "I'm having a very low-key panic attack right now."

"Deep breaths," Jean encouraged, coming over to sit beside me. "You got this. I have complete faith in you."

"I tripped and fell on almost every routine you showed me," I pointed out, tearing my gaze away from the blank wall to glare at him.

"You still managed to get through them." Jean spoke tenderly as he placed a hand on each of my shoulders to calm me down. "And you only had a day to practice. That's impressive."

"It's not." I was being fatalistic and knew it, but my brain had become stuck on self-loathing and refused to budge. "I'm a complete failure. Why am I doing this?"

Jean gave my shoulders a squeeze. "Do you want to back out?" he asked carefully.

"Yes!" I exclaimed at once, only to have self-doubt cripple me the moment the word left my lips. "No. I mean, maybe? I don't know what I want. I'm just…scared."

I felt the thick bush of Jean's beard brush against my neck. He placed a tender kiss there before pulling me into a hug. I didn't fight when his arms encircled me. It felt good to have him take charge then, to hold me and keep me safe.

"Will you do something for me?" I heard him ask.

"I almost want to ask you to find me some GHB," I revealed, ashamed. "Or Ecstasy or…something. Anything that'll help me calm down."

"Let's try something else first," Jean replied, patting the bed. "Lay down for a minute. Will you, please?"

I didn't feel much like stretching out. Something in my gut told me that a nap wouldn't help matters much. Nevertheless, I lay back on the bed per Jean's request, settling my head down on the pillow. The tension started to slip out of my body almost instantly.

"Now then," Jean whispered softly near my ear. "The first thing that I want you to do is breathe. Take one deep breath in and let it back out. Do that for me, okay?"

I did, filling my lungs up with as much air as they would hold. It was a deep enough breath to make me light-headed. The room tilted slightly as I exhaled.

"And again," Jean said. "Let each breath out slowly for me."

I repeated the process, letting my body grow lighter each time. It wasn't long before I felt a tingle in my limbs. My body seemed lighter now.

"I want to remind you that you are in control," Jean went on, still whispering softly beside me on the bed. The heat from his body was giving me warm shivers. "You have the power."

"I have the power," I repeated, wondering why I just did that.

"Yes, you are in control." Jean's voice was like melted butter flowing over me, heating me up from the inside. "You always are in control. Go on the stage or don't. Stay here or go home. These are your choices and your decisions. No one else's."

Privately, I realized he was right. I was doing this because something strange had happened. We needed proof before we could go to the police. I wasn't willing to embarrass myself for money, but I would do it to help others.

For some reason, it felt like I had my priorities backward but that was a puzzle to sort out later.

"Now," Jean resumed. His voice seemed further away compared to before. "I want you to relax. Just think about how good it feels to relax your tense muscles. To let go of all that stress and worry."

My body began to feel lighter. I wasn't sure when, but at some point after Jean began talking, I closed my eyes. They remained shut while Jean continued to talk.

"Feel your body drifting, rising." It really did feel as if I were floating up off the bed. "Floating. Carrying you up into the air. You have no need to fear falling. You're being taken away from everything that could harm you. Everything that might be troubling you."

I couldn't remember now if I had started out facing down on the bed or sunny side up. "Let go of your troubles and your worries," Jean whispered. "And just relax. Feel how amazing life is now that you no longer have all that stress and worry in it."

"Mmm." A moan escaped between my lips. "I feel…"

I couldn't finish the thought. The will to form complete sentences was slipping away from me. I was sure that was a bad thing, but I couldn't figure out why. It seemed like not being able to talk should have worried me more.

Jean was right, however. It felt too good to let go. I had been holding in so much stress and worry about this thing. In fact, I had been anxious about embarrassing myself before the previous night. Simply coming to the bathhouse had put me in an anxious mood. I was far too hung up on what other people thought of me.

"This is all you need to do," Jean revealed, whispering in my ear. "All you need to think about is taking the time to relax."

If I got any more relaxed, I would be a dead man.

"And I want you to remember what it felt like to dance." The request came out of left field for me, but I didn't protest. "Go back to when you were on top of the table dancing with that other man."

I could see Brandon's face so clearly in that moment. He was laughing and smiling right next to me. I could almost count each tooth in the top and bottom row. They practically gleamed in the low lights.

"Remember how it felt."

My body moved so easily. It was perfect, like I had been born to dance.

"Remember how powerful you were in that moment."

It was true. I had never felt more alive. My blood raced as my heart pounded from the thrill of it all.

"Remember how everyone was watching you. How much they loved seeing you move."

Every single eye around that table had been on me. They stood there staring while Brandon and I danced together. We held their gazes together in the palms of our hands.

"I want you to remember all of those feelings. Each time you hear the music play, go back to that moment. Go back to when you felt powerful and strong. Full of confidence."

The music was playing again. I could hear it.

"When you hear the music, you'll remember."

I could feel it right now. The music was coming through the walls. It rose up out of the floor and down through the ceiling. I was covered in it, bathed by it.

"Remember that you have the power."

I did have the power. I always had the power.

"Now open your eyes."

My eyelids fluttered open, blinking. The room was oddly quiet. I could hear sounds coming through the walls faintly, but there was no music. I wasn't floating in the air either. My body remained flat on the bed. I hadn't moved an inch from where I was the whole time.

"Feeling better?" Jean asked.

I raised up slightly. He was sitting on the side of the bed near my feet, watching me closely. An unreadable glint shined brightly in his eyes. I wasn't sure why, but my gut told me something significant had happened.

And yet, my hole didn't feel stretched to fit an express train.

"A little, yeah," I answered. It was a moment before I realized what I just said. "Actually, yeah. I do feel okay. Better than I was before, anyway."

"Good," Jean said, getting up off the bed. "Because you go on pretty soon. We need to find Michael and let him know you made it here safely."

Nervousness flooded my stomach. Nevertheless, I climbed up off the bed and stood. Butterflies batted against the inner walls of my abdomen, but I didn't protest when Jean went for the door.

"Let's do this," I agreed, surprised by how bold I sounded.

"That's the spirit," Jean said encouragingly.

I changed into my stripper gear while Jean stripped down. Our clothes went into the small safe built into the underside of the bed. Jean then secured a towel around his waist and motioned for me to follow. I quickly closed the gap after making sure the door was locked and secure. One break-in was enough for me.

We followed a familiar twisting path through the maze of corridors that made up the bathhouse rooms. It wasn't long before we were back in the main hallway with the stairway heading up to the third floor. I could hear moans and other sounds as we passed by.

"Sounds like the guests are putting the Slurp Room to good use," I said without breaking my stride.

"That's the sex dungeon," Jean reminded me, pointing back at the door frame we just passed. "That's the Slurp Room."

I turned in the direction Jean was pointing now. Sure enough, the sounds of gagging and deep slurping echoed out through the open doorway.

"Let's hope they cleaned up all the barf from last night," I said, continuing on with Jean at my side.

"I'm sure they did," he replied confidently. "They're usually good about that sort of thing in these places. It's bad for business if customers slip and fall on hurl. Or other bodily fluids."

"Grounds for a lawsuit too, I'm sure," I added as we headed up the stairs. "Imagine the face of the judge having to preside over that case."

Jean laughed. "I'm sure they've heard stranger," he said. "But you're not wrong. It is pretty hilarious."

We continued the climb in silence. One thing was for certain, though. Going up and down all of these stairs was going to do wonders for my workout. I was getting in some great calisthenics. My upper thighs were on fire by the time we reached the top.

"A couple things," Jean said suddenly as we approached the door. "Before you go out there."

"Okay." I stopped and turned to face him. "Hit me."

Jean's expression was a little bit more serious than I would have liked. "First," he began, ticking off on a finger. "Be friendly and open, but don't ask a lot of questions. If I'm right, they'll be on the lookout for that."

"Okay..."

"Second, don't volunteer a lot of personal information," he went on, ignoring my nervousness. "You live here in the city. You're trying out something new while between jobs."

"Less than a year ago," I pointed out, "that would've been the truth. Shouldn't be hard for me to spin a story around that."

"Exactly," Jean agreed. "The best way to lie is to stick as close to the truth as possible."

I wondered how Jean knew that. He said it with such confidence.

"Oh," he added before I could press for details. "And mention that you have a boyfriend."

"Why?" I asked automatically, only to feel guilty afterward. "I mean, I can. Sure, but is there a specific reason?"

"Yes." Jean's face was almost grave as he leaned forward. "So that I don't get too jealous."

I thought for sure he was joking, but the intense way that Jean kissed me made me think otherwise. He gripped me tightly in his arms, holding me into him. I could feel that he was very happy having me in his arms, too. It felt like the towel he wore was going to fly off any second.

I was spared from any such embarrassment, but only because I was wearing the blue g-string Jean had picked out. One hand slid down the back to cup my cheek in his meaty paw. His tongue pushed past my mouth, forcing its way down my throat.

The rough treatment surprised me, but I wasn't fighting him off. It felt good to know he wanted me, that Jean was being possessive. I liked that he was going to feel a little jealous of me dancing for strangers.

"Sorry," I said, once I managed to push him away. "But you don't get any further without tipping first."

Jean seemed surprised for a second, but then he laughed. "Good one," he said. "Don't be afraid to get assertive. Especially with the ones wanting something for nothing."

"I remember," I assured him. "Now let's get this over with."

Jean opened the door and let me go first. "Your public awaits," he said. "Mustn't keep them waiting on the night of your debut."

"Right," I muttered, feeling the nervous butterflies in my belly bat against the fleshy walls of my insides. "Can't have that, can we?"

"Nope!" Jean said, giving me a slight push.

I shot a dirty look over my shoulder at him. The nudge did the trick, however, much as I was loathe to admit. Taking that first step was the hardest. None of the nervousness abated, but I was able to remember how to move my feet.

We had gotten to the bathhouse much earlier than before. I needed time to prepare, according to Jean, and getting there earlier meant that I wouldn't see the packed house until it was time for me to go on.

He was right, of course. The deck area was nearly deserted. I spotted Chrissy Sinz setting up in the booth that had been put aside for him. He was already dressed for the occasion. A day-glow jock strap concealed an ample package and that was it. His tattoos were once again on prominent display as he moved about, checking his equipment.

I debated going over to say hello. Jean seemed to read my thoughts. He was suddenly behind me and whispering low into my ear, tickling the lobe with his thick whiskers.

"We've got a few minutes," he reminded me. "If you want his autograph."

I blushed, which was concealed thanks to the low lighting of the deck, but Jean knew my body's mannerisms too well.

"It's okay if you were a fan of more than one porn star," he added teasingly. "I knew from the start that you're a porn slut."

My foot connected with his by total and complete accident. "I am not a porn slut," I declared defensively. "I just…was wondering if he was anything like how he acted in his movies. That's all."

"Take a chance and find out," Jean suggested, nodding toward Chrissy.

I debated a moment more. Uncertainty seemed to be the running theme for me of late. After a moment of hesitation, I took a tentative step forward. My heart began beating faster as I approached the booth.

Up close, he was remarkably similar to the way I remembered him from the movies. It didn't look as though the tattoos had faded. Chrissy was also in remarkable shape. A tiny bit of body fat covered the edges of his muscles. It wasn't enough to be called flab. If anything, it made him look healthy and—for want of a better word—normal. He lacked the photoshopped gym look that so many porn stars tried for, but it was clear Chrissy kept up a very strict fitness regimen.

"Hi," I blurted out once I was close enough.

Chrissy barely glanced up at me. "'Sup?" he greeted in that thick Chi-Town accent he always sported in his films, confirming at least one thing for me. "You new here?"

"Stripper," I confirmed, fighting back embarrassment. "My first night…here, I mean. I just started."

"Should be a good night for tips," Chrissy said. He was avoiding eye contact, reserving most of his attention for the turntable in front of him, but his voice never wavered. "You new to the game?"

Apparently, Chrissy could multitask. "Is it that obvious?" I wondered.

"Eh, I've been doing this long enough to know how to spot fresh meat," Chrissy revealed, turning away from the turn table long enough to toss me a knowing smirk. "Don't be too hard on yourself if it turns out this isn't the right gig for you. Not everyone can cut it."

"Yeah." My shoulders slumped a little. "I have a feeling this is only gonna be temporary."

"No shame in that," he replied casually while adjusting several knobs. "What'd you do before this?"

"Before quarantine?" I flashed back briefly to my life before Jean, which felt like watching stills of a previous incarnation. "I was a massage therapist."

"COVID sucks ass," Chrissy declared, to which I wholeheartedly agreed. "I know a lot of people who didn't bounce back right away. Don't kick yourself down just because you gotta do what you gotta do. Hear me?"

I nodded. "I've been getting similar advice," I said, thinking back to the impromptu therapy session during yoga. "Anyway, I just wanted to come over and say hi. This…is a little embarrassing, but I was a big fan of yours."

"Thanks." Chrissy glanced up long enough to smile at me, but I couldn't help but notice how the grin never quite made it all the way up to his eyes. "I appreciate that."

Being Jean's boyfriend had an effect on me. I wanted to know whether or not the lack of warmth in Chrissy's eyes was due to him being distracted. After a brief second of indecision, I decided to try again.

"*Saddles Blazing* was terrific," I went on, turning up the fanboy in me a little. "I wasn't a huge fan of the threeway at the end. But I'm guessing that wasn't your call."

"Just doing what the script asked me to," Chrissy revealed. A dangerous smirk spread across his face then. "The bottom for that scene was a prissy lil' bitch. Never liked him much, so topping the hell outta his ass was fun."

He looked up at me again. The smile was gone from his face. I could see the same coldness in his eyes as before. They never changed when he spoke again.

"Might wanna go ahead and find Michael," Chrissy told me point-blank. "He's not the sort of fellow who likes to be kept waiting."

"Oh." It felt like I was being given the brush-off. "Right, I should do that. Um, do you know where he is by any chance?"

Chrissy nodded once at a spot behind me before going back to his equipment. "In the pool area with the others," he said, cussing once at something that was apparently wrong with his turntable. "Last time I saw him, least."

"Thanks," I said, turning to go. "See you around. You're a great DJ, just so you know."

Either Chrissy didn't hear me, or he didn't feel the compliment warranted a response. I decided to leave it be and walk away. Jean was waiting for me near the door to the pool area.

"How'd it go?" he asked, getting the door.

"Weird," I answered, keeping my voice low as I went in. "He acted cool enough. Didn't seem to mind me bringing up his porn career, but…"

"But?" Jean asked when I hesitated, following close behind me.

"I dunno." I was struggling to put my thoughts into words. "He's kind of intense. There's this strange aura about him. He wasn't mean or anything, but he didn't come across as particularly friendly either."

"Hm, interesting."

We were crossing the pool area. The air once again smelled of chlorine. Soft blue lights reflected off the shimmering water, giving the whole space an eerie glow. I spotted a knot of people huddled around what looked like a table. They all wore speedos, cluing me in that these were the men I would be working alongside for the next few days.

Most of them had other accessories on as well, keeping with the theme of it being Halloween. One wore an oversized leprechaun hat with a paper four-leaf clover covered in green glitter. Another had plastic red horns sticking up from his dark hair.

Brandon was among them, stuffed in-between the hard bodies. An open sailor shirt hugged his upper body like it had been tailored to fit him. His package was concealed by a bright blue speedo with anchors on the sides. It showed off his amazing ass well—but, then, so did the way he was bent over slightly.

It looked like Brandon was reaching for something. He seemed to sense my approach and turned around, breaking into a big smile at the sight of me.

"Hey, you made it!"

I smiled back, slowing to a stop while Brandon raised up. One or two of the other dancers turned when he called out. They each gave me a look before going back to whatever it was they were doing.

As Brandon approached, I saw a Twizzler in one hand. The table was apparently some kind of crafts stand—and an unhealthy one at that. Brandon took a bite out of his sugary treat as he came close.

"I was worried you might chicken out," he said, holding the free hand out to shake mine.

"I thought about it," I admitted, accepting the gesture.

Brandon pulled me into a hug, giving me an unexpected squeeze. I could tell he was getting excited by me being so close. When we pulled apart, however, his face seemed a bit fixed—stiff, like he was holding something back.

"I see your boyfriend came to chaperone," he went on.

"I'm here in a business capacity," Jean responded coolly from behind where I stood. "Think of me as his manager."

"You won't need a handler for this." Brandon was trying to be reassuring, but I noticed he spoke directly to me and not Jean. "The point is to loosen up and have fun."

I decided to change the subject since my boyfriend being there was apparently a bone of contention for him.

"Did you get those trick 'r treating tonight?" I teased, nodding at the snack in his hand.

"What?" Brandon looked down in confusion at first. "Oh, right. These are for quick energy. We have to move around a lot and it helps to be hopped up on sugar."

Jean had mentioned this to me and I completely forgot. "And here I was led to believe that a stripper's nonstop energy came from speed," I retorted, feeling foolish.

"Shh!" Brandon said in a mock whisper, placing a finger over his mouth. "It's a trade secret. No one must ever know."

"My lips are sealed," I said agreeably.

Brandon giggled. "For now, anyway. C'mon, I want you to meet the others."

I held back when Brandon laced his fingers with mine. A quick look over one shoulder told me that Jean was fine, though. He merely nodded once, indicating that I ought to play along.

Having been given his blessing, I followed. It occurred to me that this was the exact kind of behavior I had been fighting against. I wanted to be independent, not relying on Jean to make decisions or give me instructions on what to do. The past few days had consisted of nothing but that, however.

And yet, I was totally out of my element. Was it wrong that I was taking advice from someone who knew better than me? I didn't think so, but it made me question myself.

"Guys," Brandon called out, getting the other dancers' attention. "Come meet Rafael!"

One after the other, the dancers rose up from the table and turned. I noticed several were munching on Twizzler sticks as well. One must have been famished because he had wadded up two and crammed both into his mouth at the same time.

It was rather like watching a YouTube video of a cow chewing cud. I had been around strippers before thanks to Jean, but once again, something salacious and exciting was rapidly losing its mystique for me.

Brandon went still as the other dancers sized me up, raking me up and down with their eyes. "Oh, that reminds me," he added out the corner of his mouth. "Did you ever pick a stage name?"

I swallowed down my fear. "Papa Vega," I answered, hoping no one laughed. "It was…very last minute."

Brandon smiled. "Trust me," he said, placing a tender hand on my shoulder. "I've heard way worse. Especially from first-timers."

"I can change it," I offered.

"Don't you dare," a voice from over by the table called out. I turned to see a twink no more than five feet tall stepping around the table to greet me. "I love it."

The twink had light brown hair that was cut very short. It would have been a military buzz cut if not for the very slight mop that had been left on top. A pair of dazzling blue eyes peered out below the tuft of bangs to lock with mine as he approached.

He wore a red speedo with a checkered shawl around his shoulders. An empty wicker basket was clutched tightly in one hand. Like everything else about him, it was small. I realized that this guy was supposed to be a variation on Little Red Riding Hood.

The other hand stuck out in a gesture of friendship. I felt a heat radiate from him as we shook, though. It made the air around his body sizzle. There was something captivating about him—charismatic, like spotting a wild coyote out in the desert. He wore a rakish grin the whole time. On the whole, I felt like he would be a lot of fun to hang around with on a late Saturday night.

"Name's Austin," the young-looking twink said, flashing me a wink to go with his impish, knowing smile. "Nice to meet you. Happy to have you on board."

"Thanks," I said, feeling relieved. A tension I hadn't been aware of flooded out of me. "Glad to be here. I think."

It hadn't occurred to me that I was nervous about making a good impression. The others hanging around over by the table seemed more amicable now. I had a sneaking suspicion that I had just passed a test of some sort.

"First night jitters," Austin said knowingly, turning around and waving for me to follow him. "It happens to everybody. That's why we're fueling up. Come get something light in your stomach."

"He's right," Brandon agreed, trailing along obediently. "It'll help."

The others stepped aside to make space for me. I was touched by the gesture. The table was in full view now and I could see the bounty that had been laid out. It was like a kid's Halloween feast. In addition to Twizzlers, there were sour balls, jawbreakers, gingersnaps, and some type of candy bar in yellow wrapping I had never heard of before called Coffee Crisps.

"You wanna avoid those," Austin advised, catching me staring. "Chocolate stains your teeth and will give you bad breath."

"Dunno who thought those were a good idea," Brandon added, eyeing the candy bars disdainfully.

"Must've been one of the new people from downstairs," Austin replied, waving the issue away with one hand while the other snagged a sour ball from the bowl. "It happens."

"Downstairs?" I wondered, doing as Austin and Brandon advised by avoiding the candy bars and taking a gingersnap instead.

"From *Treats*," Brandon explained quickly, sucking on a jawbreaker. "Most of the employees here are on the first floor."

"Doing something or another," Austin added, rolling his eyes. "Oh, before I forget! Here, you'll need at least one of these."

Austin reached across the table for another bowl, picking up something round at flat in a square plastic wrapper. To my embarrassment, I realized it was a condom. With all the sugary goodness on the table, I had skimmed past those, assuming they were another part of the spread.

"Thanks," I said, taking one out of the bowl. "I mean, I don't plan to hook up tonight, but the sentiment is appreciated."

"They're not for recreational use," Austin told me, placing the bowl back down on the table.

"The bathhouse asked us to wear them as part of the show," Brandon explained. "Sorry, you should've been told already. They wanted us to promote safe sex practices."

"Oh." I looked down at the orange condom in my hands. "What do I have to do, exactly?"

"During your routine," Austin answered, still sucking away fervently at the sour ball between his cheek and gum. "You put the rubber on."

I waited, looking around at the other faces, expecting there to be more. "That's it?" I asked when no one spoke. Everyone seemed content to let Austin or Brandon do the talking. "I just wear it while I dance?"

"Make sure everyone sees you slip it on underneath your speedo," Austin verified. "But yeah, that's pretty much all there is to it."

"You don't have to wear it the whole night," one of the other dancers informed, breaking the silent streak among them at last. "Just for a little while. Take it off when you go on break."

A blond muscle jock with a crew cut wearing a camouflage speedo and military vest stuck a beefy hand out. "Sorry about the silent treatment," he said, squeezing my hand tightly when I shook his. "Name's Jax, by the way."

"Trip," a slender African-American wearing a Black Panther mask pushed up off his face added, waving my way. I noticed he had beautiful eyes too. "Nice to mee'cha."

"Dante," said the studly Italian by his side sporting the devil horns.

"Kiwi," another gym bunny with a heavy Australian access introduced, nodding. This guy had on a very skimpy version of a cowboy ensemble. "Good to know ya."

"Marcus," came the last one, a cocky brown-haired jock of short height with deep green eyes that held a tenderness to them behind his swagger. He was the one wearing the great big leprechaun hat.

I assumed they were all going by their stage names. That was fine with me. I had no desire to be called "Vega" or "Papa" for the rest of the night, unless it was by tippers.

"Nice to meet you all," I replied, figuring it never hurt to be polite. "Like I said, my name's Rafael. Feel free to keep calling me that instead of my stage name. Or 'Raf' if you'd like."

"You've got a great name," Dante said, sounding sincere. "Wish I'd thought of that for my stage name."

"What you do for a living?" Trip asked me, making light conversation.

"Ah, I used to be a massage therapist," I explained. "Before COVID happened. I might go back to that again. For now, though, I…work in a bookstore."

"Cool," said Jax, nodding as he chewed on another Twizzler. He was the one that had shoved two into his mouth at once. Thankfully, this wasn't a repeat performance. "Where at?"

"Here in the Castro," I said, taking another gingersnap. "The pay is lousy, but I really enjoy working there."

"You'll like stripping then," said Marcus, grinning cheekily. "It pays way better. Can't beat the hours either. Getting to party all night and sleep late."

I wasn't as enamored of the idea as Marcus apparently felt I should be. However, the whole point of me being here was to work undercover. Of course, I had no clue how to go about doing that. So far, all we had done was chit-chat over unhealthy junk food.

"Sounds good," I said, playing along.

"Here's hoping there are better tippers soon," Trip said, giving Austin a look. "It's been slim pickings thus far."

Austin looked nonplussed as he snagged another sour ball. "The big money's coming," he told Trip nonchalantly. "You'll see."

"It did seem like there was a bigger crowd waiting to get in tonight," I threw out, finishing my gingersnap.

"Good," Brandon replied, smiling at me. "Lots of horny men with fat wallets ready to make poor life choices that'll drastically affect their lives."

"At least for a month or two," Dante added.

"That's what we're here for," Austin joked, dusting his hands. "So, let's divide up who goes where. Brandon, you wanna stick by the new guy for tonight and show him the ropes?"

"Glad to," Brandon answered, placing one arm around my shoulder.

I blushed. "Go easy on me, okay?" I pleaded softly. "I have no idea what I am doing."

"You seemed to know last night," Brandon whispered back, moving in close enough for his words to brush against my ear, making me shiver. "Do like you did before. Listen to the music and go with the flow."

I nodded, glancing back over one shoulder to look for Jean. He had been quiet this whole time. It became clear why once I had looked around the whole of the pool area.

Jean had taken off. My face turned into a scowl for a moment. The odds were good he had gone to snoop around somewhere while I mingled. Jean seemed convinced something was off about *Treats*, so it was logical that he would investigate further.

Still, I would have preferred for him to stick close to me. As Brandon put it, there were a lot of horny men showing up at *Treats* tonight. More than a few would be handsome. Several were certain to recognize Jean from his porn career.

My mind flashed back to the trio that lured him away from me on the dance floor last night. A man as well-endowed as Jean roaming a bathhouse was like sending a slab of beef out among hungry wolves.

The thought of someone making a play for Jean while I wasn't there filled me with unexpected jealousy. Here I was about to shake my ass for total strangers while worrying about him having a casual hook-up. Austin, meanwhile, was still giving out orders. I shook off the green glow that had descended over my aura and focused, remembering that I was supposed to be paying attention in case something unusual came up.

"You two are on the second floor," Austin said, speaking to Brandon and myself. "Jax, you take the first floor with Trip and Dante. Marcus, you and I'll handle things up here."

"I want the pool tonight," Marcus declared insistently. "There's way better tips on this end."

"Whatever," Austin said. The right corner of his mouth twitched slightly. "I'll hold down the fort on the dance floor."

Talk of the dance floor reminded me of my conversation with Chrissy. "Do you guys always dance with a DJ?" I asked, looking around. "Or is it usually pre-recorded."

"Depends on the show," Brandon told me, keeping his arm around my shoulder.

"Sometimes there's a DJ," Austin said, licking his fingers. "If the club hosting us is too cheap to spring for one, we bring our own music."

I became momentarily distracted watching Austin clean the sticky syrup off his fingers. The way he ran his tongue over each digit was oddly arousing. It was like he performed a sex act even though there was nothing overtly sexual about it. Somehow, he managed to mesmerize me momentarily without trying.

"I'd watch out for that guy if I were you," Marcus was telling Austin. I forced the spell off me that Austin had inadvertently woven and listened. "I get a bad vibe off him."

"How come?" I asked before I could stop myself, eager to look at something other than Austin.

Dante was the one who answered. "Dunno if you know," he said in a conspiratorial way. "But that guy? He used to do porn."

I wasn't sure what to make of that. It sounded as if Dante were implying that doing porn was a bad thing. I couldn't see how. It wasn't as if any of us could point fingers.

"Yeah," Marcus added, carrying on. "And he had a terrible reputation to boot. Real nasty temper. Had some sort of feud with a director. Making all kinds of shitty accusations."

"Sinz is cool," Austin insisted. "Just keep your head down and your dick hard. Let the man do his job so we can do ours."

"Yeah, we'll be doing our job," Trip said, crossing his arms. "Don't you worry none."

"C'mon," Brandon said suddenly, jerking his head toward the pool area entrance. "We oughta get downstairs."

"Right," I said, feeling as though I missed something. "Lead the way."

A nagging thought pushed at the back of my head, but I couldn't quite place it. "So tell me this," I asked as we headed out together. Brandon was holding me close and I had yet to break contact. "How is it everyone here can eat like an eight-year old on Halloween night and still stay skinny?"

Brandon laughed. "It's only on nights like tonight," he replied, guiding me toward the stairs. "And we have to pay for it the next day. Twice the cardio in return for having enough sugar to power us through hours of shaking our groove thing for the masses."

I looked Brandon up and down as we descended to the second floor side by side. "It doesn't show," I said, jealous now of his two-percent body fat.

"Of course not," Brandon revealed. "That's the whole point!"

"Ah, I see," I said, thinking back to that night at the Nob Hill Theater. "Magicians never reveal their secrets."

"Neither do strippers," Brandon said knowingly as we reached the second floor together.

The party was in full swing. Despite getting there early, the other guests had cranked things up considerably compared to last night. Brandon and I walked past two men—one with an impressive muscle paunch while the second was in his twilight years—jerking each other off.

A few feet down, a bear had a twink down on his knees in the side corridor. The twink was gobbling down on the bear's thick cock like he was starved for a meal. The bear, on the other hand, had rested his back against the wall and was staring up at the ceiling as though he were witnessing God.

"I'm still not used to this," I said, quickening my pace a little.

"It passes," Brandon assured me. "I was like that when I first started. It seemed too surreal, men getting their nasty on with one another out in the open."

"Were you…" I hesitated when we passed the sex dungeon. Two beefy, hairy men had a third tied up on a St. Andrew's Cross and were taking turns spanking him. "I mean, I'm assuming you're gay. Right?"

Brandon laughed. "What gave it away?" he teased, smirking. "I thought all us fags had gaydar."

"Mine's in the shop," I explained. "Plus, it was never a hundred percent accurate. I was wrong about my best friend, for example. Though, that might've been my own lustful thoughts mucking it up."

"I've been there." Brandon sounded sympathetic. "But, yes, to clarify, I am definitely gay."

"Good to know," I said, remembering then that I was supposed to be grilling my co-workers for information. "I'd love to talk more later, if that's okay."

"It is." Brandon's voice seemed to deepen, making it harder to hear above the thumping of the beat playing on the sound system. "I'd like that a lot."

Brandon made sure he was looking me straight in the eye. Unfortunately, we were turning a corner. I clipped my shoulder on the bend in the wall and stumbled.

"Ugh," I groaned, shame-faced. "See, I am way too uncoordinated to be a stripper."

Brandon reached out to catch me. I felt his hands on my biceps, and all at once, the electric current between us was back. It shot straight down into my dick, making me hard in seconds. It happened so fast that I actually felt pain.

"Oh…" I let out slowly. "Oh, um…hi."

A great big smile spread out across Brandon's face. "Hi," he said, though he was no longer looking me in the eye. "Was that for me?"

"Looks like it," I said as fresh waves of embarrassment washed over me.

I was desperate for a change of subject. Brandon was still staring down at the tent my cock was making in my speedo. The fabric looked like it might tear open. Without a doubt, I would die of humiliation if that happened.

Slowly, Brandon raised his head up. "Can we finish this later?" he asked me seriously. "We still have a show to do."

"I…"

My eyes darted around. I hadn't seen Jean anywhere. He still hadn't come back from wherever it was he wandered off to.

"Maybe…" I said for some reason—probably a very petty one. "I have a boyfriend."

"I remember," Brandon said, moving in closer to put his warm, tingling hand on my chest. "Maybe I don't care. You should think twice about dating someone who is willing to leave you all alone with total strangers."

I felt a need to defend the love of my life, even if Brandon wasn't totally wrong. "I can take care of myself," I said. "He's a big boy and so am I."

"That…" Brandon's eyes traveled back down. "I can see."

His hand left my chest, albeit slowly. I felt the spot where his flesh touched mine tingle with naked heat, almost like a sunburn. Brandon surprised me by taking my hand.

"C'mon," he instructed, giving my arm a slight tug. "We're gonna be late. Austin runs a tight ship, just so you know. He won't like it if we're not where we're supposed to be."

I said nothing as we walked along through the corridors. My eyes continued to wander, taking in the sights. We passed several men on full display, walking around with their towels thrown over their shoulders. I spotted a couple down another side corridor making out.

The truth was, I was keeping an eye out for Jean. It wasn't that I was worried about finding him with someone else. That thought hadn't even occurred to me. And besides, it was ridiculous for me to be jealous. The first time I saw him was on my laptop screen watching him have sex.

What concerned me was the fact that I hadn't seen him at all.

Granted, he could have gone back to our room or wandered down to the first floor. Brandon and I weren't exactly giving the building a full sweep, after all.

So, there might have been some jealousy mixed in after all. I pushed it down and hurried so that Brandon and I were walking beside each other.

"Where are we going, anyway?" I wondered. It felt like we had been walking for a while, even though *Treats* wasn't that big of an establishment. "Did Austin tell you?"

"Right here." Brandon stopped in front of a dark red curtain. "The viewing room."

"Room" was a bit of a misnomer. It looked more like a corner of the building that had been sectioned off. I took a peek inside through a crack in the curtain and spotted a semi-circle of couches.

A large ottoman stood in the center. Beyond that, hanging on the wall, was a massive flatscreen television. It was currently playing a scene from Mustang Studios. I recognized it as one of their hits from back in the early twenty-tens.

"We're…" My tongue got in the way of my words momentarily. "We're…performing here?"

There wasn't a vacant seat in the whole viewing area. Naked men sat in the seats with their eyes glued to the screen. Almost all of them were in some state of arousal. Quite a few were openly jerking off.

"Yup," Brandon confirmed.

"So…" I was still having trouble using my words. "What do we do now?"

"Go inside," Brandon stated matter-of-factly.

"Just…" I couldn't believe it. "Just walk in there?"

"Yup," Brandon said again. "Go right inside."

"And dance?" I dunno why it felt like such a foreign concept suddenly. "Right there? In front of the screen?"

"They can see us best there," Brandon replied.

"What if…" I was making excuses and knew it. "What if someone gets pissed? You know, like in a 'down in front' kinda way?"

Brandon chuckled. "You think any of these men would rather jerk off to porn than have two real live studs shake their asses in front of them?"

"They might!"

It sounded flimsy even to me. Brandon placed a hand on my shoulder and clapped me there twice before giving it a squeeze. He was pitying me.

"Deep breaths," he told me.

I did as he asked despite feeling that it wouldn't work. To my surprise, some of the edge melted off me. I breathed in and out a few more times for good measure, letting the tension in my body drain away.

For some reason, doing so reminded me of earlier when Jean had me lay down on the bed in our rented room.

"I'm ready."

It wasn't quite the truth. My legs didn't shake when I made that first step. I was able to work my way around the furniture without stumbling or falling on my face. More than a few faces perked up when Brandon and I came into view.

I was still nervous as hell, though, as he and I climbed up onto the ottoman. A few spectators whooped and cheered, which surprised me. Brandon began moving first, so I followed his lead. It was easier to get into it once he established a rhythm for me to follow.

"There you go," Brandon encouraged in a low voice, keeping me close to his body—not that we had a lot of space to ourselves on top of the ottoman. "Just relax and go with the flow."

The music was helping a great deal. I found myself going back to the last time Brandon and I danced together. Our bodies fell back into sync with each other, grinding to the repetitive beat.

The men around us moved in closer. All of their eyes were on us. I was in awe of how captivated they were. My body held them in a trance while I gyrated. Any lingering doubts or fears melted off of me, drifting away into the aether.

"I've never felt so free before," I breathed out, turning around to face Brandon.

"And you never want it to end, right?" Brandon guessed, pulling me into his warmth.

"Never!"

I didn't care if our audience heard us. I wanted this feeling to go on forever. When their hands came up to touch us, I didn't recoil. I could feel their caresses all over; tender, almost hesitant. It was like Brandon and I were being worshiped.

"You're amazing," I told him as our bodies moved together.

"No, you are," Brandon replied, looking back at me like I was some kind of specter from on high. "You're even better than last night."

I laughed. "I had time to practice," I told him. "Last night was me acting on the fly."

"Keep at it!"

There was adulation in Brandon's eyes as he reached out to touch me. His hands felt different than the dozen or so pawing at us from below. I could tell which hands were Brandon's by how hot they felt. His fingers carried that familiar electric current. I felt gooseflesh grow in their wake.

Like before, my cock sprang to attention. I had been in a semi-erect state for a while now, but it was Brandon's touch who awoke me to full mast. My hardon strained against the fabric again, fighting to get out. A wet stain appeared on the front, which in turn smeared over Brandon's perfectly sculpted abs.

"Mmm!" Brandon traced two of his own fingers over the slimy trail I had left on him. "Looks delicious."

To my shock, he placed both fingers into his mouth, licking them clean. "Thank you," he whispered to me.

A reckless abandon took hold then. "Want more?" I asked, making it sound like a challenge.

"Absolutely." Brandon pushed his groin into mine and I could feel his arousal. "Please?"

It was sweet of him to remember his manners. "Get down on your knees," I told him. "I've got plenty, but you have to take it all."

Brandon obeyed at once. He was down on his knees astride the ottoman in the time it took for me to blink. I felt his fingers hook the front of my speedo, giving the fabric a quick, swift tug. My cock sprang out at once, waving back and forth in his face.

A few droplets of precum went flying. I watched, staring down through a surreal, dream-like lens over my eyes as they splashed against his face. Brandon stuck his tongue out and lapped hungrily like a canine.

"Tastes so sweet," he groaned, his voice muffled by the noise of the beat we had been dancing to. "I need more. Please, sir?"

A thick, viscous string hung down from the tip of my cock. It swung back and forth as I steadied myself on the ottoman. This situation had gotten ridiculously out of hand. It baffled me how fast things escalated.

I had to remind myself that I had a boyfriend. Jean could walk past any second. There was no telling what he would say. The last thing I needed was to be caught cheating on him while a dozen or so men ran their hands all over my body.

"Brandon…"

I started to protest, but Brandon's hands were already moving up. I watched—like I was hypnotized—as Brandon took hold of my engorged cock. As his tongue stuck out, I felt the electric current between us go live. My balls began to churn, swelling to almost twice their normal size.

Brandon lapped up the thick thread of precum hanging off the tip of my uncut cock. The sight made me gasp. I was breathing like I had run a marathon. His fingers, though barely moving, felt like they were slender electrodes.

"Oh gods!" I cried out, realizing with horror what was happening.

Something inside my balls was boiling. I felt them jerk upward, hard and fast. The room started to swim. I couldn't hold my balance.

The first rope of white-hot cum exploded out of my piss slit, flying through the air in an arc. I watched, both mortified and aroused, as it splashed across Brandon's face. The cum landed at an angle, covering one eyebrow and traveling all the way across his nose down to one corner of his mouth.

"Fuck!"

My scream echoed off the walls, drowning out the music. A second rope went sailing onto Brandon's face, followed by a third. I felt a second hand on my balls and knew at once that Brandon was the one cradling them. None of the other hands felt as electric or as warm as his.

The crowd might have still been touching me. They were certainly pawing all over Brandon, but for all my senses cared, there was no one else besides Brandon making contact with my flesh. His hands were the only ones that existed while my balls drained themselves all over his face and chest.

I came and came again, painting him white. Rope after rope of thick cum flew through the air, landing with a heavy splatter. His face looked like it had been dipped in candle wax. Several of my ropes had decorated his chest. Those drizzled down towards those amazing abs of his, settling into his cum gutters.

"Brandon…" I gasped out. "Brandon, please…stop!"

Brandon was running his tongue all over his face now. He lapped at my essence like it was the tastiest treat on earth. I hadn't seen him look this hungry when we were standing by the table full of junk food.

For Brandon, the best treat this Halloween was delivered to him straight out of my nuts.

"More!" he begged, jerking my cock.

"Give him more!" someone cried out.

"Cum again," another man cheered. "He's begging you for it."

I opened my mouth, to speak or to scream. There was too much fog around my brain for me to be sure which. I was still on cloud nine after having an intense orgasm all over my dance partner. Worse, it had happened in front of eyewitnesses. There was no way in hell I could ever live this down.

I wanted to run, but my legs felt like jelly. They were trembling as I watched Brandon clean himself up. There was not an ounce of my seed wasted. He scooped up every last drop and fed it too himself. A few of the men around us helped out, eagerly gathering up my cum to shove it past Brandon's lips.

Judging by his expression, Brandon didn't mind one bit.

"Help!"

Thankfully, the spell was broken by the sound of someone screaming. "Help, please! Is there a doctor in the house?"

I turned as the curtain sectioning off the viewing area parted. A naked man of about thirty came charging through. His eyes were wild and his hair was unkempt. He was sweating as well.

This wasn't due to being on a bad trip, though. I could tell right away that the fellow was sober. His eyes were clear and his movements were concise. He never stumbled or staggered once, and he was moving too fast to be out of it.

I could also tell he was panicked. "What's wrong?" I asked, letting go of my shame for the moment. It was, however, the perfect excuse to get down off the ottoman. "Did something happen?"

"Are you a doctor?" he asked me.

"No, I'm not a doctor," I answered, moving in closer to him. "Is everything all right? Is someone hurt?"

The man jerked a thumb over one shoulder. "Someone upstairs collapsed," he said. "I think they're dead."

My mind immediately started reeling. "Jean!" I screamed, breaking into a run.

Chapter 8

Finding out that your boyfriend has died while you were blowing your wad all over the face of a guy you barely know—in front of eyewitnesses—is cause for life reevaluation.

Fortunately, at least for me, that was not the case.

I stood alongside a number of others. We were all crowded back around the walls, making as much space as possible. This wasn't a whole hell of a lot since the corridors inside of *Treats* weren't very wide. The EMTs kept asking for people to clear out so they could wheel the body to the employee elevator on a gurney.

I stared down into Marcus' lifeless face as it passed us by. Jean kept a hand on my shoulder the whole time, reassuring me with his presence. Whatever guilt I felt was put on the back burner for the time being. I needed to memorize his face, commit every feature to memory.

Someone had placed his leprechaun hat onto the gurney beside him. The gesture made me tear up. Even still, I continued to stare—to etch every part of him into my mind—until he was gone. Only then did I bury my face into Jean's side and sob.

"I believe you," I whispered.

There was no way for me to tell if Jean heard me. The thumpa-thumpa of the house music still played over the sound system. Praise be to the gods, though, someone turned it down.

Jean squeezed my side, letting me know he heard. "I know," he replied, his own voice eerily calm. I knew him well enough at this point to know he was anything but, however. "I know."

"I didn't before," I confessed tearfully, breaking away far enough to look up at his stony, steely expression. "Not really. I thought…hoped you were imagining it."

"I wish I was," Jean said quietly. "This time, I'd have rather gotten it wrong."

We stood there together, giving one another mutual comfort. I could feel my conscience peck away at the back of my brain the whole time. This was not where I wanted to confess my infidelity, though. There were far too many strangers around us, most of whom were still very much naked. The party atmosphere had crashed and burned, but the dress code for *Treats* remained intact.

Some part of me felt that was funny and I hated myself for it.

"Marcus' face," I said quietly. "You saw it. It was so…"

My voice trailed off. It was so hard to describe, to put into words how twisted Marcus' expression had been. His face was contorted into a grimace of utter agony. Dying had not given him any sort of peace. Whatever killed him, he had been in terrible pain the whole time.

"Poison, I think," Jean stated coldly, his face still a mask of quiet anger.

"You think?" My mind reeled back to earlier by the crafts table. "In one of the candy?"

"That would be my first guess," Jean replied. "Did you see him ingest anything else?"

I shook my head at once. "Not while I was there," I answered. "Which, granted, wasn't that long. We all went our separate ways not long afterward."

Jean started to speak, but then remembered we were very much not alone. The crowd in the hallway did not disperse right away. Men stood around, slowly congealing into small groups. The space began to fill up with the excited sounds of whispered chatter. The gossip would be hitting the social media sites in moments, assuming it had not already.

Once upon a time, I would have been right there with them. Doing so felt disrespectful, though. I had met Marcus personally. We barely knew one another, but we worked together. It felt like that ought to mean something.

And besides, I had left my phone in the safe of our room.

"Let's find some place quiet," I suggested. "Our room?"

"My thoughts exactly," Jean said, taking the lead.

I did not protest, keeping myself snuggled inside the crook of his arm. It felt wonderful to be in physical contact with him. I desperately needed that after the panic attack I had at the thought of Jean being the one found dead. Seeing that it was Marcus was only better by comparison.

"Hey!" a voice called out.

Jean and I didn't stop right away. I was under the assumption that whoever it was had been calling for somebody else. My attention was on finding our room and seeking asylum.

"Hey, Papi Vega!"

That managed to make me slow to a stop. Turning around, I spotted a figure in the dim light pushing their way through the sea of bodies. As they drew close, I made out Brandon's face.

"Brandon!" I exclaimed.

Impulse seized me. Before I could talk myself out of it, I left Jean's side. Both arms reached out to pull my dance partner into a hug.

"I'm sorry," I whispered miserably, crying fresh tears into his shoulder. "Gods, I am so, so sorry!"

He smelled of fresh soap. Brandon had taken the time to wash himself off in the last hour. I was happy that the trace remains of my betrayal were washing down the drain. And I felt like a miserable, horrible human being for feeling glad of that—and for feeling glad at all.

"It's...this is all so fucking crazy." Brandon sounded like he was near panic himself. "First Jason and now this!"

I didn't know what he was talking about. He seemed to need my comfort more than anything else, though. I gladly gave it, squeezing him tightly so that he knew I was there.

Brandon held me back. I could feel the strength in his body. He was only slightly smaller than I was, but there was power behind his frame. It felt like he could have broken me in half if he wanted. For the moment, Brandon was content to cling to me, accepting the shelter that I provided.

"Sorry to interrupt," Jean's voice broke through, cutting across like a cold knife. "But maybe we should take this somewhere else."

Slowly, Brandon pushed me away, separating the two of us. "I overheard the two of you talking," he said, staring past me with hard eyes at Jean. "You think something is going on, right?"

Jean didn't answer immediately. I turned around to face him, finding an unreadable expression on his face. He wasn't quite staring at me or Brandon. Rather, he seemed fixated on the spot between our bodies. It was as if something lay there that was only visible to him.

"Let's go to our room and talk there," Jean suggested.

Brandon nodded. "Lead the way," he said.

I kept close to Jean the whole time. There was no way I could navigate the bathhouse in my current state. Despite having become more familiar with it, it still felt like a maze with the narrow hallways and dim lights.

Fortunately, Jean knew the way. Brandon kept close on my heels the whole time. I could almost hear his footfalls above the rhythm that continued to play. Were I in a better mindset, I might have thought he was worried we might ditch him. All I wanted right then, though, was to find shelter.

"Okay," Brandon said sternly, sliding the room door closed behind him. "Start talking."

I took a seat on the bed. Jean remained standing. Brandon kept vigil over the door, watching both of us closely. There was a steeliness in his eyes that I hadn't seen before.

"A few days ago," Jean began, "there was a shooting outside of Trader Joe's."

Brandon raised one eyebrow in surprise, as did I. I hadn't expected for Jean to start there.

"Go on," Brandon said, resting his back against the door, which rattled conspicuously.

"The security in this place is terrible," I muttered, taking us off subject. "No wonder someone got into our room last night."

"We'll get to that," Jean said, touching my shoulder tenderly. "First, though, I think we should go back to the day when we were shopping."

"How come?" I wondered, feeling a bit lost.

"Because," Jean began, looking over at Brandon. "I have a hunch. Did the young man who was shot happen to work for Stud Stable?"

This question bothered me. Jean and I both knew about that already, that Blu was a dancer for Stud Stable. We had been to the website, after all.

Jean wasn't the only one who had a hunch. I suspected he was fishing to see whether or not Brandon would be honest. Speaking of, Brandon didn't answer immediately. When at last he did, it was to nod once. His eyes never left Jean the whole time. I watched as Brandon folded both arms over his chest protectively.

"Jason," he said. "That was his name. He went by 'Blu' on stage, though."

"He was shot by someone riding a motorcycle," Jean went on. "We were there when it happened."

"I wish I had been. I would've…" Brandon stopped speaking suddenly. "Never mind. You think Jason's death is mixed up with Marcus'. Am I right?"

"Two dancers working for the same company die within a matter of days," Jean pointed out. "By unnatural causes."

"But not in the same way," Brandon pointed out. He sounded a bit like a cop at that point, very crisp and professional. "Jason was shot. Marcus dropped dead while performing, if the gossip I overhead has any weight to it."

"It's a little premature to tell," Jean said. "But I think it could have been poison."

Brandon went quiet, thinking on that for a good minute or so. "We were all standing around the crafts table together," I spoke up, breaking my silence. "Could somebody have put something in one of the candy?"

I watched Brandon bite his lower lip thoughtfully. "It's possible," he said hesitantly. "But I have trouble buying that one of the other dancers did it."

"Why?" Jean asked pointedly.

"What's the…" Brandon stopped himself. "Well, let's just say we're a pretty tight group. If someone had a problem, they'd rather hash it out than resort to poisoning someone."

"You don't think someone might get jealous that another dancer was bringing in better tips?" Jean challenged.

Brandon snorted. "Does it look like the guests here came prepared to tip?" He shook his head. "Sure, some bring cash, but for the most part, we'd be doing this pro bono if it weren't for the cash machine downstairs."

"I figured," Jean said.

"Michael never said anything about that to me," I recalled, thinking back. "Well, he didn't say much to me besides what time to be here."

"You're new," Brandon explained. "Think of it as a grace period. Before the company brings you on full time."

"Oh." I decided it didn't matter either way since I was actually working here undercover, so to speak. "Okay, so let's go back to the fact that two dancers have died in less than a week."

"One by a shooting," Jean ticked off. "And the other by what could have been poison."

"By someone with a vendetta against Stud Stable," Brandon finished. "I still say it isn't one of the dancers. We've all got too much to lose by turning against one another."

"Could it be a rival company?" I offered.

"Or an obsessed fan?" Jean added. "Someone who felt slighted by one or more dancers?"

Brandon hesitated again. "I could almost believe that," he said, pointing to Jean. "But a stalker would probably only target one person. Not the whole group."

"And a rival company wouldn't resort to murder," Jean went on, shooting my theory down. "I hope not, anyway. So who has what to gain by doing this?"

I looked back and forth, watching from the sideline as Jean and Brandon mulled over the question. "It's a little uncanny," I commented. "How well you two work together. I feel left out."

Brandon and Jean reacted at the same time. Jean seemed surprised while Brandon's face turned downward into a solid frown.

"We should talk to the police," Brandon decided. "Austin won't like it, but to hell with him."

It was Jean's turn to hesitate. "I haven't had the best experience with cops," he said. "They tend to think that I'm some sort of criminal mastermind."

I rolled my eyes at this. "They accused him of murder not long ago," I explained for Brandon's benefit. "After a porn star was found dead at the Nob Hill."

"I heard about that," Brandon revealed, reaching for the door. "After you."

Brandon stepped aside so that we could pass. I stood up to leave, but Jean held back. His eyes were narrowed slightly and I could see underneath the thick, bushy beard he wore that he had a stern expression.

"We don't have proof," Jean reminded. "You think the police will take the word of a stripper, a former massage therapist, and a retired porn star?"

"Maybe not," Brandon admitted, looking away. "But none of us are equipped to deal with a murder conspiracy."

I watched as Brandon moved to walk out the door. "If you won't tell them, I will," Brandon stated. "To hell what you or they think. At least I'll be doing something about this."

I looked at Jean. He was staring at me, waiting to see what I would do. When I turned back to face the doorway, Brandon was gone.

"He's right," I said, hating myself at that moment.

"I know you think so," Jean said softly. "If you want to go with him, I won't blame you."

I didn't like how accepting he sounded. It seemed so unfair. I felt like I was making a bigger decision than simply choosing to go speak to the police. It felt like I was picking Brandon over my boyfriend.

That wasn't the case, but it said a lot about what my conscience thought of the situation.

"There's…something I have to tell you," I began, settling down on the bed again. "And, you're probably gonna be real pissed at me afterward. But not because I still plan to go tell the police what we think is going on."

My voice must have sounded grave. Or, maybe it because I looked so thoroughly miserable. There was no mirror in the room, but what little light the room offered reflected from the flatscreen television. I could see myself dimly there. One might have thought my dog had died.

It wasn't a great metaphor considering a real live human being was murdered moments before.

"What's wrong?" Jean asked, sitting down on the bed beside me. "Did something happen?"

I would have preferred it if Jean remained standing. "Yeah," I answered miserably, moving over so that there was a gap between us. "I…"

There were no words. I had no idea how to explain myself. This kind of thing had never happened to me before, and I was completely out of my depth.

"I…" A lump formed in my throat. "I came on Brandon!"

An impulse seized me. Suddenly, the best thing to do was to put it all out there. I began talking very quickly, fearful that I would lose my nerve otherwise.

"I didn't mean for it to happen. We were dancing together in the viewing area and all of the men around us got up and moved in real close. And they were touching him and me at the same time. And I could feel all their hands on me. And then Brandon got down on his knees. And I don't know how it happened but I got really worked up and suddenly I was just shooting all over his face and chest and abs and it got everywhere and I am really so very sorry!"

I was sobbing. It took me a minute to realize that the horrible choking sounds were coming from me. Quickly, I buried my face in Jean's chest. My heart couldn't bear to see the look that I knew was going to be on his face.

"I'm sorry," I sobbed out. "I am so, so sorry!"

Jean's arms were around me in an instant. I tried to push them away, figuring I didn't deserve to be comforted by him. He wasn't taking "no" for an answer, though.

"Shhh!" Jean whispered insistently, patting me on the back. "Shhh! It's okay! Really, it is okay, love. You haven't done anything wrong."

"Wrong?" I tried to raise back. "I blew my wad all over a guy I barely know while another guy was being murdered. And for a second, I thought that it might have been…"

The words trailed off. It hurt to put the thought out there. That had been one of the most horrible moments of my life.

"What?" Jean pressed, confused.

"I thought…" A hiccup escaped me, which could have been funny under other circumstances. "I thought you might have died. I thought it was you who was dead."

Jean was pulling on me. Between the hysterics and guilt, my brain was in a total fog. I decided to just go along with whatever it was he wanted.

To my surprise, Jean pulled me into his lap. I sat with my legs across his, feeling his warm, strong arms wrap securely around me. Tenderly, he put my head on one shoulder, holding me there.

For the next few minutes, we stayed that way. Jean rocked back and forth slightly. I heard him mumbling something in Spanish. It was a song, and even though I didn't recognize any of the lyrics, it sounded beautiful.

Jean was half-Latino. His mother's side of the family originally came from Puerto Rico. I had known that long before we met. Hell, it was part of the reason why I became so enamored of him as a teenager.

The other half of his family was a mixture of Greek and Italian, but he spoke Spanish better than I did.

"I love you," Jean told me after he had finished singing.

"I love you too," I said back, holding on to him as tightly as I could, afraid he might let go. "Do you do everything well? Because that sounded amazing."

"I had singing lessons when I was a kid," Jean explained dismissively, turning the subject back toward the unpleasant point. "And I'm not upset with you, for the record."

"I'm a cheater," I stated, wanting to crawl under the bed.

"You're in a gay bathhouse, sweetie, in case you've forgotten." He almost sounded amused there. "Something like this was bound to happen."

I rose up so that we could face one another. It wasn't courage that spurred me on. Rather, I was deeply confused and a little bit offended.

"What?" I wondered. "You think I have no impulse control?"

Jean didn't need his much-lauded—by me for the most part—deductive prowess to tell I was hurt. "Let me ask you this," he began delicately. "What were you thinking back then, in that moment?"

"I…" I went back to when Brandon and I were dancing. "I wasn't thinking anything," I answered truthfully. "The music was playing. We started dancing. Guys were groping us."

"And you went with the flow?" Jean surmised.

A fresh wave of shame washed over me. "Yeah," I confessed, feeling miserable all over again that it was that simple.

"This is a bathhouse," Jean stated. "And yes, I know you know that. But I don't think you fully grasp what that means."

"It's a place where guys go to get off," I replied, scowling at being thought of as naive—even though it was true. "I knew that before we came here the first night."

"But you've never been to one before now," Jean pointed out, shifting a little on the bed. "And that's probably my fault. I should have gotten your toes wet before throwing you into the deep end of the pool."

I wasn't sure where this was going. "I'm an adult," I reminded him.

"It was my choice in the end to agree to come here. You didn't make me."

"But I shouldn't have left you alone."

I thought back to how it had felt seeing that Jean basically abandoned me to the wolves. "Yeah, maybe." I wasn't sure that I liked passing the buck off to him, even as it made me feel slightly better.

"You are new to this kind of thing," Jean went on. "Is what I'm saying. I've had a lifetime to adjust. This kind of place can have an effect on you. It's the atmosphere."

I considered carefully what Jean was saying. Guys strutted around in the nude regularly. Fetish gear and a semi-wet towel were the only articles of clothing permitted. Touching a total stranger's cock and balls as they passed by in the hallways was considered normal. Even now, as we had this discussion, the faint sounds of men fucking each other drifted through the walls.

"It's like…" I tried, considering my words carefully. "It's like a whole other world."

Jean nodded. "Exactly," he said knowledgeably. "The rules of society don't apply here. What we're taught is right or wrong goes out the door. Men come here seeking pleasure and that's what they find."

I was beginning to follow along at last. "And in a Puritanical society," I weighed in. "Not to mention years of Catholic guilt, we learn that pleasure is a bad thing."

"Then you come to a place that's all about pleasure," Jean continued, pleased that we were on the same page at last. "Where you let go and do whatever feels right."

It clicked into place for me. I was a virgin, at least in the sense of being inexperienced. Jean had known about that already. He brought me to a world where gay sex was wild and uninhibited. It was a world he had spent fifteen years in. Surely, in that time, it had changed how he viewed things like commitment or monogamy.

"You got caught up in the moment and something happened," Jean stated. "I'd be a pretty poor boyfriend if I didn't know it could happen."

I could feel a blush creeping up along the back of my neck. "And an even worse one," Jean went on, "if I held a grudge over it."

"I honestly didn't mean for it to happen," I swore.

"I believe you," Jean said, taking my hand. I watched as he placed a tender, loving kiss on the back of my palm. "And I love you. To be honest, it sounds kinda hot."

That was the point where the creeping blush consumed my whole face. "It was," I admitted, looking anywhere but at his face.

"This whole party was about us having fun together," Jean reminded me. "Loosening up after being in quarantine for so long. Getting back out into the gay world."

"Yeah." I still couldn't quite meet Jean's eyes yet. "But I wish I could have gone in more slowly. Do something fun that wasn't with a guy I barely know, and in front of eyewitnesses."

"Duly noted."

Jean patted me on the thigh. "Let's go find the police," he decided as I got out of his lap. "We can make the attempt to tell them that we know. If they don't believe us, we'll keep looking for proof that will change their minds."

I smiled, big and broad. "Thank you," I said, wrapping both arms around him once he stood up. "I love you so much, Jean."

Jean responded by kissing me full on the mouth. "I love you too," he said, his eyes burning with an unreleased animal passion. "Now let's do this so we can finally have a little fun for Halloween."

I took Jean's big hand into mine and squeezed it. "Yes, sir," I said, guiding us out the door together.

Chapter 9

Inspector Audrey Wong of the San Francisco Police Department did not look amused.

"You think there's a conspiracy at this place," she began, speaking very slowly and clearly, "to murder strippers."

"Exotic dancers," Brandon clarified, even though we had all used the term "stripper" to describe ourselves at some point. "Or go-go boys, if you prefer."

One eyebrow of hers raised up. "Go-go boy is the less offensive term nowadays?" she asked, and for the first time, she honestly seemed amused. "That's new."

To be fair, she had been in a foul mood when we found her. Having three nearly-naked men—one of whom sported a towel that did positively nothing to conceal his endowment—approach her with an outlandish murder conspiracy theory didn't put the scowl on her face. It was clear she would have rather been anywhere else this late at night than a gay bathhouse.

I couldn't tell if it was due to homophobia or simply being tired from staying up so late, but I was willing to give the lady the benefit of the doubt.

"May we talk privately somewhere?" I asked, hoping she would accept that I was being sincere.

Inspector Wong gave me a rather droll look. "Private?" she asked before glancing around. "In this place?"

Jean helped by taking several steps back. Inspector Wong

immediately zeroed her gaze on him. I suspect she automatically thought he was making a break for it.

However, Jean stopped after a couple of paces and tested a door on his left. "This one is clear," he said, after peeking inside the room.

Brandon and I waited while Inspector Wong let out a heavy sigh. "Fine," she said, throwing both hands up. "Let's get this over with."

Brandon and I both stepped aside to let the inspector pass first. She stopped a couple of feet short of the door and stared.

"You think four people can fit inside there?" she asked of Jean.

My boyfriend shrugged. "It's been done before," he replied plainly.

Brandon took a peek next. "Yeah, we can fit," he told her, smiling the whole time. "Easy-peasey."

"You know what?" said the inspector in response, shaking her head as she marched through the opened sliding door. "I believe you."

Each one of us filed, one after the other, into the room numbered two-forty-five. "This may be the only time that happens tonight," she added, closing the door behind me. "So don't get used to it."

The three of us had a seat on the bed. This was done out of necessity as the room was incredibly cramped. I instantly appreciated the fact that Jean and I sprung for a luxury room at Treats. It appeared that the standard-size room was far less accommodating.

There was no television for one thing. In fact, the only piece of furniture was the bed we had claimed. I did notice that the room offered the same safe built into the underside of the bed. That was something, at least.

Inspector Wong leaned against the wall in front of the door. I couldn't tell if she was preventing us from leaving or simply didn't feel there was another part of the room for her to fit in. Our legs stuck out far enough from the bed to almost touch the wall. Getting around them would have been a challenge, even for a woman of her average size, and there was nowhere to go beyond that save for right into a wall.

Jean was using the silence to study the inspector. I decided to do the same, running my eyes quickly over her shapely hips and big feet. Chestnut hair hung down past her shoulders in an old-fashioned Betty

Paige haircut. She was dressed in plain clothes, wearing an inexpensive suit that didn't quite suit her figure.

"Start from the top," she told us. "And make it fast."

All three of us started to speak. "And," she added, cutting us off. "One at a time."

Brandon started to speak again, only to cut himself off. He glanced my way, as though asking for permission. Jean cleared his throat, intending to take the floor, but he was interrupted by someone knocking.

"Oh for fuck's…" the inspector groaned as the door rattled uneasily on the rollers. "What is it?"

Inspector Wong flung open the door, revealing a squat, wrinkled old lady on the other side. A pair of beady eyes and a graying permed hairstyle stared right into the police inspector's chest. I had to tilt my head slightly so I could see.

"I dunno what I was expecting," Brandon whispered to me. "But it wasn't that!"

The inspector shot Brandon a dirty look over her shoulder before turning back to our new guest. "Sorry," she said, sounding as though she meant it. "Can I help you?"

"Estelle Boylston," the elderly lady said in response, speaking in a voice that made me think she had a two-pack-a-day smoking habit. "Department of Health and Safety."

Inspector Wong didn't immediately relent, which surprised me. "Can I see some identification?" she asked, keeping her tone polite.

The health and safety inspector managed to not look completely offended. She did, however, roll her eyes slightly while reaching into the back pocket of her jeans. The trousers hung loosely on her hips, and came dangerously close to slipping off while she rooted around in her back pocket.

"Here," the elderly lady snipped, flashing an ID badge at the inspector. "Happy now, hon?"

"Thanks," Inspector Wong said, pulling out her own badge. "Common courtesy. I'll show you mine since you showed me yours."

"Thank you, precious." Estelle's voice practically dripped with sarcasm. "I'd ask if I could come in, but it looks as though you're busy."

"I'm questioning these three," Inspector Wong explained, refusing to rise to the bait. "It shouldn't take long. Do you wish to speak with me?"

"Someone said there was a cop on the premises," Estelle explained, reaching into a different pocket for a pack of cigarettes. "Thought I should have a word. Officially, anyway."

"Ah, there's no smoking on the premises," Jean chimed in.

Estelle had been about to pluck a cancer stick out of her crumpled pack. When Jean spoke up, she shot a dirty look at him. I felt a shudder run through me. She was giving me the creeps, but Jean did not waver.

"He's right," Inspector Wong confirmed, taking Jean's side. "This establishment does not permit smoking. You'll have to take it outside, I'm afraid."

Estelle shoved the cigarette back into the pack. "Goddamn regulations," she cussed, squeezing the blue box of Native American Spirits in frustration.

She had a surprisingly firm grip. "Any word yet on what made the hooker croak?" Estelle asked Inspector Wong point-blank. "My superiors will want me to verify that it was natural causes and not part of some new outbreak."

"We'll have to wait for an autopsy," Inspector Wong answered. "Is that why you're here?"

Estelle snorted. "Honey, we've just been through a pandemic," she reminded. "You've got something like two or three hundred fudgepackers crammed into a three-story building for a week. Sharing bodily fluids and fuck knows what all else."

Now I was slightly offended. "Which is perfectly legal," I reminded, getting the attention of both women.

"And for the record," Brandon added, speaking out clearly. "Marcus wasn't a prostitute. Not that it is any of your businesses."

"Or that there's anything wrong with that," Jean added.

Inspector Wong's eyes had darkened when she turned to face us.

"Actually," she said in a steely tone. "It is police business. Was Marcus a prostitute?"

"No," Brandon answered coolly. "He was a dancer. And I don't appreciate the insinuation, inspector, that he was. Or that being a prostitute might have contributed to his death."

"He didn't die while having sex with someone," Jean pointed out. "He was performing for his audience."

"Like it matters?" Estelle grumbled. "He's still dead either way."

Brandon turned to where he could see Estelle properly and shot her a reproachful glare. There was so little room to maneuver in the room that Inspector Wong managed to block him from view. It must have done the trick, however, because Estelle looked taken aback for a second.

"Out of respect for the dead," Inspector Wong said, playing peacemaker. "We will not make insinuations about the deceased. And…" Her eyes drifted toward the three of us briefly. "It is confirmed that the potential victim was not a professional sex worker."

"Thank you," Brandon said stiffly. "Again, not that it would have mattered if he was."

"Acknowledged," Inspector Wong told him crisply. "Now, Mrs. Boylston, I believe it was? If you'll just give me a few minutes? I'll be with you as soon as I'm done here."

"Take your time," she replied, looking each one of us over. Her eyes lingered a second longer on Brandon. "If I was in a room this small with three studs, I wouldn't wanna leave either."

A smile tugged at the corner of the inspector's mouth. "That's fair," she agreed, reaching for the door. "And I'm sorry if I'm keeping you."

"Like I said, don't worry about it," Estelle told the inspector calmly. "I'm stuck here for as long as this little shindig goes. They insisted someone be on hand to make sure some semblance of public safety is observed."

"Must be why they were asking for people's V-cards at the front," I said, more to myself than anyone else.

"Oh." Inspector Wong, meanwhile, sounded interested. "You've been here all week then?" she asked Estelle. "Have you noticed anything unusual?"

"Besides the blowjob room needing a mop?" Estelle joked. "Nah, nothing out of the ordinary. Just a bunch of fags bumping uglies every hour on the hour. At my age, that's not gonna make me shed any gray hairs."

"Still," the inspector pressed. "I'd like to have a word with you afterward. If you don't mind."

"Suit yourself," Estelle replied, backing away. "I dunno if I'll be much help, though. I called in sick last night. But if you still wanna chat after you're done with the three naked stooges in here, I'll be outside having a smoke."

"Sounds good," Inspector Wong said, sliding the door closed. "And I appreciate it."

Once the lock snapped into place, Inspector Wong turned to the three of us. "Now," she began, once more making me feel like a disobedient student. "Start talking."

It took a bit for us to get the whole story out. Inspector Wong kept asking us to repeat certain parts while she jotted information down onto her phone. We hadn't bothered getting our story straight beforehand. More than once, Jean or I would backtrack to cover something we had forgotten.

And then, there was the fact that all of this was happening in a bathhouse. None of the walls were thick. It sounded as though the party had resumed. The music certainly seemed louder now, which made talking harder.

None of that compared to being interrupted by what were clearly the sounds of men having sex.

"I haven't heard about the shooting outside Trader Joe's," she admitted, thinking hard. "The report should be on file. You say that—"

"Fuck me!"

Inspector Wong tried to continue. "You believe he worked here?"

"He did," Brandon chimed in. "I can verify that. His name was

Joshua, but he went by Blu when on stage. We got the word not long after he was shot."

"Now a second dancer who works for the same company has died." It looked like Inspector Wong was beginning to take us seriously. "That's unusual, I'll admi—"

"Harder, Daddy! Breed me!"

Inspector Wong cleared her throat while Jean bit down on his lower lip. I would have liked to take this somewhere else. Unfortunately, the rest of the bathhouse was sure to be the same, if not more so.

"How long will it take for the autopsy?" I asked.

"Should be about two to four hours," Brandon answered, to the surprise of everyone. "I, uh…watch a lot of crime shows."

Jean gave Brandon a suspicious glare, which was mirrored by the one Inspector Wong had on. "Right," she said, punching something into her phone. "Actually, he's right. The thing that doesn't fit—"

"Goddammit! Right there!"

Inspector Wong was getting flustered. "The thing that doesn't fit—"

"Ahh! Ohhhh! Fuck! Oh, I'm cumming! Shit!"

"Go on," Jean encouraged. "It's just sex. Tune it out and focus on the important part."

Inspector Wong was not amused. "I know how to do my job," she told Jean crisply. "And I don't need advice from a retired porn star."

I was ready to be offended, but something occurred to me. "Hang on," I interrupted before the inspector could continue. "How'd you know that?"

Brandon didn't look surprised. "Isn't he?" the stripper next to me wondered.

"I am," Jean readily admitted. "Been retired for about a decade or so. But Raf happens to be right. Neither one of us brought that up, far as I can remember."

"We didn't," I said, feeling confident about something for once. "I'm sure of it."

Inspector Wong blushed then. "My roommate liked your movies," she revealed while pursing her lips. "I recognized you from the DVD covers. She—"

"Gimme that hot piss!"

Jean was pleased with himself. "I'm surprised you could tell it was me," he said over the sounds of another man cumming hard from somewhere beyond the walls. "That was a while ago."

Inspector Wong gave Jean a hard look. "It wasn't that long ago that your face was in the news," she reminded. "Accused of murder, as I recall."

Brandon gave Jean a hard look, but Jean was unfazed. "And found innocent," he reminded Wong calmly. "The person who committed that crime was arrested. They even confessed."

"True," Inspector Wong acknowledged. "Still, it does feel odd that you would be in the same spot where a murder took place—"

"Put the other one in me!"

"—again," Wong finished, no longer willing to allow the salacious cries around us to interrupt her train of thought.

"That…" I paused, considering the circumstances of both instances. "Yeah, okay. It is a little weird, but neither of those instances were our fault."

"Harder!"

"Does this happen a lot?" Brandon wondered, leaning sideways into me slightly, making me jump when our shoulders touched.

"Very good question," Inspector Wong said, looking at me strangely. "I'd like to know that as well."

"It doesn't," Jean reassured her. "It's only been a problem for us lately."

"Since we started dating, actually." I thought about that for a moment. "Which isn't a good sign for a relationship."

Jean looked worried for some reason. "Having second thoughts?" he whispered to me beneath the thrum of the house music. "I mean, right now, really?"

"I'm not," I assured my boyfriend, giving his hand a squeeze. "It's not like you to be worried about that."

Jean acted like he wasn't completely convinced. He was looking past me, but I became distracted when another cry rang out.

"Deeper! Oh fuck, go deeper!"

Inspector Wong actually facepalmed. "I cannot wait to get out of here," she said through two rows of recently cleaned teeth that were clenched together. "I am going to slug that fat bastard of a captain for this."

"What for?" I wondered. "Isn't homicide your…beat? Do they still call it a 'beat'?"

Her eyes went steely again. "None of your damn business," she said flatly. "I mean, about my career. Yes, they still call it a 'beat'. Though, traditional beat policing has gone back to community policing with more foot patrols and…why am I telling you all this?"

"Suck my fat fucking cock, bitch!"

"'It's plot exposition. It has to go somewhere.'" Brandon was smiling as he said this, which made me suspect he was quoting something. "Sorry. I always did love the *Great Muppet Caper*."

"*The Muppets Take Manhattan* was better," Jean retorted loftily.

"I was always partial to the *Muppet Family Christmas* mysel—and again, why am I telling you these things?" Inspector Wong appeared to be nearing the end of her rope. "What is it with you three?"

"Cumming! Cumming again!"

"I think we're all trying to tune out the fact that the four of us are the only ones not having any fun tonight," Brandon offered as the clear sounds of a man emptying his balls deep into another guy echoed through from our left.

"Why can't women have places like this?" I overheard Wong mutter. "Men get all the luck."

"I suspect that they do," Jean replied, having heard her as well. "They just don't advertise as well."

"You want this load, boy? You want Daddy's load inside of you?"

"Fuck it." Inspector Wong wearily put her phone away. "We're done here. Make sure you stay in town for the next few days. I may have more questions."

"I work here," Brandon reminded. "The company doesn't leave until after November the first."

"Same goes for me," I added, even though I had no intention of traveling with Stud Stable. "Just call or swing by here if you want to talk to us."

"Wonderful."

I watched as Inspector Wong undid the lock on the door. It rolled smoothly to the side this time. A trio of very naked older men walked past as she stepped out. All three seemed surprised to see her, but none of them said anything.

"Come on out," she ordered, waving us on with one hand. "Someone else will probably need to use this room soon enough, I'm sure."

"Eh, they'd just do it in the Viewing Room," Jean replied casually as he strolled out with his towel only halfway secured around his waist.

"Or the dungeon," Brandon pointed out, following Jean.

"Or here in the hallway," I added, pointing farther down where a twink was getting hammered up against a wall by a hairy daddy bear type.

Inspector Wong couldn't resist staring. Her hand hung idly on the door. I moved to the side so that she would get a better view, noticing how her mouth opened wider with each passing second.

"Jesus," she breathed out.

"Welcome to a world without rules," Jean whispered in her ear as we filed past, leaving Wong to her own awakening as a voyeur.

I was young, but had been around enough to recognize when a sexual kink was being born.

"What do we do now?" I asked once we were far enough away.

We were having to maneuver around a lot of bodies. The hallways felt more congested. Men stood around shooting the breeze or jerking each other off. Doors had been left wide open in lieu of an invitation so that strangers could walk in for a blowjob or quick fuck.

Others were fucking openly out in the hallway. The three of us had to work past two such couples, neither of which slowed down. The man getting his hole pounded by a young jock reached out to pinch Brandon on the nipple. Brandon merely smiled and firmly removed the hand.

"Sorry, can't stay to play," he told the guy being so vigorously railed. "Got somewhere to be now."

"You're a popular man," I noted, continuing on with Jean toward the stairs.

"Comes with the territory." Brandon brushed off the compliment. "So how're we supposed to get on the third floor? The police will have sectioned it off."

"That explains the crowd," I said, giving a naked couple making out as wide a berth as possible. "Some of these people must have come from upstairs."

"We wait for the forensics people to leave," Jean explained, keeping close so he would be overheard. "Once they clear out, there won't be anyone guarding the place."

"They might put one of the bathhouse employees on duty," Brandon pointed out, following close behind me. I could feel his breath on my neck. "Cops always make a mess."

"He has a point," I told Jean, ignoring the feeling.

"You both work here," Jean reminded. "Just say you're employees and I lost something. You're both here to watch while I look for it. Easy enough."

It wasn't the most ideal plan I had heard, but it could work. "I keep forgetting that," I confessed. "It feels weird to say out loud that I'm employed here."

"Try bringing it up in front of your grandparents," Brandon said, laughing. "That was actually not the worst New Year's party we had, come to think of it."

"Tell me about it later," I said as we at last rounded the corner toward the stairs. "I'll tell you about the time my mom outed me to her sister during Thanksgiving dinner."

There was indeed a cop guarding the stairway. Most of the other guests paid him no mind. One or two gave him approving looks. They might have thought he was wearing fetish gear. No one gave the officer a hard time, though, or hit him up for sex.

The gun on his belt probably acted as a deterrent, but that might have just been me.

"It doesn't look like he's going anywhere," I noted.

"We can camp out here," Jean suggested. "Wait him out."

"And if he gets suspicious?" Brandon pressed, not taking his eyes off the cop.

Jean studied Brandon for a minute. "Blend in," was his answer. "What else?"

I realized what Jean meant when he reached out to pull me in close. We were standing in a hallway full of naked men who were openly touching and fondling one another. The fact that all three of us had been keeping our hands to ourselves was incredibly conspicuous.

"You're joking," Brandon said incredulously.

Jean clamped his mouth down hard over mine, kissing me deeply. I wanted to protest, but it didn't take long for me to be swept up in the moment. It felt wonderful to be held by him. One hand ran down the length of his chest and abs, feeling the raw muscle buried underneath a thick forest of dark hair.

"The more the merrier," Jean said after disengaging from my face. "Or at least, the less salient we all are."

I had to agree. "Come closer," I said, waving Brandon toward me. "It doesn't have to mean anything. We just need to look like we're having fun."

Brandon held back a moment. "Fine," he decided, taking up the spot on Jean's other side. "This had better work, though."

His reluctance confused me. I was certain Brandon was a member of the club. A straight guy wouldn't have been so happy to have my load spray all over his upper body. It may have been that Jean wasn't his type.

If that was the case, Brandon managed to hide his disinterest once we got started. Jean held both of us close to him, reveling in being the center of attention. I imagined that this was what it felt like to be cast in one of his movies. So many porn actors got to worship his heavenly body, feeling the power and strength in his muscles, and run their fingers through his hair.

Looking over, I saw that Brandon had buried his face in my boyfriend's pit. He was breathing in deeply while licking his pink tongue out to taste the essence soaked into the dense fur there. One hand slid across Jean's chest, taking hold of mine.

Brandon met my eye for a moment, giving my hand a squeeze. Slowly, he moved it lower. I went willingly, gripping my boyfriend's cock in my fist. Jean let out a low groan which rumbled through me like thunder. I spread the viscous, sticky precum leaking there all over my palm and began lubing him up, using it to slick the full length of Jean's manhood.

While I jerked Jean off, Brandon went back to worshiping his pit. He came up for air periodically, using the time to kiss along my boyfriend's bicep. Jean obliged by flexing, which Brandon appreciated. I could see his own package strain against the fabric of his speedo.

My eyes went past him to the stairway. The cop was still on guard, but our little performance had gotten his attention.

"He's still there," I whispered while kissing Jean's ear. "And I think he's watching us."

"Good," Jean replied while Brandon began salivating over his pectorals. "Let's not disappoint."

The cop shifted back and forth, resting his weight on a different leg every couple of minutes. He was doing this to adjust his hardon without being conspicuous. I had seen guys do that so many times in the past—and had attempted it myself.

There was no point in concealing mine. In addition to the circus tent that had sprung up in my speedo, I was leaking like an old faucet. Brandon was having similar troubles. His hips rutted up against Jean's leg like a puppy in heat. We had passed the point where this was putting on a show to blend in. A line was crossed and the three of us were dancing off into the sunset.

This was especially true for Jean. His cock had risen to full mast. There was no mistaking that he was enjoying himself. He had enough sausage hanging between his legs to put The Butcher Shop in Showcase Square out of business.

"I think he's about to leave," I whispered.

It didn't look like Jean or Brandon heard me. They were kissing, slow and sensually. Jean was taking the lead while Brandon let out these adorable whimpers. His hips were still rocking up and down Jean's thick upper thigh.

I felt an unexpected stab of jealousy, oddly reminiscent of last night. That felt like a lifetime ago, before my impromptu career as a stripper started and a co-worker died on stage. It had been an eventful Halloween for me.

Things appeared to be getting even more eventful. It wasn't as though I was being ignored, mind you. Jean had one arm around me and was stroking my back. I felt his touch everywhere that his hand could reach.

Once in a while, he would brush the back of his thumb down my neck, trailing it along my spine between my shoulder blades. It was his way of letting me know that he was enjoying the handy I was giving him. I licked and kissed along his check, mimicking Brandon from a moment ago, but my eyes kept wandering back to watching them kiss.

"Hey!" I exclaimed suddenly, giving Jean's arm a shake. "He's gone."

Jean didn't hear me, but he reacting to me letting go of his cock. "Mmm, what?" he asked, looking a little dazed. "Gone?"

I pointed down the hall. "The cop that was guarding the stairway," I reminded, sticking my lower lip out just a little. "He left."

"Oh... oh!" Jean whipped his head around. "That's right. We were waiting on that, weren't we?"

"That was what I thought," I said, giving his arm the barest of slaps. I couldn't be too mad after hosing Brandon down with my cum ropes earlier. "You seemed distracted, though."

"Let's not waste time." Brandon was suddenly all business, wiping the drool off his mouth. "He could come back."

Brandon took the lead this time. I hurried after him with Jean by my side, getting ahead by a foot or so thanks to the hardon he still had.

We rushed up the stairs to the pool area and ducked under the police tape, taking the steps two at a time. There was police tape blocking the entrance, but Brandon and Jean each swept it aside.

"Spread out and look around," Brandon said once we ascended to the top. "The cops will have searched the place already. See if they left any evidence behind."

"Yes, sir." Jean's tone was almost mocking. "You're the boss."

"Be nice," I whispered to Jean. "He's trying to be helpful."

"Anything that looks out of the ordinary," Brandon went on, still speaking in that jarringly authoritative tone. "Don't pick it up. Let me know, but leave it where you find it."

It sounded like Brandon had really gotten into those crime shows. I did as he requested, however, keeping my eye on the floor for anything usual.

A party had definitely gone down up here. There was no question of that. The evidence was all around us and we were strolling right through it. I kicked who knew how many bottles of lubricant left lying on the floor with my sandalled feet.

And then, of course, there were all of the puddles of lube, cum, and who knew what else that I slipped on.

"I don't envy the forensic team having to sweep this," I muttered, having to regain my balance yet again.

One reassuring sight was the number of condom wrappers scattered everywhere. The event promoting safe sex had done the trick. In all the craziness of the night, I had forgotten that Brandon and I were supposed to put condoms on for the crowd to remind them about being safe.

A surge of guilt took hold, but I reminded myself that Brandon and I hadn't engaged in actual anal intercourse. If only technically, we still set a good example. I could live with that, but that old Catholic guilt was still a tough bitch to beat. I was silently cursing myself when a razor-sharp voice snapped me out of it.

"Hey! The fuck are you three doing?"

I whipped my head around, scrambling for an excuse. My first assumption was that Inspector Wong had come back and caught us red-handed disturbing a crime scene. Wide-eyed with worry, I watched the figure in the shadows emerge.

It wasn't quite that bad, but it still wasn't good. "This is a restricted area," the elderly woman whose name I recalled being Estelle Boylston shouted in the same gruff, smoker's tone as before.

"We work here, lady." Brandon's reply was curt and to the point. "Someone lost their room key. We offered to help find it. Since it doesn't look like we'll be working the rest of the night."

"Yeah," I agreed. "That's all."

I was a horrible liar and knew it. My assumption about Brandon being the same way had been proven wrong. The words flowed right out of his mouth, as though he had rehearsed it.

Which, to be fair, he could have.

"Do you have any problem with that?" Jean added, coming into view.

"Yeah," Estelle said, jerking a thumb back toward the stairwell. "Take a hike. Bad enough one poor fellow dropped dead here. The cops don't need you mucking up any evidence."

"The cops left," Brandon said plainly. "How do you think we got up here?"

Estelle marched right up into Brandon's face. "Listen, twink," she said threateningly. "If you're so sure, why don't I run downstairs and drag her back up here? See what she thinks of the three she spent over half an hour questioning snooping around."

"Didn't she want to talk to you?" I asked, thinking back.

Estelle glared at me hard. "Couldn't find her," she replied. "Now march!"

Brandon wanted to argue more, but Jean played peacemaker. "Let's go," he offered, taking me by one hand as he walked past. "We can ask the front desk to give the guy another key. It'll be fine."

I walked with Jean. Brandon held back for a moment more. He seemed intent on winning a staring contest. Estelle was no pushover, however. She could glare with the best of them.

In the end, Brandon followed us.

"Well, that felt like a waste," I heard him mutter as we descended the steps back to the second floor.

"Not completely," Jean revealed, surprising me. "I didn't have much time to look, but there was something off to the side from where Marcus was dancing."

"How do you know where he was dancing?" Brandon wondered, stopping when we exited the stairway onto the landing.

"A couple of singles were scattered around on the floor," Jean explained. "Marcus must've dropped them. Or else they fell out of his speedo when he collapsed."

Brandon nodded. "Okay, that makes sense," he said. "What'd you find?"

"Something important," Jean revealed, keeping his tone low as he leaned forward. "I think I know what killed Marcus. And neither of you is going to believe this."

Chapter 10

"I don't believe this."

Inspector Wong was staring at the three of us from across her desk. We had all agreed to meet up at the precinct where she was stationed the next morning. Wong hadn't left her address, but a quick search on Google told me where to find her.

Brandon was there, having gone home after speaking with Michael and Austin. He was staying at a hotel not far from the Castro. He wanted to be there too, but asked that we make it later in the morning so he could grab a little shut-eye.

"Called it," Jean muttered smugly.

"No," Inspector Wong explained, looking thoroughly unamused. "I cannot believe you broke into a crime scene and disturbed evidence. After being questioned by a cop."

"We didn't break in," Jean said simply.

"There was no one guarding the stairs when we went up," Brandon added.

"That means it was okay to go up, right?" I pressed, trying to sound as confident as they were.

"The police tape wasn't a clue?" Inspector Wong asked, the edge in her tone getting sharper.

"We found something," Jean told her. "Something we think the forensic team missed. I think it'll corroborate with the autopsy report, if you're interested."

Inspector Wong let out a dry smirk. "Okay, let's hear it," she began sarcastically. "What murder podcast or true crime series has convinced you that you're some amateur sleuth in the making?"

Jean folded both arms. "Marcus died by poisoning," he stated as fact. "Cyanide, I'm guessing. And it wasn't administered to him through the mouth."

I watched as Inspector Wong's eyes went wide. "How did you know that?" she demanded.

"There was a condom wrapper lying off to the side," I began slowly.

"Big deal," she replied, cutting me off at the quick.

I got the feeling that she was waiting to hear more, however. Jean glanced over at me and nodded once. I returned the favor and continued.

"I know," I went on. "There were hundreds of them. Jean found one that smelled of bitter almonds. It was near the spot where Marcus collapsed, but a little off to the side."

"Which is probably how it was missed," Brandon added. "Best place to hide a needle is in a stack of other needles."

"Someone slipped cyanide into the condom," Jean picked up, carrying the conversation on his own now. "This is just a guess, but I think they used a syringe to inject the poison into the packet so that it didn't look disturbed."

Inspector Wong had her eyes on Jean. "So, you just walked around the deck area sniffing condoms?" she asked him pointedly. "Until you found something suspicious?"

I balked, but Brandon laughed. Jean, meanwhile, glared at Inspector Wong ruefully. I expected for him to fire off a sarcastic retort, but my boyfriend was strangely silent.

Brandon waited a moment before speaking, needing time to recover from his giggle fit. "Does that line up with the autopsy report?" he asked, sounding as though he already knew it did.

"It…" Inspector Wong grimaced. "Cyanide was found in Marcus' bloodstream," she confirmed, reaching into her desk drawer for a folder. "Toxicology confirms that it was the cause of death."

The file hit the top of her desk hard. "Seems he didn't swallow the poison, though," she told us. "Just like you said. They found the poison around his groin region."

"How does someone die from cyanide poisoning that way?" I wondered. This was the part that confused me. "If he didn't ingest it—"

"Cyanide can be absorbed through certain areas of the body," Inspector Wong explained, flipping the file open. "Areas where the skin is soft and especially absorbent. Like the eyes or—"

"The sensitive foreskin area," Jean finished. "Or the scrotum."

"Why go through that much trouble to poison someone?" Brandon wondered. "There was candy left on the table. He could have just eaten it."

"That's the million-dollar question, isn't it?" Wong replied. Her eyes drifted back and forth between the three of us. "I don't suppose you saved that condom?" she asked, tenting her fingers.

"We didn't," Jean admitted.

"Figured that tampering with a crime scene wouldn't go over well," I added.

"Plus, the health inspector showed up," Brandon added. "Wonderful lady."

Inspector Wong's expression turned thoughtful. "I wanted to talk with her last night," she said. "But someone told me she had left."

"She didn't," Jean said. "We saw her while up on the third floor."

"Interesting." Inspector Wong tightened her lips. "Well, what you found does line up with the autopsy. I'll have one of the boys go back to *Treats* and look around."

"The condom is gone, I'm sure," Jean said. "They would have cleaned the place thoroughly."

"I like to be sure," Inspector Wong said, standing. "Thanks for coming by. But do me a favor and stay out of this from now on. This is a police matter."

We were being shown out. I got up first, figuring it was best not to argue. To be honest, I was relieved. The cops were on the case now. There was no more need for us to look into the matter.

"Before you go, though," Inspector Wong said, surprising me. "I'd like to have a word with you for a moment, Mr. Vásquez."

I had gotten out of my seat. The inspector's request made me freeze up. Swallowing the curse on my tongue, I turned back toward the inspector. Jean and Brandon hung back, waiting to see what I would do.

"Alone," she added pointedly.

The sigh I let outweighed enough to sink the Balclutha. "Go on ahead," I told them, being firm. Neither one moved right away. "I'll be right behind you. This won't take long."

I gave Inspector Wong a look, letting her know that it wouldn't. Jean and Brandon stood behind me a moment more. Getting irritated, I waved my hand like I was scaring away a fly.

"Shoo!" I ordered.

That got them to leave, albeit with extreme reluctance. "Do I need a lawyer?" I asked Inspector Wong point-blank once they were out of earshot. "Because I can have a lawyer here in minutes. There happens to be a very wealthy benefactor living with me. She'll certainly accommodate."

The inspector didn't appear fazed, but I suspected she heard threats like this daily. "Not necessary," she said, trying without success to be reassuring. "You aren't under suspicion."

"My boyfriend agreed to cooperate with the police not too long ago," I told her flatly. "He wound up being labeled a person of interest."

Inspector Wong folded her arms. "Like I said," she told me. "You're not under suspicion. And I suspect that there is a lot about your boyfriend that would greatly interest any officer in charge of a murder investigation."

I ignored that, figuring that it was a jab at Jean's porn career. People tended to do that. There was something about doing porn that automatically made authority figures in our society assume the worst. Jean had to live with it for his entire adult life. I didn't understand how he tolerated it so easily.

"I think I should still have a lawyer present," I said, still standing. "If I'm going to be questioned?"

"You're not," Wong said. "I need your help."

That got my attention. "Say again?" I asked, bemused.

She seemed to find my reaction funny. "Have a seat, please," she asked, gesturing to the chair I had been commanding moments before. "As you put it, this won't take long."

Slowly, I settled back down into the chair, watching her the whole time. "To be clear, you were downstairs on the second floor," the inspector began. "Eyewitnesses corroborated this. And you had no motive to poison the victim."

I nodded, wondering where she was going with this. "That's true," I agreed.

"And as for the first dancer's death," she went on, settling in behind her desk and crossing one leg over the other. "It looks like that was just a case of bad timing."

"Worse timing for the victim," I pointed out.

"No arguments there." Inspector Wong watched me closely. "I'd like for you to keep an eye on things for me at *Treats*. If you're willing to cooperate, that is."

The surprise on my face must have been evident. "You want me to spy for you?" I asked, stunned. "You know, you're the second person to ask me that."

Inspector Wong was very interested. "Oh, really? Who was the first?" she all but demanded, tenting her fingers together.

I thought back to what she said about my boyfriend. "You wouldn't believe me if I told you," I said, my words carrying an edge to them. "But, I'm going to have to decline. Stripping, it turns out, is a dangerous business. Two people have died already."

"Which is precisely why I need your help," Inspector Wong argued. "You work there. I can't put my finger on it, but there's something shady about that place."

I gave her a droll look. "It's a bathhouse," I reminded dryly. "And— far as I can tell—you're a straight woman. It's bound to look a little sussy from the outside."

"No, it's more than that." Inspector Wong sounded very sure of herself. "I can feel it. There's more going on there than a simple murder case."

"Death by condom doesn't sound simple to me," I retorted.

A smirk tugged at her mouth. "Well, you've got me there," she muttered, flexing her fingers once before setting them down on the armrests of her chair. "Someone went to a lot of trouble to commit murder and I'd love to know why."

Jean had practically said those same words to me. It was how this whole mess had gotten off the ground. I was supposed to be keeping tabs on the place for him. And now, the police were asking me to do the same thing.

"What if I refuse?" I asked hesitantly.

Inspector Wong shrugged. "There's not really anything I can do about that," she said. "But two people have died. Doesn't it bother you?"

She was attempting to play to my conscience, and it was working. "Dammit," I grumbled. "Yes, I want to know why. Neither of them deserved that."

"Then help me." Inspector Wong leaned forward a little. "I'll do my damnedest to protect you."

I highly doubted that, and it surprised me. I was becoming a lot more cynical as I got older. Maybe I had seen too many dead bodies. Most people go through life seeing none outside of a funeral home. This would be my third murder victim.

"I should start keeping a tally," I muttered.

"Sorry?" Wong asked.

"Nothing," I said quickly. "Sure, let's do this."

Wong reached out to shake hands. Nervously, I extended mine across her desk and accepted, feeling like a Faustian bargain was taking place. Wong was trying to hide it, but I could see she was pleased.

"Gimme your number," I said, going for my phone. "I'll text you if anything else goes down while I'm at work."

"You could just call," she pointed out before rattling off her digits.

I entered the inspector into my list of contacts. "I'm a Zoomer," I said, looking a little smug around my phone at the older woman. "Phones aren't for calling people."

Inspector Wong waited while I gave her my own number. She actually wrote it down on a piece of paper with a pen. I couldn't fathom why.

"Why is that?" she asked me, wearing a genuinely bewildered expression when she raised up. "I've always wondered. I mean, they're phones."

I ignored the question, partly because I didn't know the answer myself. "Make sure you recycle that paper," I told her, getting out of the chair.

Inspector Wong made a face as she realized what she had done. "Yeah, whatever," she said dismissively, pointing in the direction that Brandon and Jean went. "The other Planeteers are waiting for you."

I had been about to leave for the second time when something she said made me stop short. "The who?" I wondered.

"Never mind," she told me. "Get out of here. And make certain you call me if anything happens. Got it?"

"Will do," I told her, giving Inspector Wong a wave as I finally made my exit.

Jean and Brandon were waiting for me near the entrance. Neither one looked particularly happy. I was about to add to that, and puzzled over the best way to break the news as I approached.

"Well?" Jean asked insistently.

"What did she say?" Brandon added in the identical tone, which was surreal.

I slowed to a stop and opened my mouth. "It looks like I'm working with the police now," I blurted out, instantly realizing after the fact that this was a bad way to break the news.

Brandon and Jean each stared. "What?" they both exclaimed simultaneously.

I watched as they shot one another a glare afterward. "I'm afraid it's true," I said, regretting the decision already. "And something tells me it will only get worse from here."

Chapter 11

"I don't like this."

Brandon's words only just registered with me. I was exhausted and felt gross. Actually, "gross" didn't begin to describe how I felt. I was covered in sweat from head to toe. Handprints made from lubricant marked my body. I had been surrounded by men jerking off while watching me dance for hours.

"I don't think I'll ever be able to go without saying the words 'I need a fucking shower' again," I replied, leaning against a wall for support.

We were standing together on the ground floor across from the lockers. I needed a break from dancing. Brandon offered to go with me. He had been keeping close to me all night, maintaining as much of a constant vigil as he could.

I suspected he was doing so per Jean's request. The truth was, though, I didn't mind it. Having Brandon around made me feel better about spying for the cops. I didn't feel so alone knowing he knew what I was doing there.

That, and Austin made it easier by putting us on the third floor together. We were all abstaining from the "safe sex" portion of the evening. Having a stripper drop dead from a poisoned condom might have been a touch ironic, but it made all of us skittish about touching the damn things.

"It's one of the downsides of this job," Brandon confessed, looking up at me from the scrap of paper he was holding. "About this, though…"

I held a hand up and took a long pull from the bottled water he had brought me. The plastic container was half-empty by the time I came up for air. Droplets fell from my face, splattering all over my chest. The cold made me shiver.

We were, of course, almost nude. Brandon and I had on matching orange speedos. The front was decorated to look like a jack-o-lantern. The material shined in the low light of the bathhouse, giving off a spooky aura by design.

They were kind of cute, honestly. Brandon definitely wore his better.

"I really do need a shower," I insisted. Actually, it sounded more like I was pleased. "We can finish talking in there if you want. But I will scream if I don't get cleaned up soon."

"Fair point," Brandon said, folding the small piece of paper up. "Lead the way."

I took the helm, walking the length of the corridor to where it intersected. Sounds came from the whirlpool room on the left. It seemed guests were yet again ignoring the sign warning about there being no contact allowed.

The showers were on the right up ahead. I took the turn and strode past the employee elevator. It was, as Michael had said, marked as being for staff only. I thought I heard it "ding" as we were walking past, but the need to feel clean again overrode any curiosity I might have had to see who was riding in it.

A whiff of soap and chlorine hit me as I stepped inside, mixed with the steam filling the air. The showers were communal, naturally. Shower heads stuck out from a set of pillars in the center of a tile room. There were brass hooks on the wall down a small side corridor to hang towels on.

I stripped out of my holiday-themed speedo and left it hanging on one. Enough moisture from my body had been absorbed in for it to make a slight squishing sound. Wincing, I turned away and made for the nearest spray.

There was only one control for each shower head. I felt hesitant for a moment, not wanting to hose myself down in an ice-cold bath. The need to be clean returned in full force, unfortunately. Bracing myself, I pressed the button and steeled myself, expecting to be doused in an Arctic rain.

Surprisingly, the water was warm and incredibly soothing. It grew even warmer as I stood under the spray for a moment, washing the aches and stiffness away. Dancing for hours was exhausting. I was really grateful that my mother let me be a swimmer instead of taking ballet.

"Gods, this is bliss," I whispered, stepping away long enough to get some soap out of a dispenser. "Why the hell is the hot water in this place so much better than the house?"

Silence greeted me. There was no one else in the shower area at the moment. I had come by earlier hoping to wash off before the party started. There had been two guys fucking over by the wall, though, so I ended up putting it off.

"Brandon?" I called out, confirming that I was alone.

Brandon was nowhere to be found. I was surprised, and a little nervous, but decided not to make a big deal out of it. I was a big boy, after all. Showering by myself wasn't a huge deal, even if there was potentially a murderer lurking somewhere nearby.

That was what Jean and Inspector Wong both thought, at least.

"Hey!" a voice called out, getting my attention. "You in here?"

I turned to find Brandon entering the steam-filled room. He had taken off his speedo as well. Naked, he looked incredible, and I had to remind myself not to stare.

"Guilty," I said, continuing to lather soap on my body from head to toe. "The water in here feels great. Better than where I live."

"Better than the hotel where I'm staying," Brandon concurred, turning on the shower head next to me.

The warm water was doing an excellent job massaging my muscles. My legs no longer cramped quite so much. There was a spot between my shoulders that also didn't ache. I was enjoying the heavenly treatment when the water unexpectedly turned off.

"The hell?" I wondered, staring indignantly at the shower head.

"The water never lasts long," Brandon explained. His turned off a moment later. "You have to keep hitting the button over and over. It's kind of a trade-off."

"Oh." I wasn't sure why that was a feature, but it didn't matter. "That's better," I said once the hot spray was back on. "Thanks for the tip."

Brandon shrugged. "You'd have figured it out without me," he pointed out. "Glad to see you're holding up well under pressure."

"Heh, feels like I've had a lot of practice with that over the past couple years." My eyes wandered over to Brandon again, taking in his muscular form. "Where'd you go, anyway?"

"Huh?" Brandon seemed startled by the question. "Oh, I ran into one of the guys in the hallway. Just needed to ask him something real quick."

That made sense. Austin had once again assigned most of the dancers to the first floor. I hadn't run into any of them thus far, but Brandon evidently knew where they were. This seemed a bit lazy on my end, I would admit. My job—my other job—was supposed to be keeping an eye on things here.

The sad fact was, however, there wasn't much to report.

Plenty was happening at *Treats* that night. It was a Saturday night and Halloween was right around the corner. Men had poured in through the front door, eager to strip down, get set, and get wet. We had passed so many occupied rooms with doors hanging wide open. Quite a few of those had two or more guys inside fucking like there was no tomorrow.

Others openly jerked their cocks while watching porn. Their doors were an open invitation to join. I noticed that some of the other guests took them up on that. Brandon and I would walk past later on to find the doors shut. Deep moans and heavy creaking from the beds mixed with the beat playing.

And then, there were those who never bothered to shut the door at all.

"The night's half over," I noted, checking a digital clock on the wall outside the shower area. "Got any plans afterward?"

"Sleep," Brandon answered firmly. "Once I have a word with Austin, it'll be time for me to hit the hay."

I found that a bit strange. "Does anybody ever actually check in with Michael?" I wondered. "He always seems busy. But does he have anything to do with us?"

Brandon shrugged. "Yes and no," he explained. "Michael works in conjunction with the company in charge of the bathhouse. He's a liaison, I guess you could say. Austin is the one who calls the shots, at least for our little family."

It felt strange to think of the group as a family. Then again, I had seen a lot of found families in my short time. Being that they were all in a profession people found questionable, it made sense that the group might feel closer to one another than their other friends. The fact that they were on tour probably cemented it.

"I wanted to talk to you about that note," Brandon went on, getting my attention. "The one you found in your speedo?"

I had been emptying out the singles our devoted fans tipped us with. Our speedos came with a small pocket on the side, just big enough to hold things like the room key. Nestled into mine was a note folded up along with a lone dollar bill. Someone had slid it in there while I was dancing. It explained why I had felt something poking me in the sensitive flesh for over an hour.

"'Meet me in the Dark Maze after your shift'," I said, quoting the extremely brief message from memory. "It's not the most romantic proposal I've ever heard."

"I'm serious," Brandon said, sounding just that. "This kind of job? You will attract your fair share of weirdos. It comes with the territory."

"Plus," I added, "there's the fact that someone was killed here last night. 'Dark Maze' doesn't exactly scream safe space right now."

"That too," Brandon agreed. "So you're not going?"

"I'm not going," I told him, keeping my head down and my eyes aimed at the tile floor while I rubbed the soap off my legs. "Cross my heart."

"Good." Brandon went quiet for a moment. "It's just…I got worried is all. You being here for your own reasons. You might feel the need to prove yourself."

"I don't have anything to prove," I said, still bent over. "And a Dark Maze doesn't sound like it would be my kind of thing. I don't even remember what that is."

Brandon considered this. "It's similar to the sex dungeon," he explained. "Like a cross between that and the Slurp Room. The equipment is roughly the same, but there's almost no light."

"Sounds like you'd spend most of your time bumping into people," I said pointedly as the water turned off. This time, I didn't reach for the button. "Not my idea of a good time."

"It's lit well enough to see," Brandon said, turning the water off himself. "The whole idea is anonymous sex. Some guys like the idea of getting to fuck without consequences."

"I can see that," I replied, standing there dripping. "But it's not for me. Right now, my goal is to dry off. And…" I looked around the space we both stood in. "…there are no spare towels here."

"Try the front desk," Brandon said, pointing toward the door. "They'll hand one out to you if you ask."

"Great." I stared down at the puddle forming around me. "If you need me, just follow the wet trail."

I left the showers and Brandon's gorgeous naked self behind. The small corridor with the brass hooks was right around the corner. A couple towels had been left hanging. Some other guests had made use of the facilities and forgotten them—or had gotten distracted by all the fun going on.

I debated using one, but decided against it. Knowing what all went down at this place, it wasn't safe. Towels could be used for more than drying off. Sure enough, one of them looked a bit stiff. I kept my hands to myself and searched for the jack-o-lantern speedos instead.

They, however, were nowhere to be found.

"Brandon?" I called out, peeking my head around the corner into the showers. "Did you move our speedos by any chance?"

"Move them?" Brandon had been wiping down is front, which meant his back was pointed toward me. I was momentarily distracted by the fine, fine ass on the man. "Not me, why?"

"Um…" I had to wait for my brain to reboot. "They're gone."

"Gone?" Brandon's forehead wrinkled with confusion as he walked around to where I stood. "Yup, that definitely constitutes as 'gone' in my book," he said, staring at the two empty hooks. "They're not on the floor anywhere?"

"Don't think so," I said, checking the area by the sinks just in case. "They're not over here either."

"Someone took them," Brandon concluded. He didn't sound especially perturbed. "One of the guys could be playing a prank on us. Or we've got an obsessed fan wanting a souvenir."

I stared at him. "You sound way too at ease about this," I remarked. "It's concerning."

"Like I said." Brandon gave me a clap on the back as he walked past. "It's part of the job. You'll get used to it eventually."

"Lucky me," I muttered, still dripping wet as I left the showers behind.

Fortunately, the desk past the main door wasn't far. I left a trail of moisture all over the floor as I walked back toward it, but this was why sandals were so important. The guy behind the desk was nice enough. He passed a towel to me underneath the window without giving me a hard time.

Given that I was naked, he must have thought I was just another guest. I thanked him and dabbed myself dry out in the open. Enough people had already seen my goods. It felt foolish to be modest at this point.

It occurred to me that I was undergoing a sort of change. Jean had said that places such as this had a vibe about them. There was definitely something different about me now. Being naked wasn't as self-conscious for me as it once was. At least, I didn't feel as self-conscious right now behind the walls of *Treats*.

Most likely, the same would not be said if I somehow ended up going for a stroll through the Castro in the nude.

My body still ached something terribly. The shower helped, but my legs still cramped something awful. There was a little time left before I had to go back on. I decided to make use of the facilities. It seemed silly not to, since they were available and I was on break.

The whirlpool room was up ahead and to the left. I peeked inside first, having learned my lesson the first time. Guests appeared to take the *No Physical Contact* sign on the wall as a suggestion and not a hard line.

I half-expected to find another orgy going on. To my relief—and somewhat surprise—the whirlpool was empty.

"Thank fuck," I breathed out, entering the room properly.

Hanging the towel on a hook, I slid in under the churning surface. It didn't look as though anyone had used the whirlpool for a while. That helped me relax, since Jean assured me the pool was drained and cleaned regularly.

There was a health inspector snooping around too, so it seemed likely that the bathhouse would be following company ordinances closely.

Speaking of, I had been in the water for maybe five minutes when a set of footfalls made me open my eyes. Estelle Boylston was standing in the entrance. On instinct, I checked to make sure she couldn't see much below the belt.

"Don't bother," she said, entering the area without a care. "At my age, I've seen it all, remember?"

"Seemed polite," I said, embarrassed for checking and not sure why. My brain could be weird about modesty, it seemed. "How goes your night?"

"It goes." She sounded tired, and given how late it was, that didn't shock me. "Mostly, I'm wishing I could have a cigarette."

I watched her pull something out of her back pocket. Estelle tore into the plastic paper wrapping and took a bite. I smelled the faint whiff of chocolate in the air around the chlorine.

"Candy bar break?"

Estelle nodded as she chewed. "My last vice," she said. "Coffee Crisps. I've been trying to quit smoking. They say the best way to lick an addiction is by replacing it with something else."

"Never heard of those," I mused. There was an itch in the back of my brain, though, and it took a moment for me to understand why. "Hang on a minute. I have seen those before. Upstairs, on my first night."

"My private stash," she said, devouring more of the sugary treat. "Thought I'd share a few, but the skinny bitch in charge told me they'd make everyone's breath smell like shit."

She must have been referring to Austin instead of Michael. I recalled being warned about that very thing.

"Little ungrateful, if you ask me," she went on, still chewing. "They don't sell these in the states no more. I have to special order them from Canada."

I wasn't sure what else I could say. The idea of coffee and chocolate in a candy bar form sounded delicious. Sadly, though, I was due back upstairs in a bit. The last thing I wanted was to do was dance in front of strangers with bad breath and chocolate stains on my teeth.

Still, dancing for so long made one hungry.

"What you got planned for the night?" she asked, before I could beg a Coffee Crisp off her.

"More dancing," I replied, settling back while the churning water massaged my tender body. "Might go to my room for a bit first and relax."

Estelle nodded. "You go do that, then," she said casually, turning to walk back out. "I've gotta make sure people are at least keeping their bodily fluids inside the rooms."

Given what I had seen of the place, Estelle was fighting a losing battle. "Good luck," I called out after her. "You'll need it!"

The whirlpool was heavenly. I settled in for a bit longer, stretching my legs out to give them the massage they so desperately needed. A couple guys strolled in after a bit, nude of course. Both were insanely hot, like they lived and slept at the gym. They evidently knew one another too, since they entered while in the midst of a conversation.

I wanted to tune them out, but kept one ear open. Spying was the whole reason why I had taken this job. I eavesdropped for a couple of minutes.

"—can't believe one of the dancers died last night," one guy said as he settled into the frothy water.

"I wasn't here," the other responded, joining him. "Too bad I missed it."

I tried to keep the scowl off my face, but was unsuccessful.

"Think it was drugs?" the second one went on.

The first one nodded. "Probably an overdose," he theorized, setting his back against the inner rim. "You know their type. They're always on something."

"Yeah." The second guy let out a derisive snort. "Like guys who do porn. They've all got the 'gift' or something just as bad."

My hands clenched into fists momentarily.

"Still," the second one went on, waving his hands along the surface. "Some of them aren't bad looking."

I thought about Brandon and his sculpted perfection. My cock instantly stirred to life even though I was tired. If Brandon was what these two considered "not bad", it made me wonder how they ranked men in general.

"Might be worth fucking," the second guy continued, "at least once, anyway."

The first guy sputtered. "Yeah," he teased in a mean-spirited tone. "Just make sure you run to the clinic right afterward."

They laughed, long and cruel, which echoed off the walls. Having heard enough, I stood up. Water dripped down off my body. The movement caught their attention and I watched as their eyes raked over me. Judging by their expressions, neither one was impressed.

That suited me just fine. I'd have sooner put my dick inside of a wood chipper than have either one of them touch me. Taking a second look, there was something about their faces that seemed artificial. I realized that they'd both had work done.

"What about you?" the first one asked. "Would you fuck one of the dancers?"

"Don't have time," I replied curtly, moving over to claim my towel. "I'm due back on stage soon."

I let those words settle while I dried myself off. "No way," the first one said, watching me. "You're not really a dancer, are you?"

Turning, I displayed my ass for them to ogle next. "You tell me," I challenged, feeling my anger rise. "Or is the fact that I'm sober and healthy too much of a twist."

The second one snickered, but the first guy went quiet.

"His name was Marcus," I told them both. "I didn't know him that well. But he didn't die of an overdose."

Looking back, I saw that they were both staring. "Someone murdered him," I informed, my words dripping with venom. "He died of cyanide poisoning."

Their eyes doubled in size. "Really?" the second asked.

"Yes."

Having said my piece, I turned to go. When I was at the door frame, curiosity took hold. I looked back to find the two chatting quietly among themselves.

"Fuck you both," I said flatly and turned to go.

The run-in with the two basic bitches had cemented something for me. I made my way past the employee elevator to the stairs, never slowing my pace. The Dark Maze was on the second floor. That much I could remember clearly.

Okay, so I might have lied a little bit to Brandon. It wasn't a clear plan in my head at that point. I had only been seriously considering going to meet whoever left that note in my speedo. There was a possibility, however thin, that somebody had information about Marcus' murder.

Sure, it felt like a cliché out of one of Auntie Mags' books, but I was working with that I had.

To my consternation, I took a wrong turn once I reached the second level. This took me into the labyrinth of doors that made up the bathhouse rooms. Turning around, I headed back the way I came.

Things in the Slurp Room were proceeding accordingly. I didn't hear any gagging this time. A few guys were making good use of the sex dungeon's equipment too. I spotted one guy being railroaded from both ends while laying back in a sex sling.

The Dark Maze, it turned out, was not far from the Viewing Room. I simply had to turn right at the end of the hallway. A set of mirrors ran along one side of the corridor. There was a bench on the other end, which had been claimed by a trio of older men. All three were watching each other jerk off.

"Wanna join?" one called out to me as I strode past.

"Maybe some other time," I replied politely, continuing onward.

Following the sign, I turned right. The entrance to the Dark Maze veered to the left automatically. A huge sign had been hung up on the wall, shaped like the kind used to warn drivers of road work.

Caution: Open Manholes Ahead was emblazoned on it in bold letters.

"Cute," I noted, mildly amused by this.

Turning left, I entered what turned out to be a room that was almost completely dark. Black lights kept the area lit well enough to maneuver. The term "Dark Maze" was turning out to be an apt description, though.

"Oh, wow…" I breathed out, startled.

It being hard to see wasn't stopping me from getting an eyeful. I found myself standing in an open area. There were booths all along the walls. In-between them stood full-length mirrors. All of the booths had gloryholes—the long kind that ran down about a foot or so.

Men stood around the booths, naked and hard, while thrusting their dicks through each available entrance. Slurping sounds could be heard inside. I realized that each booth had at least one man inside.

Sawhorses with rubber padding were laid out in the center. A couple of those were occupied. Men wearing hoods to cover their faces knelt with their asses pointed high in the air. A line had formed in front and behind them. They were being penetrated hard by men through each orifice.

A second sex sling was set up over in a corner. It was surrounded by gloryholes as well. One man lay across it, face up, with his arms and legs bound. He was being put through the ringer by a much younger man. Each thrust produced a plea for more from the tied-up turkey lying on the leather seat.

His cries were almost lost in the room. There was so much grunting and cussing, men groaning as their cum went flying. It was like a symphony.

Worse, or better, the room appeared to be built for carrying these sounds. They reverberated off the walls, bouncing back and forth to the point that it was hard to gauge their source. It didn't seem to matter either way because everyone else was grunting out the exact same thing.

"Fuck."

I wasn't sure what else to say. There was so much happening at once that my brain couldn't absorb it. Every which way I turned, men were getting their rocks off. The air stank of sweat and sex. Bodies were thrusting together in a rhythm of their own. Cries rang out, begging for more of the same rough, indifferent treatment.

It was all so much to take. I could feel it starting to overwhelm me. My brain switched into autopilot. Blood roared in my veins. I could feel my heart beating like a drum. My cock had swollen to full mast, getting harder with each heavy thud in my chest.

Slowly, I walked the circumference of the room. It was a really, really good thing I was wearing sandals. The floor didn't look safe to walk on with bare feet.

"*More!*"

"*Harder!*"

"*Fuck yeah!*"

The words came together easily, even though they were being shouted by different men. It was as if we were all being put under a trance. I was late to the party, but going under the spell of this place took no time at all.

In that moment, I wanted to be a part of it. To hell with having a boyfriend. This was freedom at its most primal. Everyone here did exactly what they wanted. If they wanted to be used, they could be. If they wanted to get off, nothing was holding them back.

"More!" someone cried out from inside one of the booths. "Fuck! Give me more cum!"

The men gathered around were doing just that. I watched one buck his hips into the gloryhole hard enough to shake the cabinet. The guy inside didn't appear to mind, however. I could hear him slurping up this latest volley of cum like he was dying for it.

Another cabinet was occupied. I could tell because the door was shut. Only a couple men had gathered around. Again, as if in a trance, I approached.

It would be so easy for me to feed my cock through one of the available holes. I could pump my load inside and the fellow on the other end would take it. Hell, he might even beg for it like the other one did. It didn't have to be intimate. We didn't have to exchange names or numbers, make promises to call each other afterward.

He was here to be used. And my cock was hard.

It was that simple.

A pair of arms grabbed me before I could take that last step. Some part of me deep inside felt a surge of relief. The rest of me was pissed off, though. Someone was keeping me from what I wanted. The id section of my brain roared with deep rage.

"Let." I stated the words with acid in my tone. "Go. Of. Me."

A light kiss, playful and teasing, was planted on my cheek. "Oh, come on," I heard Jean's voice in my ear. "You don't really mean that, do you?"

I let myself relax, breathing in the smell of sweat and hard sex coming from all around us. This didn't help my current state of mind, regrettably. I was as hard as I could remember being. My body felt alive, like it was being fed an electric charge.

A part of me was grateful that Jean showed up to stop me, but another part was royally pissed. I didn't want to behave myself anymore. This was total freedom, to do whatever the hell I wanted.

"You almost went over to the booth," Jean whispered in a teasing, knowing way as he placed wet kisses along the back of my neck. "Naughty! Naughty!"

Shame tried to boil up from within. I could feel it and steeled myself. He had every right to be hurt, but his tone didn't reflect that. The instincts burning inside of me were too strong for regret to take hold.

Instead, I spread my legs slightly. "Fuck me," I told him. "I need you inside of me right now. Before I do something stupid."

Jean chortled. "I think that line's already been crossed," he growled out. I could tell how horny he was, in his voice and by the thick, heavy cock pressing into the small of my back. "You've jizzed all over another guy. And you were about to get a blowjob from a total stranger."

"I know." I rubbed myself against him, hoping to entice Jean into giving me what I so desperately needed. "Fuck me."

Jean's armed squeezed me. "Just like that?" he asked. "No apology? No promise not to ever do it again?"

Anger filled me. "Fuck me!" I demanded, standing on my tiptoes. "Fuck me right now!"

Jean shoved me forward. The movement surprised me, and I might have landed on my face were he not still holding me tightly in his arms. Jean marched forward, maneuvering us both over to one of the booths.

"You're gonna get exactly what you need," he snarled in my ear. "Dirty little slut boy!"

I had unleashed a monster, it seemed. There was no warmth in Jean's voice. He actually growled, low and deep, as my body landed on the side of the booth.

It was then that I remembered I was still naked. Jean had aimed me right at the gloryhole. My cock slid through without resistance. I felt a stranger's hand touch it a second or two before this warm, hungry mouth descended over it.

"How do you like that, huh?" Jean demanded, keeping me pinned.

"Mmm! Ohhh!" I cried out. Whoever was in the booth, they belonged there. Hell, this guy could charge cash for his oral skills. "Fuck! He's so fucking good."

"Good." Jean's voice seemed to calm a little. "Hold still."

Jean kept one arm wrapped securely around me, keeping me pinned against the booth. I wasn't trying to get away, not when the human hoover inside the box was doing such a splendid job of keeping me aroused. Jean fumbled one-handed with something for a moment. I was enjoying myself too much to care, not until I felt a warm, slick liquid touch my hole courtesy of his fingers.

"Open up," he told me, probing my sphincter. "Now."

I wanted to obey, but the quality of head I was getting made it difficult to think. Jean settled the matter himself by kicking my legs wide apart. I felt like I was being frisked by a cop.

"Uhhhh…" The sound stretched out of my throat just like my hole did. Jean had lubed me up and was pushing inside. "Oh, thank fuck!"

His cock felt amazing, as always. Taking it was so intense, but the resistance was gone. My body wasn't fighting the invasion this time. It welcomed him home like he belonged inside of me.

I rocked backward, spearing myself on his massive cudgel. Primal instincts were in charge. I wasn't fighting this anymore. Some part of me had screamed in protest during this whole journey. Jean had brought me here to loosen up and I stubbornly refused.

Not anymore, though. Now, in the heat of the moment, I was ready to abandon everything I had been taught about what was right.

This time, it was simply about pleasure.

"Fuck me!" I practically screamed.

That declaration spurred on the stranger in the booth. He began to really suck my cock in earnest. I helped by rocking myself back and forth, thrusting back onto Jean before rearing forward to slam my cock through the gloryhole.

The scream had drawn the attention of numerous pairs of eyes. I could see faces turn to stare while I took thirteen inches of male perfection inside of my stretched hole. Slurping sounds came from the inside of the booth. I was hitting it hard enough with my thrusts to rattle the cabin.

"More!" I demanded, of both my lovers—the one who slept in bed with me each night and the faceless stranger. "Give me more, please!"

Jean seized me by the throat, griping me tightly as he drove himself forward harder. "You dirty little slut," he hissed, pounding me into the booth. "This is what you need."

"I need it," I whimpered, letting go. "You need to fuck m—oh, fuck! Yes, that's it. Right there!"

Jean knew how to pleasure my body. It didn't take much, given his girth as well as the ample length of him. There was a reason he had been scouted for porn, after all. The man was a living legend—not to mention proof that "all men are created equal" was a bold-faced lie in certain contexts.

It was more than that, however. He knew how to time his thrusts, knew which angle to tease and torment my prostate. I could feel him reaching that second g-spot inside of me. His cock always reached places no other man had touched before.

"Ughh! Ahhh! Fuck, that's so good!"

Jean gave my throat another squeeze. "Feel him sucking you so good," he whispered huskily as he thrust. "Taking your cock while you take mine!"

"Yes!" I answered immediately. "Oh, he's so fucking good at it!"

The guy in the booth took that as a compliment. His hoovering my cock intensified. I couldn't hold myself back. He knew just how to pleasure a man's dick. One hand squeezed the upper part of my balls while the other stroked me at the base. His cheeks were positioned to create a vacuum, inhaling my cock each time Jean pounded me forward.

"More!" I pleaded.

"You're always gonna get more," Jean assured me, never ceasing his assault on my tender hole. "You're mine."

Both hands braced against the cabin. I didn't want us to break the damn thing. It struck me as weird that I would care in the heat of the moment, but I did. The bathhouse would charge us a fortune. Plus, we would undoubtedly be banned, given the only partially-deserved reputation for ruining equipment with our destructo-nookie.

"I'm yours," I swore.

Jean bucked his hips into me hard enough that my limbs collapsed. "Always," he swore as I was slammed up against the booth completely.

More men turned to watch. A couple of them stepped forward out of the gloom. I could feel their eyes rake over my sweat-soaked body. They were stroking themselves furiously.

This is what pushed me over the edge. "Fuck, I'm gonna cum," I warned, trying to back away.

Jean kept right on pounding me. Pinned against the booth, I couldn't move well enough to slip off his cock and pull my dick out of the gloryhole. The stranger in the booth didn't seem to care either.

"Ohhh! Ohhh!" I cried out as my balls churned. "Oh, I'm gonna… fuck, it's…cumming! Cumming! Oh shit!"

My load shot forth out of me like a fountain. I felt it flood the inside of the hungry stranger's mouth. Some tiny part of my brain that was still functional wondered if he would spit it out.

Those fears were totally unfounded, though. Above the din of Jean's thrusts and the rattling of the cabinet, I could hear him hungrily slurping each rope that I shot. He drained it all down like it was his last meal.

"Gods!" I screamed.

For some reason, this destroyed the last vestiges of my resistance. I felt it crumble around me, leaving the wanton whore I had become on display. My cock didn't go down. I was as hard as I had been when we first started.

"Take it," I ordered the stranger, resuming my thrusts. "Take it, you filthy little fucking whore!"

Jean laughed. "That's it," he said, driving himself forward so that we were pressed together. "Use that fucking mouth."

"Take my fucking cock," I commanded, wanting to give the unknown man the full experience.

I was back to rocking myself onto Jean's massive cock. Each inch that slid inside of me set off an explosion. My skin felt so alive. It tingled with every part of me that made contact against Jean's own hairy, muscled flesh.

The first guy jerking off while watching us blew his load. It flew in an arc, splattering all over the floor near my feet. Sweat creased his forehead as he doubled over, bent in half from the intensity of his orgasm.

"Good boy," Jean whispered in my ear. "You did that. Watching us made him cum. Does that excite you?"

"Yes," I answered immediately without hesitation. "I want to make them all cum."

My main priority, though, was getting my rocks off again. I pushed forward, driving my still-hard cock down the stranger's throat. He gagged, barely audible with all the noise going on, but didn't resist.

"Remember," Jean whispered as I bucked back onto him. "Right now, he's just a hole. Use him to shoot your load."

I did just that, slamming my hips once more into the cabinet. It rattled and shook with my thrusts. The guy inside gagged and slurped, hungry for another load from my balls. Thanks to Jean's cock buried deep inside me, that didn't take long.

"Fuck!" I screamed as Jean bruised my prostate again. "Cumming! Goddammit, cumming again!"

The stranger inside gulped down this second load. Seeing me force my cum into a complete and total stranger again drove another viewer over the edge. One of the guys jerking off nearby blasted his cream into the air. It landed on his feet and the floor, splattering the toes of the two beside him.

"Fuck, that's hot," Jean said.

"It is…" I grunted out, impaling myself onto my boyfriend's cudgel. "I wanna make them all cum."

"Yes." Jean sounded as enthused by the idea as I was. "Let's really give them a show!"

Jean timed his thrusts so that each delicious stroke brought me closer to yet another glorious climax. My balls churned the entire time.

I could feel the cum inside of them boil. There seemed to be no limit to the number of times I could shoot.

I was elated with the discovery of my new sex toy. The mystery man in the booth pressed his mouth all around the gloryhole. All I had to do was feed him each time Jean drove me forward.

"Gag on it," I ordered.

"Take my cock," Jean ordered me.

The stranger in the cabinet slurped and gobbled down the cock feeding him the cum he so badly needed. My balls emptied their load down his throat, which set off another chain reaction. Two more men blew their wad from watching me cum.

One of them had range on his load. He managed to splash it on me. I should have been grossed out, being cum on by a man I didn't know. The feel of his hot jizz spraying my hair and all over my back and side had the opposite effect, however. I came yet again, hosing the stranger's throat down with my cum.

"Cum in me!" I cried out, speaking to Jean. "I want them to cum on me while you're breeding me!"

Jean didn't so much as flinch. Turning his head, he nodded at the three remaining men who were watching us, stroking their hard cocks. One after the other, they stepped forward, closing the gap separating us.

I was surrounded on one side by three men, all of whom looked ready to shoot. A solid wall stood to my right. The booth was in front of me where a stranger slurped greedily on my cock. Jean held me from behind, rapidly hammering his thick slab of meat in and out of my poor battered hole.

"Fuck," I cried out, feeling more cum well up. "Here I cum again!"

I was pinned in. All three men looked ready to shoot. My balls unloaded for the final time with a jolt. I came so hard that it actually made my nuts ache. This would turn out to be my biggest load of the night. The guy inside the booth choked and gargled. Clearly, he hadn't expected me to blow so much after having cum so many times.

"Drink it!" I commanded the stranger, slamming my cock through the hole. "Drink it all down, you slut!"

Cumming pushed the others over the edge. It was like a domino effect. In a moment, one let out a howl and sprayed his jizz across my back as well. I could feel myself being hosed down in the dark by another man—another that I didn't know the same of.

"Aww, shit!" he cried, his voice carrying a slight twang to it.

Jean pushed in again, hitting that one spot so deep inside that only he had ever been able to reach. I yelped, bucking slightly, as the next one shot his cream across my side. He was gasping, his breath ragged, as his seed covered the short gap between us.

"Fuck yeah," he groaned, buckling at the knees.

The last one took a step forward. He was already on shaky legs, but managed to aim his load at my ass. My cheeks were coated with his cum, and fuck if there wasn't a lot of it. He managed to cum the most. I could feel it leak down in-between the crack of my ass as Jean picked up the pace.

"Cumming," he warned me, slamming those muscular hairy thighs into my smaller frame. "Get ready!"

"I'm ready," I promised, pushing back to meet his thrusts. "Breed me!"

He roared, the loudest of them all. The next thrust pushed me so hard that my body flattened against the booth. The entire cabinet shook as Jean unloaded inside of me.

"Fuck!" he screamed, yelling loud enough to drown out the house beat playing over the system. "Goddammit! Fuck!"

"Ahhh!" I howled. His cock always expanded, swelling to an even bigger size when he came. "Ohhh! Fuck! Fuck! Ahh! Shit! Fuck me! Fuck!"

I was cussing up a storm, certainly not the sort of language I would use at my mother's dinner table. The entire core of my being was painted with Jean's virile seed. There was enough cum to knock me up with septuplets.

My body stayed pressed up against the booth for a while. I wasn't sure how long. The stranger inside kept running his tongue in circles around my swollen head, licking my foreskin clean. I stayed there, arms and legs spread, making an X figure. My hands clung to the sides, holding on for dear life while my boyfriend finished claiming me.

"Fuck!" he screamed one final time as his climax abated.

I was covered in cum from several men I didn't know. My boyfriend had delivered to me one of the wildest, nastiest fucks I had ever had. A man whose face I hadn't seen had a full belly of cum from my balls. I had cum several times inside of him and didn't know what he looked like.

Perhaps I should have felt ashamed. In that moment, it was the total opposite. I had never felt more alive or free in my life. Every cell in my body vibrated with excitement. I never wanted it to end.

"Take me to our room," I told Jean, not bothering to keep my voice down, "and fuck me again."

Jean gave me a slight squeeze. "Don't you have to go back on?" he asked, taking a step back to give me space.

It was just enough for me to turn around. I reached up for him, planting a hard kiss on his mouth. We held one another there for a moment, kissing deeply while the others stared. I thought I heard a door open, but couldn't care less.

"Fuck me," I demanded. "Fuck me for the rest of the night."

Jean seemed surprised. I took hold of his arm and pulled him along behind me. He was mine by right and I was making certain everyone there understood. The others stepped aside, parting like the Red Sea to let us pass.

As we left, a man reached out to touch me on the shoulder, getting my attention. "Dude," he said, looking amazed. "You're a fucking animal. You just kept cumming and cumming."

"Thanks," I said, meaning it, but having no patience for anything. "Sorry, but my boyfriend and I have somewhere else to be."

At once, the stranger from the booth stepped aside. Curious, I turned to get a glimpse of his face. He was older, of Chinese descent, and had a slight stubble on his chin—which was coated with slobber and my cum.

"Make sure you eat the rest of that," I said as we walked toward the door.

The man from the booth laughed. "Oh, don't worry," I heard him say while dragging Jean along behind me out of the Dark Maze. "I will!"

I kept a firm grip on Jean's arm as we walked back toward our room. Jean followed along behind me without protest. If my assertiveness bothered him, he gave no indication.

Along the way, we passed a couple going at it up against a wall. I recognized ThiccBlackDaddy sporting the same type of leather fetish gear he had on the night we met. He did a double-take as I struggled to squeeze past.

"Sorry," he said, pushing the twink he was railing up against the wall. "Better?"

"Much," I said, remembering enough of my manners. "Thanks."

Nothing more needed be said beyond that. ThiccBlackDaddy went back to hammering his cock inside the twink—who, judging by his moans—was more than pleased by the treatment. I pulled Jean along behind me and we continued down the darkened corridor to our room.

We had decided against splurging this time around. The room rented by us was far more compact and had fewer amenities. It was, I had realized, the same room Inspector Wong used to question us last night.

That, I would come to understand later, should have been a red flag. I was in too big of a hurry to care, however. In my haste, I managed to forget about losing my key as well. It had been in the speedo that went missing.

"Here," Jean said, reaching for his spare.

"Don't bother," I said impatiently, spotting where the door was cracked. "It's open."

For the first time that night, Jean held me back. "That's odd," he said, taking hold of my arm. "I thought I locked it."

"Never mind," I told him, giving his arm a tug. "It's not like we had anything of value in there this t—Oh!" My voice cracked as I stared, having slid the door aside. "…my god."

The inside of the room was trashed. It looked even worse than when our first room was destroyed. Holes had been punched into the walls. Plaster was torn out and lying in shreds all over the floor. The mattress had been flipped over and ripped to pieces. Even the pillow didn't survive the purge.

None of that mattered, though. That was the least of our concerns. A body, lying slumped in the corner, stared back. I looked into the stiff, shocked expression of Estelle Boylston.

She was dead.

And in her hands, two orange speedos were clutched tightly. I didn't need Jean's deductive prowess to figure out who they belonged to.

Chapter 12

"Okay, let's hear it," said Inspector Wong tersely.

Mercifully, I was clutching a cup of the strongest coffee that Auntie Mags' fancy French coffeemaker could brew. Otherwise, Inspector Wong might have found herself on the receiving end of some serious morning grumpiness. It seemed unwise to antagonize the police inspector, especially since she hadn't arrested me or Jean.

The words "as of yet" lingered in the back of my mind. "Let me caffeinate," I pleaded, taking a sip of the warm bliss in a cup. "We've been up most of the night."

"Late stripper hours?" Wong teased, though she held back saying anything more.

I drank several gulps of the liquid nirvana. Cream and sugar, in ample amounts, had been added already. Auntie Mags knew how I liked my coffee. She hadn't lingered after bringing everyone a cup—merely gave Wong a scathing look and told Jean and I to call if we needed her. Then, she was heading up the stairs to work on her latest novel.

"Yes," I freely admitted, setting my cup down on a coaster. Inspector Wong's cup was already camped out on one atop the coffee table. "And something about police questioning as well."

Jean held a cup of tea. For some reason, he abstained from coffee. It was one of the great mysteries about the man I would never understand.

His ass rested on the armchair of the recliner I had claimed for myself. I needed him close to me right now. One hand automatically reached up every so often to touch him, reassuring myself that he was there. Seeing him wasn't enough.

"Standard procedure," Inspector Wong replied, trying to sound nonchalant. "You were one of the last ones to see Estelle Boylston alive."

A shudder went through me. I was having a difficult time picturing Estelle as anything but dead. My mind kept flashing back to her body sitting squat, slumped over slightly, with a gruesome expression on her dead face.

Like Marcus, she had died in agony. No one deserved that.

"And the fact that eyewitnesses can confirm our whereabouts," Jean added, gripping his tea cup tightly, "is the reason why we haven't been indicted?"

Inspector Wong stared at Jean for a moment. "Estelle was found in your room," she pointed out, studying Jean closely. "Which had been ransacked."

"It happened before," Jean said.

I reached for my cup again, desperately needing more coffee. "The first night we were there," I confirmed, holding the cup a moment to warm my hands. "At *Treats*. Someone broke into our room and trashed the place."

"The owner threatened to sue for damages," Jean added.

"Come to think of it…" I turned, looking up at Jean. "The room where we found Estelle looked an awful lot like the first one. They were both torn up in the same way."

"Like they were done by the same person," Jean said, smiling slightly as he sipped his tea.

Inspector Wong frowned. "You're saying that Estelle wrecked your room?" she pressed. "That seems pretty far-fetched." She was, however, considering it. "I'll have to pull photos from the police report, assuming there was one, but the room Estelle's body was found in looked worse than something that had been raided by the FBI."

"We've got pictures of our first room," I told her.

Jean was already reaching for his phone. "We took them after finding the room that way," he explained, pulling them up. "The bathhouse manager wasn't convinced. Not until Brandon vouched for us."

Inspector Wong stretched an arm across the coffee table, taking the phone from Jean's extended hand. She leaned back in her own chair, studying the screen while swiping with her thumb.

"They do look similar," she admitted, flicking her eyes up at Jean and I momentarily. "Yeah, I could believe this was done by the same person."

My body fell back into the chair. I could feel my head reeling. It seemed so utterly out there, too wild to contemplate. And yet, the longer I considered the possibility, the more it made a strange sort of sense.

"I think…" I began, hesitant about voicing my theory aloud. "I think…that Estelle might have been the one who killed Marcus."

Inspector Wong couldn't keep her poker face up. "Say again?" she asked me. "You think a woman in her fifties poisoned a stripper?"

Jean reached for a coaster, placing his teacup down atop it on the coffee table. He was smiling the entire time. In fact, he looked incredibly pleased about something.

"Go on," he told me encouragingly. "Make your case."

Nervously, I looked from him back to Inspector Wong. She was watching me as well. I felt as though I were being sized up.

"A lot of this is just guessing," I admitted, putting my own coffee cup down. "But…"

I took a deep breath, composing my thoughts before continuing. "To start off with," I said, speaking directly to Inspector Wong, "I assume the toxicology report came back on Estelle Boylston."

Inspector Wong hesitated, then nodded. "Cyanide," she revealed flatly. "Just like the first victim."

"Second," Jean corrected. "If you count Blu."

"Who?" Inspector Wong's forehead wrinkled in confusion. "There's a third body?"

"He means the guy who was shot outside Trader Joe's," I said, making a grim face as I thought back to that morning. "But he didn't die via poisoning."

"I have a theory about that too," Jean revealed, wearing a thin smile. "But you go first. I want to hear your thoughts on this."

"I'd be lying if I said I wasn't curious." Inspector Wong sat back, tenting her fingers together. "What's your theory, detective?"

I thought long and hard about how to phrase what was swirling around in my head. "Both rooms were trashed the same way," I began, figuring I would start there since it was something Inspector Wong seemed to agree on. "It stands to reason they were done by the same person."

"Right," Wong said, nodding once.

"Estelle is…was," I corrected myself, "the health inspector. She had access to all areas of the bathhouse. She could have easily gotten upstairs before the party was in full swing."

"Putting the cyanide in the condom," Jean said, still smiling.

"You're suggesting," Inspector Wong interjected, "that she didn't care who was poisoned. That it was a random killing."

Something nagged at the back of my mind. "Not exactly," I replied, deciding to go with the impulse. "I think she definitely meant to murder one of us. One of the dancers, I mean. It didn't matter to her which one, though."

The room fell silent. I used the time to try and organize my thoughts more. The pieces were there, but they weren't falling into place on their own. I could feel it.

"Brandon and I bumped into someone," I said, flashing back. "Our first night there, when he and I were trying to lose some guys that wouldn't take a hint, I bumped into someone in the hallway on the second floor by the stairs."

"You think it was Estelle?" Wong asked.

I thought back to that night again and nodded. "Yeah," I answered, feeling slightly more confident. "At the time, I wasn't worried about it. It was only for a second. But they were Estelle's height and build."

"Was she in a hurry?" Jean asked me.

"And in a foul mood," I added, reaching for my coffee cup again. "I smelled cigarette smoke too. Not far from our room. Estelle mentioned that she was trying to give up smoking. She ate these candy bars instead to curb her craving, but she could have relapsed. And…"

My voice trailed off as another thought occurred to me. "Come to think of it," I went on. "Estelle said that she wasn't at Treats that night."

I looked over at Inspector Wong, and then up at Jean. "But she knew about the vomit in the Slurp Room," I finished. "How?"

Wong made a face. "That place is disgusting," she stated, a fact that I chose to overlook for the moment. "And she could have easily heard about that from someone else. It was probably a part of her job."

"That sort of thing isn't uncommon," Jean revealed. "I doubt the staff would mention it to her unless she asked. And it seems unlikely that she would, unless she had been there."

"Again," Inspector Wong interrupted, making a sour face. "Gross."

"So she lied about being there," I said, not wanting to lose my train of thought. "Why? Unless she was worried about needing an alibi."

"She needed an alibi for breaking into a bathhouse room?" Inspector Wong challenged. "But not one for murder?"

"Estelle had one," Jean pointed out, going for his tea. "As far as she was concerned, anyway. She was nowhere near Marcus when he was killed."

"And she had no reason to kill him," I threw in, taking a sip of my coffee. The caffeine was helping me to think better. "As far as anyone knew, they had never met."

"Meaning," Inspector Wong said pointedly, going for her own coffee, "she had no motive."

"She had motive," Jean insisted.

I leaned back in the chair again, resting my tired head against the softness of the headrest. "Fuck if I know why, though," I admitted, giving up.

"I think I can fill in a few gaps," Jean said, holding his own cup in his hands. He looked pleased, which wasn't shocking. "If neither of you mind."

It didn't surprise me in the slightest that Jean had figured everything out. Inspector Wong was less than pleased. She took a long drink from her coffee, like she needed it, before putting the cup back down on the coaster.

"Fine," she declared, throwing both hands up. "Let's hear this. A stripper and an ex-porn star think they've solved two murders."

"Three," Jean corrected again, sipping his tea. "But we'll get to that."

Inspector Wong stared hard across the table at Jean, but my boyfriend wasn't about to let that faze him. I listened, hoping that this would finally start to make sense.

"Let's start with Estelle's death," he said, cracking his knuckles. "Raf, you said that Estelle ate candy bars, right? To help with her nicotine cravings."

"Um…" I thought back to the conversation she and I had in the whirlpool room. "Coffee Crisps, they were called. They came in a yellow wrapper."

Jean smiled, looking even more pleased. "I saw a candy wrapper in our room," he said, giving my arm a squeeze in thanks. "The one we found Estelle's body in."

"So?" Wong asked, clearly confused.

Jean leaned forward, locking eyes with her. "Blu was eating a Coffee Crisp the day that he died," my boyfriend revealed. "Inside Trader Joe's."

"Great for him." Wong was growing irritated. "He bought it in the store."

"No, he didn't," I cut in, thinking quick. The coffee helped with that. "Estelle told me. I remember her saying that she had to special order those."

"They don't sell them in many places here in the United States," Jean said, looking pleased with me. "She would have to order them from Canada."

"And there were Coffee Crisps on the table!" I was getting excited now. "My first night at Treats. The others warned me not to eat them. Said it would give me bad breath."

"Which is why Estelle had to resort to poisoning a condom instead," Jean said, keeping his gaze fixed on Inspector Wong. It was her he had to convince, not me. "She wanted one of the dancers to die during their performance, or just before."

I watched as Inspector Wong bit down on the tip of one thumb, deep in thought. "You're saying she poisoned Blu, the stri—the dancer at Trader Joe's. But then someone shot him?"

Jean nodded. "Most likely Estelle," he explained. "Estelle wanted to send a message. Blu probably stole one of her Coffee Crisps—the ones she had laced with cyanide."

Judging by her expression, Inspector Wong didn't buy into Jean's theory, but I was starting to see what he meant.

"She meant for Blu," I began, "or one of the other dancers, to die that first night. But Blu snagged one of her poisoned candy bars and left earlier that day."

"They would have set up beforehand," Jean said, nodding at me. "And if Blu dropped dead somewhere else, the police would get involved."

"So she makes it look like a random shooting?" Inspector Wong still didn't sound convinced. "I guess there's no point in checking for poison. Not when the victim has several bullet holes in him."

"It wouldn't matter if you looked now anyway," I told her. "Cyanide disappears from a corpse after about a day."

Inspector Wong and Jean both stared at me. "Auntie Mags told me about it," I explained, draining the last of the coffee from my mug to hide my embarrassment.

"Your aunt knows about cyanide?" Wong asked, sincerely confused.

"She writes murder mysteries," Jean explained, gesturing toward a bookshelf against a wall behind the inspector.

Wong turned around. I watched as her eyes swept across the long row of titles, growing wider with each passing second. Wong was slightly unsteady when she looked back at us.

"Your aunt," she began shakily, "is Margaret Sherrinford?"

Jean looked extraordinarily giddy. "You're a fan," he pegged smugly. "Aren't you?"

"Never you mind," she dismissed, herself blushing at the cheeks.

"Back to this wild theory of yours. I'll admit some of it seems plausible, if outlandish. But you've yet to give me a reason for why Estelle Boylston would murder anyone."

"And then there's the matter of who killed her," I pointed out.

"That's easy." Jean sounded confident, of course. "Estelle was blackmailing the dancers."

That, I would admit, was not something I expected to hear Jean say. Inspector Wong was caught off-guard as well.

"What?" I asked.

"What?" she demanded.

"Estelle tore up both rooms," Jean explained, speaking more quickly now. "Because she was looking for something. Something she assumed one of the dancers had hidden in a room at the bathhouse."

"Like what?" Inspector Wong challenged. "Extra tips?"

"Something smaller," Jean said, shaking his head. He was all business now. "Something you could fit inside of a small pocket inside of a speedo."

"Yeah, that's the part that confused me," I readily admitted. "Why were Brandon's and my speedo in the room with her body?"

"Because she thought one of you might have what she was looking for," Jean told me. "And when she didn't find it, she decided to search the room where the two of you were seen together."

I thought back. "The room where Inspector Wong questioned us?"

"Bingo," Jean said, pointing at me.

"And then, what?" Inspector Wong demanded. "Someone poisoned her?"

I could tell Wong was intrigued, despite the disdain in her voice. "No," Jean replied, raising up. "She poisoned herself."

"She committed suicide?" I asked, utterly lost now.

"Not quite." Jean took a deep breath. "Remember, Estelle was getting desperate. She was desperate enough right from the start to murder two people. And she hadn't found what she was looking for."

A memory flashed in my mind, of Estelle going for one of her Coffee Crisps while talking with me.

"She needed a fix," I said, feeling like I was on the right track at last. "A cigarette, or something. But she was trying to quit. So she—"

"—ate one of her candy bars," Jean finished.

Wong stared at the two of us for a long time. I anticipated her saying something sarcastic. She had made her contempt for the two of us clear already.

"We didn't find candy bars on the snack table," she began, startling me with how serious she was being.

"She would have taken them," Jean said. "To conceal her hand in the murder."

"I guess," I began, mulling over what we had deduced so far based mostly on conjecture. "She lost track of which ones were poisoned and which weren't."

"And didn't realize her mistake," Jean concurred. "Until it was too late."

Inspector Wong thought this over for a bit. "Okay," she said after a full minute. "You have a possible theory—really, more of a hypothesis—on why the murders took place. So here's the point where I blow a hole in all of that."

I waited. "Go ahead," I insisted when Wong didn't continue immediately. "We're listening."

Inspector Wong flexed her fingers, releasing them from the tent she had been making. "What," she asked the two of us, "was the point?"

"Like I said," Jean answered enigmatically. "Estelle was trying to blackmail the other dancers."

"With what, though?" Inspector Wong asked through gritted teeth.

"Sweetie," I told Jean, touching his arm tenderly. "Don't antagonize the nice homicide investigator. Just tell us what you found out, please?"

Jean complied. I listened, as did Inspector Wong, while he explained everything. Neither one of us said a word during the exposition. When Jean finished, I opened my mouth to speak, but Wong beat me to it.

"You have got to be kidding me," she said flatly.

Chapter 13

"I still can't believe it," I said.

We were standing in the hallway beyond the entrance to *Treats*. It was the middle of the day, so the bathhouse wasn't terribly crowded. I felt like this was a good thing. Two murders couldn't be good for business. The arrest of every stripper working there would definitely give the place an unsavory reputation.

Assuming the notoriety didn't boost membership sales.

Jean and I stood side-by-side. It had taken a day for Aubrey Wong to get all the paperwork filled out and the arrest warrants to come through. Her investigation of the bathhouse proved everything Jean deduced as dead-on accurate. The bathhouse personnel had let her in so she could have another look around, even though she didn't bring a warrant.

Inspector Wong had come back looking absolutely dumbfounded. "It was where you said it would be," she had explained. "The only thing now is getting a warrant so we can make the arrests."

"Better hurry," Jean had advised her. "Before they skip town."

Monday morning, the day before Halloween and two days after Estelle Boylston's body was found, nearly every member of Stud Stable was led out in handcuffs. Jean and I stood by watching as uniformed officers led them out through the main doors. Most of them gave me nasty looks. They undoubtedly thought I had tipped the police off.

"I don't see Brandon," I noticed as the last of the crew was marched out. "Or Austin."

"Brandon can take care of himself," Jean assured me. "Austin made have gone underground."

I wanted to ask what Jean meant about Brandon, but his statement concerning Austin confused me. "Do you mean that literally or figuratively?" I wondered.

"Yes," Jean answered, chuckling. "If he isn't here, then he's on the run. I'm sure the search for him will turn up something soon."

"They should check the rooms," I said, waiting in case Brandon showed up. "This place is essentially a cheap hotel. He could have hidden upstairs."

"They will, I'm sure," Jean reassured me. "Feel like doing a little snooping?"

What I wanted to do was find Brandon. The troubling part was that I wasn't sure why. I couldn't figure out if I wanted to beg him to turn himself over or run for his life.

Brandon had befriended me. I didn't think he should get away with theft, but a part of me couldn't stand the thought of him being locked away, either.

"Sure," I decided, steeling myself. "Should we stick together?"

Jean considered that. "Seems like the safest idea," he agreed.

"Right," I said, keeping as much of the disappointment that I felt out of my voice as I could.

"On the other hand," Jean added thoughtfully. "We'd cover more ground if we split up. Make things easier for the inspector."

"Plus," I added dryly, "you'll have another chance to show off."

"Well, that too," Jean readily confessed, giggling.

I reached over, taking him by the hand. His eyes met mine as I squeezed it tightly. Jean returned the gesture by bending over to kiss me quickly on the lips.

"Be safe," he told me.

I held my phone up. "Keep in touch," I told him. "If you find Austin, don't try to play hero. Let me or the inspector know."

"Good idea," he said, nodding. "I think Austin might be a bit trickier than a crazy ex-boyfriend."

I rolled my eyes, but conceded the point. "You take the second floor," I said as we marched toward the stairs together. "I'll poke around on the third floor and then meet you there."

"Roger that."

Jean split off from me once we reached the second floor. I continued on, climbing to the top toward the smell of chlorine. My body was still stiff and sore, having been put through the ringer for the past several days. As such, it was slow-going for most of the trip.

I didn't expect to find Austin hanging around by the pool. My heart hoped that Brandon might be nearby, but that was unlikely. Going to the top was more about checking it off the list. I didn't have Jean's keen eye for details, after all. A spacious area like the deck and pool would be easier for me to cover. Jean, I felt sure, would have better success looking through the labyrinth of doors and rooms that made up the second level.

"Hey, how's it going?"

The voice startled me. I looked around, spotting DJ Chrissy Sinz in the booth. He was wearing a tank top that looked to be about two sizes too small. As a result, his biceps looked ready to burst.

"Been one hell of a day," I confessed, stepping out into the deck area.

"So I heard," Chrissy went on, pausing in the midst of inspecting his equipment. "I showed up early to prep for the big shindig tonight. Word is you had something to do with the dancers being busted."

"Wasn't me," I said truthfully. "Somebody else worked that one out."

"If you say so." It didn't sound as if Chrissy believed a word I was saying. "Any idea why they got busted?"

"Bank robbery," I told him, figuring there was no harm in him knowing the truth.

Chrissy stared at me hard for a moment. "You're serious," he realized when my facial expression didn't change.

"I'm afraid so," I replied.

Unexpectedly, Chrissy found that hysterical. "A bunch of gay strippers decide to knock over a bank together," he said, shaking his head. "Sounds like the plot to a Francine McDougall movie."

I had no clue who that was. "If you say so," I said, taking the time to look around the deck while we conversed. "This sure has been a hell of a few days."

It felt strange seeing this place in daylight. I was so accustomed to it being shrouded in shadows and black lighting. There was a certain air about it that way, like anything could happen.

In the daytime hours, the mystique was conspicuously absent. The pool looked as though it needed cleaning. There were handprints all over the surrounding glass that hadn't been scrubbed away yet. Someone had swept the deck floor, at least. There wasn't a single condom wrapper to be found.

"You know," I said thoughtfully, turning back to the booth. "I'm gonna miss this pl—"

I found myself staring into an empty booth. Chrissy was nowhere to be found.

"Okay," I said, feeling suddenly very antsy. "That just happened."

Something in my gut whispered to me that this wasn't right. There was only one way in or out of the booth. Chrissy would have had to open the latch gate to leave. That should have made enough noise to get my attention. I hadn't been that far lost in nostalgia.

Hesitant, I nevertheless worked my way around to the side. My eyes widened as I took in the scene. Chrissy was lying prone on the floor, unconscious. He could have been mistaken for taking a nap, except his head was turned at an awkward angle.

His neck didn't look broken, thankfully. For a moment, I was terrified that we had another murder on our hands. A second look showed that his chest rose and fell ever so slightly. He had been knocked out cold, but he was alive.

"Don't move."

I felt the cold press of a gun against my back. The touch caused me to flinch reflexively. Austin's voice was clear and crisp in my ear.

It appeared he had found me.

"The police are looking for you," I told him, craning my neck so I could see his face.

"I know," Austin replied, a threat of anger carrying under his reserved tone. "I've been hiding in the DJ booth. There's a small cabinet built into the underside for storage."

That news startled me. "Really?" I wondered.

"I'm small," he said, pushing the barrel of the gun into the spot between my shoulder blades. "One of the perks of being so compact. I can fit into places people don't think about looking in."

"Must be handy," I said, taking the cue.

Austin waited while I raised both of my hands up. "It is," he informed me. "Just like it's easy to fit through a network of tunnels underneath the city."

"So the cops say." Slowly, I turned around to face Austin holding the gun on me. "What did you do to Chrissy? Is he going to be all right?"

"Midazolam." Austin punctuated his answer by holding up a syringe with his free hand. "Fast acting. Puts someone under almost immediately."

"Impressive," I admitted. "Did you buy that with the money you stole?"

"Money?" Austin sputtered. "Wow, you really weren't the one who figured it out, are you?"

I had to keep Austin talking. That was the important thing. Being kidnapped had taught me something about these situations, at least. So long as Austin stayed calm and continued to talk, I stood a chance. My job was to make sure not to agitate him.

"Like I told Chrissy," I said sincerely, "before you knocked him out cold. That wasn't me."

"Yeah, well…" Austin's finger hovered over the trigger. "I'd love to know who it was. They managed to fuck up a perfectly good scheme."

"That, I'll believe." I studied Austin for a second. "What were you stealing, then? If it wasn't money, why go through all this trouble?"

"Nice try," Austin said, narrowing his eyes slightly.

Panic threatened to overwhelm me. I fought back as best as I could.

If Jean didn't find me, he would come looking up here. I needed time for that to happen, though.

"Who am I going to tell?" I asked.

Austin chewed on that fact. "Nah, I don't think I'll kill you," he decided. "Getting out of here will be tight without a hostage, even for me."

"So give me incentive to go along," I asked, hearing a tremble in my voice. "What's the deal with this setup you had? Because I haven't been able to figure it out."

That wasn't completely true. Jean had explained most of it, and I followed along well enough. There were a few details, apparently, that I had gotten wrong. I wanted Austin to fill in those gaps while also keeping him talking.

"Okay," Austin said, dropping the syringe. I watched him fish a tiny flash drive from the pocket of his cut-off jean shorts. "Know what this is?" he asked me.

"A flash drive," I answered at once.

Austin shook his head, hard enough to take his aim off me momentarily. "This is the future," he explained, training his gun back on my chest before I could move. "Why steal gold or cash when you can take away people's entire lives and put it on a tiny computer that fits right in your pocket?"

It started making sense at last. "You stole the information off the bank hardrives," I realized.

Austin smiled as the full implications of what was on that drive hit home. "Banks keep all sorts of records," he went on. "There are account and routing numbers. Credit cards. Credit scores. Purchasing history. Mortgages."

"Those are protected," I pointed out, confused.

"From outside infiltration," Austin explained, sliding the flash drive back into his pocket. "Hacking means hours and hours of firewalls and encryptions. But if you had access to the inside of a bank after hours—"

"You'd still have to get through all the security," I insisted, interrupting him.

Austin didn't seem perturbed by me cutting him off. He was having fun explaining his scheme to me. I needed to prolong that for as long as possible.

"Not when the higher ups leave their passwords lying around," Austin replied, chuckling. "No one bothers to remember those things. They'll write them down and tape them to the underside of their desks, even though they aren't supposed to."

I tried to remember the number of times I forgot my own social media passwords. It was the whole reason why I had my phone remember them for me. It was neither safe nor smart, but it sure as hell was convenient. I could believe that people working in a bank might do the same thing.

It also gave me even less reason to trust banks from here on out.

"There's saved passwords too," Austin continued, following my line of thought. "And catfishing employees so they give up information they shouldn't."

"And since you don't wipe the hardrives," I said. "Nobody knows that anything vital has been taken."

"Especially as we don't use the information right away," Austin confirmed, still grinning his smug expression. "But it is worth a fortune. The right people will pay out the ass for what is on this drive."

"And you can carry it around in your pocket." Something flashed in the back of my mind. "That was why Estelle stole my speedo before she died. She must have thought I was a part of it."

Austin scowled. "Ugh, that ugly bitch," he snarled, tightening the grip on his gun. "She really shouldn't have gotten involved."

"How did she get involved?" I wondered.

Austin shrugged. "Right place at the wrong time," he answered. "She was doing an inspection of the bathhouse and stumbled on where me and the guys were digging in the basement."

"The 'Employees Only' basement no one was allowed into," I said, nodding. "Perfect hiding place for digging into the underground network of tunnels underneath San Francisco."

"It wasn't easy," Austin admitted, shifting his weight from one foot to another. "Took a lot more of us than we thought. S'why I had to assign so many guys to the ground floor."

Jean had been right on that front as well. "But then Estelle figured it out," I said. "She decided to make a fast buck by blackmailing you."

"Said she would call the cops if I didn't pay her a percentage of what we earned from selling the information," Austin said. "Like hell I would give that bitch a dime."

"She killed Marcus and Blu because you didn't," I reminded.

That was a mistake. Austin had been relatively calm throughout our conversation. Had he not kept the gun trained on me the whole time, I would have said it was civil. Hearing Marcus' name set him off, though. A shiver of repressed rage went through his body.

"I loved that man," Austin whispered menacingly. "We all loved each other. It was us *compinches* against the world. And then…"

Austin's voice trailed off. I could see real sorrow in his face. His eyes were brimming with unshed tears. Whatever else the man was, he meant every word.

"She took him away from you," I finished.

Austin's hand holding the gun shook. "Yes," he said, his voice cracking.

"I'm sorry," I told him, meaning it. "She shouldn't have done that. Whatever else may have happened, killing Marcus and Blu was going too far."

"I was going to kill her myself," he hissed, his words full of anger and pain. "Once I figured out what had happened. But then…"

"She poisoned herself," I revealed, feeling eerily calm in that moment. "Not on purpose. She had meant to kill one of you—one of us—by spiking the candy bars with cyanide. Except no one would touch them."

Austin actually laughed, but it sounded hollow. "And then she ate one of the damn things by accident?" he asked me, lowering the gun a little. "Is that really it?"

I nodded sadly. "That's how it went down," I told him. "She died by her own hand. It may not be the revenge you wanted, but it does feel karmic."

Another empty chuckle escaped Austin's throat. "Marcus would have liked that," he confessed as the tears broke free. I watched them roll down each cheek, falling from his chin. "He had a weird sense of humor."

"I didn't know him for long," I said, reaching out slowly with one hand. "But he seemed like a nice person."

Austin didn't pull the trigger. His finger hovered above it, but he made no move to fire. I decided to gamble.

"I wish I could have gotten to know him," I said softly, placing my hand on the barrel.

Austin didn't resist. Ever so carefully, I took the gun out of his hand.

"He…" Austin choked. "You would have liked him."

I pulled Austin into me with one arm. The gun hung down by my side with the other. It felt cold, like the touch of death, and was heavy too—like the metal bore the weight of the last few days. I ignored it. Austin sobbed noisily into my chest, wailing his grief to all of San Francisco from atop the building.

I stroked his back up and down, offering what comfort I could. In that moment, nothing else mattered. Inspector Wong could handle whatever crimes Austin had committed. My job, I felt, was consoling a man who had lost something precious—something irreplaceable.

"I'll take it from here."

Brandon was standing beside me. I hadn't heard him approach. The real surprise, however, was the gun clutched in his hand. He stood in a very professional way with the Glock pointed toward the deck floor.

He was also fully clothed, something else that startled me.

"Thank you, agent."

Jean's footsteps were far less light. I heard his sandals clip-clop across the deck as he approached. He looked at me with an expression of utter relief. There was something else there as well, like he had witnessed a miracle.

"Agent?" I asked, looking from Jean over to Brandon.

Jean cleared his throat. "Meet FBI Agent Li Thong," he introduced. "Working undercover with the Bureau's cybercrimes division. They've been tracking Austin's scheme for months."

"Sorry about the ruse," Brandon—or Li, rather—said as he took Austin out of my arms. "This troupe's been breaking into banks across the country, making it a federal case. So I went undercover."

I made certain that Austin was okay before releasing him. "Okay," I said to Jean as Austin went willingly. It looked like most of the fight had gone out of him. "How did you figure this one out?"

"I'm curious to know that too," Brandon said while handcuffing Austin.

"I found him on the second floor," Jean explained. "He was looking for Austin too. Since none of the cops had found Austin on the first floor—"

"—you figured out that he must be up here with me," I finished. "All well and good, but how did you know he was with the FBI."

"Well, there was something off about him from the start," Jean said, which earned him a glare from Brandon. "But I started to suspect Brandon wasn't a humble gay dancer during Inspector Wong's interrogation."

Brandon looked abashed. "I asked too many questions," he mumbled.

"You asked the right questions," Jean corrected. "And you weren't intimidated. Most people get nervous when they get questioned by the cops. You were cool as a cucumber."

"I gave myself away," Brandon admitted.

I wasn't sure what to say. "It was…" I began, stumbling over my words. "…um, nice working with you. I guess? Thanks for showing me the ropes."

"It was fun," Brandon told me, sounding earnest. "Maybe we can do it again sometime."

"Thanks, but I'm in a relationship," I reminded, nodding my head toward Jean. "Plus, it would be weird. Seeing each other again with our clothes on and all."

Brandon smiled at my joke, but his eyes betrayed something. His hand kept Austin in a tight grip, but the other pulled me closer.

"Be careful around that one," he whispered in my ear quickly. "You don't know him as well as you think you do."

I stared back, confused. "Not sure what I was expecting," I said flatly. "But it sure as hell wasn't that."

Brandon smiled a sad sort of smile, like he was pitying me. "See you around," he said, guiding Austin toward the door. "Stay safe."

He got maybe halfway to the door with Austin when it flung open. Michael stood there, eyes wide and hair an utter mess. His button-up blue shirt was sweaty and wrinkled. It looked like he had run full-stop all the way up every flight to get here.

"What the fuck is going on?" he shrieked, looking around with a freaked out expression. "There are cops everywhere. My whole troupe's being arrested and…Austin, why does Brandon have you in handcuffs? This is no time for kinkplay!"

"Wow, he really had no clue what was happening, did he?" I noted as Brandon marched Austin past without paying Michael any mind at all.

"Not an inkling," Jean affirmed, looking amused at Michael while he stood by sputtering.

Jean and I stood together, his arm wrapped securely around me, as I watched them go. The past couple days were a blur. I felt like I could sleep for a week.

"Wanna go home?" Jean asked me.

I didn't answer him right away. "I'm honestly not sure," I said, looking around the deck area once more. "A part of me wants to put this whole event behind us."

"I can understand that," he said, giving me a squeeze. "You've had a tough few days. I hope it wasn't all bad, though."

"That's the thing," I replied. "It wasn't. Some parts were fun. A little scary at first, but I feel like being here has changed me."

"For the better?" Jean asked, wanting confirmation.

"Yeah," I admitted, giving his side a little nudge with my elbow. "For the better."

"We still haven't had dinner with your mother," he reminded me. "I did promise you that we would get back to that."

"I'll have to call her," I said, digging out my phone. "It's been a few days anyway. Maybe she would be up for doing something tomorrow night."

"Dinner on the Day of the Dead?" Jean asked. "Not a bad idea, really."

I was thinking of Marcus and Blu as I dialed. "But then, there's tonight. We had tickets for the whole week-long event here. It'd be a shame to waste them."

"It would," Jean agreed. "Why not do both?"

I laughed as the call went to my mother's voice message. "What?" I asked, moving the phone away from my mouth so it didn't record this part of our conversation. "Dinner with my mom and a sex party? That doesn't strike you as a little out of the ordinary?"

Jean waved his hand. "I play by my own rules," he said. "So should you. Let's do things our way and see where that takes us."

"Okay," I agreed, smiling. "Just lemme leave a message for Mom asking about tomorrow night, okay?"

Jean had no objections. He seemed more at peace now with the idea of sitting down at a dinner table and making polite conversation. I left Mom the message, then put my phone away.

It had been days since I updated my social media. The followers I had undoubtedly wondered what had happened to me. I would have to give them a version of the events. Not everything would go public, but I intended to tell this tale online.

Marcus would need a mention, and so would Blu. The Day of the Dead was about remembering those that had already gone on ahead of us. I wanted the world to know that those two young men had been real. They were real people who had lived, and who had been taken away from the world before their time.

"Shit!" I screamed as Jean and I reached the stairs. "I completely forgot about Chrissy!"

Chapter 14

Monday night saw Jean and I back at *Treats*.

I had expected a more subdued affair. There were no strippers to perform, after all. Michael was unable to get anyone else from Stud Stable on short notice. He was quite stunned to learn that the dancers were actually bank robbers guilty of multiple counts of identity theft.

Personally, I felt like he might not have been very good at his job.

DJ Chrissy Sinz had bowed out as well. He was suffering from a massive hangover thanks to the drug Austin pumped him full of. It took a good six hours for him to wake up. Worse, he experienced some mild amnesia as well, not remembering anything about the previous day.

This was a common side effect of the drug, according to the doctors. They advised him to drink plenty of water so the remains of the drug could pass through his system. He took their advice to heart, canceling his appearances for the rest of the week.

The staff at *Treats* pumped recorded music through the system instead. None of the guests appeared to mind one bit. They were having the time of their lives, dancing like lunatics on the deck area. The pool was jam-packed as well.

All of the hallways were crowded. Practically every room had been purchased for the next eight hours. Every facility that *Treats* offered was being made full use of.

This included the Slurp Room, which was where Jean and I wound up spending a good bit of our time. We stood at each other's side, holding hands while our cocks hung down through the gloryholes.

Below us, on the padded floor beyond the raised platforms, a mass of bottom boys crowded around us. They were worshiping our dicks, running their tongues all along the sides and licking eagerly at our balls. The Slurp Room lived up to its name that night. The space was filled with the sounds of hungry men desperate for cum.

I was surprised by the number of men interested in my cock. Jean got more than his fair share of admirers. But the men were just as eager to sample from me. We both relaxed and let them have their fun, letting the stress of the past few days float away.

It was a good way to end the party.

We got home during the early hours of the morning. Neither one of us were particularly quiet, but if we woke Auntie Mags up, she said nothing about it. Jean and I slept very late, then had a small lunch. My mother was cooking, so that meant we had to be prepared to eat lots.

Sure enough, Mom prepared a feast for everyone. She had laid out all of my favorite foods, plus a few that my brother was partial to. Speaking of which, my brother grilled Jean about his career in porn. He was keen to know more about what went on behind the scenes in the industry.

I had heard all of this before, so I kept Mom occupied so she wouldn't smack my brother across the head. I had the sneaky suspicion that he was trying to get under her skin. It was a habit of his left over from childhood that he hadn't quite shaken.

Mom did her best not to get upset. She wasn't exactly thrilled with Jean's previous occupation, but that had been years ago. On the whole, he managed to win her tentative approval. It was a lot more than Jean had expected.

"I'm not gonna get used to that anytime soon," he confided in me when we had a moment of privacy.

I gave him a droll look. "You're being paranoid," I said to him, smacking his arm lightly. "Don't let bad experiences from the past hold you back. Isn't that what you've been trying to show me?"

Jean blushed. "Saved by the vibrating," he said, which confused me.

I watched Jean dig out his phone, which it turned out had been set to vibrate. He had thought ahead so that it didn't interrupt dinner. I was pleased with him for that.

"Hello?" he asked, answering it. "Inspector Wong?"

I almost stepped back into the Tres Leches cake Mom left on the counter. "What does she want?" I asked, forgetting that Inspector Wong could hear me.

Jean obliged by putting his phone on speaker. "So, here's a good one for you two," I heard her say. "A lawyer locks himself in his office, so his wife calls for the housekeeper to bring the key. When they both get inside, the man is unconscious. The wife asks that the housekeeper to call the paramedics, who pronounce the husband dead when they get there."

"Sounds like suicide," I said.

"You'd think that," Inspector Wong replied. "Except I'm holding a physical copy of the coroner's report in my hand right now. And according to it, he died approximately an hour *after* the paramedics got there."

To his credit, Jean tried not to look delighted.

"Tell us more," he encouraged, resting against the countertop.

I reached out and plucked the phone from his hand. "After dinner," I told Inspector Wong, taking the phone off speaker. "We still haven't had cake yet."

The End

About the Author

John Luke Maxwell grew up in a place that prides itself to this day on having no cable or high-speed Internet access. Therefore, it was only a matter of time before his escape!

His family farmhouse was near the bayous of central Mississippi. Here, John learned about ghosts, witches, and other things that go bump in the night. Despite everyone's best efforts, he is more comfortable with creatures of the night than plain ol' ordinary "good Christian folk".

John has since relocated to the Pacific Northwest where he intends to party hard and live life to the fullest. He prefers hard liquor to beer and would not mind meeting Bigfoot one day. His idea of happiness is a soft boy on either side of him who love the smell of his pits.

He has a very dirty mind that crops up periodically in his writing. You've been warned!

Books by John Luke Maxwell

The Phantom of Nob Hill Theatre
Tricks 'N' Treats
Southern Faer Lust

   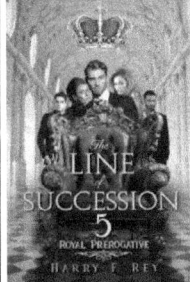

Also from Deep Desires Press

The Hookups of Hickeyhook Hall
Marco May

Jenner is gay and has a crush on Michael. Unbeknownst to him, Michael is bi and has a crush on him in return. But there's one huge obstacle in the way of professing his love. Their parents just got married to each other. Now, they're officially stepbrothers.

Both young men are determined to move on and leave their feelings behind, and what better way to do that than to dive into the challenges of starting a new life at Hickeyhook College? Their new lives are full of quirky roommates and stupid rules…and the discovery of an underground sex club with both students and staff that offers students the opportunity to cheat their way through to graduation without all the stresses of normal college life. With both young men in the club, it brings Jenner and Michael dangerously close, making it impossible to ignore the feelings they both swore to leave behind.

As sticky as their new situation is, it's about to get stickier. The powerful Dean Wicket sees the emerging relationship between Jenner and Michael and he's determined to get in the way…because he wants Michael to himself.

When the truth of Jenner and Michael comes out and the world is against them, these two men must fight with all they have to hold onto true love.

Available now in ebook and paperback!

For more hot reads, visit us at
deepdesirespress.com

www.ingramcontent.com/pod-product-compliance
Lightning Source LLC
Chambersburg PA
CBHW051340020726
47501CB00007B/2194